Auth

Hi, I'm Polly Babbington ~~and I love to write~~.
I live with my husband and family in a beautiful old Edwardian house
by the sea, with white French windows, a huge old tree out the back
and a Summer House right down the end of the garden where I spend
long days spinning stories and drinking tea.
I began writing years ago working for various online publications, my
work published worldwide and started writing and publishing books
not long after, juggling the stories in my head with bringing up babies.
These days I potter around the house writing, taking care of my family,
and plotting my next feel-good romance stories, ready to launch them
out into the world to my lovely readers.
I also love flowers, taking photos, cooking, walking in the woods, sitting
on the beach, pottering with things in the house and love nothing bet-
ter after a day of writing than an evening gardening with a drink.
You'll find me on my days off lazing in the hammock under the fruit
tree, or cosy on the sofa next to the fire, with a cup of tea and a new
book.
We live in a sweet little village complete with a gorgeous old cricket
pitch, village green with a few lovely old pubs.

Follow Polly on Instagram and Facebook @PollyBabbingtonwrites
PollyBabbington.com
For the Pretty Beach delicious simple dahl recipe and more subscribe to
Babbington Letters at PollyBabbington.com

A
Pretty Beach
Christmas

Polly Babbington

Copyright

Chapter 1

Juliette Sparkles made one last lap of the poky little flat with the low ceiling, hundreds of harsh downlights, ultra-modern double-glazed windows and shiny laminate flooring. There could have been worse places to end up when she'd walked out of her marriage, but where she was going to, a Victorian cottage with original features, the loveliest little back garden and tiny little conservatory was so very much more appealing. She smiled to herself at the thought of the cottage and clasped her hands together in anticipation.

She closed the door to the flat, walked across the tiny entrance foyer of the building, checked how long she had before the removalists arrived at the cottage and headed towards her car.

Ten minutes later, she arrived in Seapocket Lane, slowly drove along looking for a space and parked in a tight little spot right outside the cottage. She got out of her car, took her cleaning bucket filled with supplies out of the boot, pushed open the white picket gate and walked up to the half-glazed pink front door.

She peered in the bay window remembering how lovely it all looked since Sallie, her friend and now landlord, had cleaned out the place, stripped all the walls and carpets, decorated it in soft whites and vintage greys and updated the central heating system and the insulation.

She opened the door and gave herself one last little tour before their stuff arrived. Not that they had a lot of stuff. She'd left her husband with hardly anything and in the flat with its modern decor and cramped feeling she'd not had the need nor the inclination to do much in terms of decorating at all. Since she'd agreed to rent this cottage from Sallie though, she'd got a few things out of storage and slowly started to gather bits and pieces together for her new home.

In addition to her two duck-egg blue linen sofas from the flat, she'd inherited an old, round pine table from one of the receptionists at work, rubbed it down, primed it and painted it a very pale pink. She'd also added to her collection of pretty lamps and had dipped into her house deposit savings and treated herself to gorgeous down-filled velvet sofas for the conservatory.

She walked through the cottage and the tiny middle room with the window to the terrace and then into the kitchen. The old units, which in a previous life had worn a coat of bright orange varnish, had been sanded back and painted a soft grey and the floating shelves that had jutted horribly into the room were long gone, leaving a space for an old-fashioned dresser she'd seen on an online selling group.

Juliette opened a cupboard, looked inside and the smell of disinfectant hit her nose, then peering into the sparkling butler's sink and looking down at the floor she realised there wasn't a speck of dust anywhere. Sallie must have cleaned the whole place ready for her arrival. Juliette put her bucket down - she wouldn't be needing it after all.

On the worktop next to the window a small pink jug with polka dots held a beautifully arranged posy of flowers wrapped in white and tied with a pink grosgrain bow. Beside it a box of champagne and a small white card embossed with Boat House Pretty Beach was propped up against it and in small, neat calligraphy, a note.

Welcome to your new home. Hope you all love it as much as I love Pretty Beach. Sallie x.

Juliette put the card back and touched a tiny pink petal on one of the flowers and felt a tear prick the corner of her eyes.

'Hello!' A voice called out from the front door - Pretty Beach Removals had arrived.

'Hi, well here we are, ready when you are,' Juliette said, gesturing her hand around the small sitting room at the front.

'Okay, my lovely, we'll be in and out in no time with all this, just let us know where you want everything,' Jude, the owner of Pretty Beach Removals, said.

She stepped into the lean-to conservatory, worked out exactly where she wanted the new sofas to go, opened the double doors and walked out onto the terrace. Autumn was in the air, but the last of the sun was beating down on the terrace and gold and rust leaves had fallen into a huge pile onto the old patio bricks, layering the whole place in a thick carpet of russet and reds.

Sallie had told her that the cottage and the Orangery behind it had a few little sun traps where even on a cold day you could sit with a cup of tea and this was obviously one of them. She touched one of the bricks feeling the warmth from the sun underneath her hand.

She crossed over the terrace and walked all the way down the block paved pathway through the long garden to the creaky old timber gate surrounded by rambling roses. She slowly heaved it open, walked down the side of the Orangery, underneath the elderflowers and through the opening onto the beach.

Juliette stood there in the little spot behind the gate completely sheltered from the wind. Sallie was right; it was a glorious little sun trap with no one around and only the gentle lapping of the waves to keep her company.

She looked out at the sea, a fishing boat with her friend Harry dressed in bright yellow oilskin trousers went past and gave her a wave. A seagull swooped down and dived into the water and far off in the distance she could hear the horn of the Pretty Beach ferry.

Holding her face up to the sun, Juliette took in a deep breath of sea air and clenched her fists tightly to her side. Hopefully, this would be the start of a whole new brighter chapter.

Chapter 2

Juliette stood in the bedroom in the eaves all the way at the top of the cottage in Seapocket Lane. She walked over to the dormer window in the roof, pushed it open, took in a big breath of sea air and looked over the roof tiles to the glass of the domed roof Orangery at the bottom. Behind the Orangery at the end of the garden she watched the waves rolling in and out on the beach and followed the old weather vane on top of the Orangery as it swung around in the wind.

She stood there for a moment thinking about how lucky her and her daughter Maggie were to have moved out of the damp, cramped flat and now found themselves living in one of the loveliest parts of Pretty Beach, and not only that, they were right by the sea. Even though Juliette was physically exhausted and emotionally drained from the move and all it had entailed, it was elating to have the new start and moving into the cottage had somehow flicked a switch that had made her happier than she had been for a very long time.

She turned around to survey the room; it was slightly awkward where the eaves met the floor, but she knew that it wouldn't take her long to get it cosy. As she dragged her faded, vintage pale blue wool rug into the middle of the room she felt grateful that it had all been recently painted. She'd seen a photo of what it had looked like before and grimaced as the image of the bright orange stained pine room with a sad and lonely bare bulb hanging down from the middle came into her mind. In addition to that grim picture, the drab old wall-to-wall carpeting had looked tired and grubby and the fireplace had been boarded up with an old electric fire sitting on the grate.

Now, as Juliette started slowly and carefully moving furniture around the room, the eave walls were painted in a soft white, the carpets removed to reveal beautiful old timber floors and the electric fire was long gone, the surround painted in antique white. She'd had worse bases to start from since she'd walked out on her ex-husband with a suitcase and a few boxes of her things.

As she walked over to the other side of the room she silently thanked her lucky stars that the Pretty Beach removal men had been like gold - they'd lugged all her boxes of linens all the way to the top and more importantly had somehow managed to get her brass bed up the stairs. They'd struggled with the narrow steep stairs but persevered and when they'd finally got it all in they'd even put it together for her. Now, all she had to do was get everything ready and the beds made up before Maggie got home.

She pulled the huge cardboard removals box with 'linens' neatly marked on the side and started to pull out her duvet from its protective bag and looked inside to choose a cover.

She'd been waiting to use all her beautiful linens and her bed again - in the small damp flat she hadn't had the heart to use them and had bought a pretty floral cover in the supermarket and left her nice things in storage. When she'd given notice on the flat and agreed the rent with Sallie she'd washed and pressed her linens, sprayed them with a beautiful lavender spray and got them ready for the little cottage. And now here she was ready to not just put a new cover on her bed, but start the journey to a more stable life.

She pulled the ruched, duck-egg blue quilt edged with thick cotton lace onto the brass bed, flicked it up into the air and then down onto the mattress, smoothing it into the corners.

Then she pushed and pulled the two white timber bedside tables to either side of the bed, unwrapped the bubble wrap from two white-based lamps and topped each with pale-blue linen patterned lampshades.

Juliette unravelled the wool rug, lifted up one leg of the bed, pushed the rug under and then struggled with the three other legs until the beautiful rug was perfectly positioned underneath.

She pulled bed cushions out of the removals box, puffed and fluffed them up and placed them carefully on the bed and stood back. It looked lovely, her bed just about fitting under the eaves. The handle of a tiny little door to the attic poked out on the right and sitting next to it an old Bentwood chair she'd found in a skip and painted blue added to the calm, cosy feel.

She dragged a small, timber bench to the end of the bed, placed a wicker basket underneath it, put a white pottery jug with pale blue dots on the top and decided that she would treat herself to a bunch of flowers as a little personal housewarming gift for her new home.

Her new home which she could decorate as she pleased, cook whatever she fancied and after a few years of upheaval, finally have some optimism for the future.

Chapter 3

Juliette flicked the petrol cap shut, walked across the freezing cold concourse of the petrol station, went through the automatic doors, grabbed a Flake from the shelf in front of the till and tapped her card on the machine.

She pulled out of the petrol station onto the deserted coastal road to Pretty Beach and nipped along in her small midnight-blue car with the heater turned up to its fullest to warm up her icy feet - even though they were wrapped in thick socks and boots her feet always seemed to get cold on her way home from an evening shift at work.

It had been a good few weeks since her and Maggie had moved into the little cottage in Seapocket Lane and now the colder nights were on the way, and after a long shift at Newport Reef Hospital, she was ready for a night in with comfort food, a long bath and wine. Lots of wine or maybe gin, perhaps both.

The car headlights caught the glistening icy patches on the road and the thick, low fog swirled around in front of the car as she sped along. The man from the BBC coming out of her speaker informed her that it was going to be one of the coldest nights at this time of year since 1954 and she smiled to herself thinking about being all rugged up in the cottage. She turned off the coastal road and headed down Strawberry Hill towards Pretty Beach, the bunting of the Old Town welcomed her to the wharf and as she switched off the radio she felt very glad to be home.

She drove all the way through Pretty Beach, past the sand dunes, along the laneway, past the Boat House, past Holly's Bakery and saw the lights of the Orangery just behind her little cottage. She tapped on the steering wheel, and again, thanked her lucky stars that her now friend Sallie, was renting the cottage out to her for a great price.

She pulled into the tiny, one-way lane, made a most excellent attempt at reverse parking into a tight spot and turned off the engine.

Pretty Beach was silent, tranquil almost and getting ready for the quieter few months after all the tourists had gone home. The beautiful lights from the houses of Seapocket Lane glowed at every turn and a nearby porch was lit up in tiny white lights bathing the whole of the pavement in a glorious glow.

It was still a while off but the weather and the cosy lane made her think of Christmas and Juliette loved Christmas - she loved Christmas and every little thing about it and even her ex-husband's comments about helping her out by looking after Maggie while she did a late shift at the hospital couldn't dampen her spirit for the upcoming festive season.

She took a moment just before she got out of her car to look around herself and be grateful - not that long ago she had been almost desperate for some stability and structure after her quite horrid divorce, looking after the children on her own and worrying what seemed like every single second of every single day about whether she was doing a good enough job of it all. Then, when she was at what was probably her lowest point, a chance conversation with Sallie had given her hope.

That conversation and letting someone help her out had meant her and Maggie were now living quite happily in the sweet little cottage on Seapocket Lane and out of the damp, cramped, brightly-lit rental flat they'd been stuck in. Moving into the cottage had allowed her two things - some breathing space to get herself back together again, and the ability to save up further on the money she'd inherited for a deposit that she hoped would be enough to at some point buy a property for her and the girls.

Moving into the cottage had also annoyed the heck out of her ex-husband Jeremy. She'd seen the look cross his eyes when she'd opened the pale pink door of the cottage when he'd come to pick up Maggie and he had asked her just one too many nosey questions. He'd peered in at the feminine decor, the cosy rugs and lamps and she'd seen that it irritated him that Juliette was now doing exactly as she pleased with no one to answer to.

Her eyes wandered up the street - a few houses along a roof sparkled with frost and the house next door to it seemed to glisten in the light sweeping down from the lighthouse. It all looked so quiet, so still and pretty when the nights got colder and even the little sold cottage right down at the other end of the lane which had been empty for a while had a cosy warm glow from the upstairs window.

Seapocket Lane was just the sort of place she'd wanted to live when she'd first got married, but nothing she'd wanted had ever been taken into consideration and the big open plan house, with modern windows and, she shuddered, a cinema room was what Jeremy had wanted. And what Jeremy wanted, Jeremy got.

But now rid of Jeremy she could make her own decisions on pretty much everything and as she sat in the car in the cold, bright evening looking at the little cottages all around her Juliette hoped and prayed by some luck or lottery win that she'd be able to stay on the street. But after the divorce and Jeremy's clever accounting even a tiny little cottage on Seapocket Lane seemed just that little bit out of her reach.

She opened her door, locked the car, said hello to a couple strolling along with a pram and pushed open the little white picket gate to the cottage. Either side of the front door, two mini bay trees covered in tiny gold-white lights sparkled and the tiny little bee-shaped door knocker shimmered in the light. Approaching the door, she peeked in the window to get a glimpse of the little sitting room - all her bits and bobs had fitted in just right and she'd loved how cosy and welcoming it felt when she got home from a long shift at work.

She unlocked the front door of the cottage and stepped into the hallway, took off her coat, hung it on the hooks in the porch and slipped off her fur-lined boots.

'Ahhhh,' she let out a sigh as she wriggled and stretched her toes, walked up the stairs and then up the tiny steep steps to the second floor in the eaves. She dropped her uniform into the washing basket, took her dark-grey, velvet floor-length dressing gown off the hook behind the door, leant over and started to run the bath.

She poured a long stream of fig bubble bath under the tap, let the bubbles build up and then turned the taps until they were merely a dribble and headed back down the stairs for wine. She walked carefully down the steep stairs having to turn her feet sideways to fit onto the treads and hold onto the rail carefully as she made her way down through the old cottage.

Padding through to the kitchen, she glanced in at the little lanterns in the corner, the pale pink round table tucked in by the window and flicked on the under-cupboard lights in the dove grey kitchen.

Lots of things in the cottage reminded her of how her life was as this Juliette and not the Juliette who had been married to Jeremy - the pale blue Smeg fridge she'd been over the moon with when it had arrived, the polka dot tea towels, the display plates with florals all over them. Jeremy would never have allowed them to enter the house, let alone display them.

She shook her head thinking about it all and the person she was back then and even though she had much less money nowadays, she was so much happier and could, actually, spend what money she did have on whatever the heck she liked. Not that she had much spare money, but it was enough, and with her little sideline online shop, 'A Christmas Sparkle,' and her friend Sallie's kindness, she was in a much better position than she had been since the day she'd packed up her few things and walked out to give her girls the happy mum and life they deserved.

She took a bottle of wine out of the beautifully organised fridge and looked through the little pink tubs stacked neatly and labelled with their contents, grabbed one with leftover roast potatoes, popped it in the microwave, sprinkled it with seasalt and climbed carefully back up the stairs to the slowly filling bath.

Her phone buzzed in her pocket - Jeremy.

Just taking Maggie for a pizza and then ice skating - just letting you know where we'll be.

She popped a roast potato in her mouth, let out a low almost groan and lugged down a large mouthful of wine.

Oh, fabulous. She'll love that. So good of you. She messaged back between gritted teeth.

In her head she was thinking, of course he was taking her ice skating. He was the quintessential fun dad, in fact, it was almost as if he'd written the formula for it. He breezed in and breezed out of the girls' lives with gifts and showy excursions, weekends away, but loved to moan about the school fees, clothing bills or anything other than what he did at the weekends and what he legally had to pay as his contribution to his own child.

Juliette stuffed in another roast potato, put the little tub on the wicker table with her perfumes and body lotions, put the wine on the side of the sink and climbed into the tub.

She finished off the potatoes and the wine and then looked down at her stomach guiltily, she wobbled it with her left hand and it jiggled over the top of the bubbly water. After Christmas she'd watch what she was eating a bit more carefully, there really was no point with Christmas not too long away - there were too many tempting things at every turn. For someone who loved Christmas and everything that came with it, that included the food - mince pies, mulled wine, Yule log, cranberry sauce, Christmas cake, pigs in blankets. You name it, Juliette loved it - really she loved almost any sort of food, on any sort of occasion, ever. Except kiwis and celery.

She jiggled her stomach again and thought about how plump she'd got since Jeremy had been off the scene and not constantly on and on about her weight and whether or not she was exercising to 'keep herself looking nice'. Just before she'd left she'd cut up the gym membership card he'd forced her to subscribe to, started a new life on her own and happily put on more than a few pounds.

The thing with Jeremy wasn't as bad as she had convinced herself it was when she was in the marriage, the problem with him was that he was very particular about many things and especially about how the wife on his arm looked. He had liked her to be a size eight, actually he would have preferred a six - she lay there in the bath, looking at her stomach, sipping on the glass of wine, and wondered what Jeremy thought about her size now.

She smiled to herself looking at the lovely pudgy bits on her knees - she was a good four sizes bigger than when she'd walked out the door on Jeremy and oh how she had bloomed - blossomed into the floaty, ruffled dresses she loved which showed off her curves and her still tiny waist, blossomed into all the girly pink things in the house she was never allowed before and blossomed into her longer, darker beautifully curled hair and pretty pink lipstick.

Soaking in the bath musing it all she thought about how as she had begun to allow herself to eat again, allow herself to enjoy food she hadn't been near in years, she'd realised that she had, in fact, been hungry for ten years and it had impacted many areas of her life. It had dawned on her that the thing she'd read about in one of the magazines in the waiting room at work about the correlation between carbs and happiness was actually true.

She leant over the bath, hooked open the tiny cupboard, pulled out a Ziploc bag, picked her phone out of her dressing gown pocket, put the phone in the bag, zipped up the bag and sank back down into the water.

Facebook first. She scrolled through the Christmas groups she loved, whittled down over the years to her favourite three - hardcore, full-on Christmas junkies, just like her who were already well into their Christmas decorating even though for most people it hadn't even got going yet. Santa Jones, her online friend in Whistler had posted a picture of her outside Christmas trees which were more professionally designed than the inside of most homes and Laura from Sydney had posted a picture of her ten million dollar 'shack' on one of the best beaches in the world decked out in masses of coloured lights. She liked them both and made little comments, trailed a load of pink love hearts underneath her comments and promised them she'd be posting her latest vintage finds as soon as she had the time to take the photos.

Just as she leant over to the tap to top the bath up with hot water a message came in from her daughter Bella.

Hi Mum. You are NOT going to believe this. I only went and aced that assignment!

Well done. I'm not surprised though.

Not only did I ace it, I topped the year! The whole of the year, for the whole of the course at Oxford.

As I said Bella, I'm not surprised - you've been doing that since the day you were born.

You always say that!!

That's because it's always true.

I'm so happy.

You should be the amount of work you've put in. So proud of you sweetie. I hope you're going to take a break now.

Very funny. I've got another assignment coming up and then all the social stuff. I'll send you the dates. Spk later, I'm on the way to work.

Love you, stay safe.

Juliette smiled to herself, swiped up to close the app and clicked onto the BBC website to see what recipes they had for when her friends Sallie and Ben were coming over for dinner.

Chapter 4

Juliette finished off her cup of tea in the pink polka dot mug, put it neatly in the dishwasher, pulled her knee-high cream crochet socks with the velvet tops up to her knees underneath her uniform trousers and slipped her feet into her fur-lined clogs.

She grabbed her huge tote bag, big pale pink wrap coat and hot chocolate, did the wrap belt up on her coat, opened the fridge, took a packet of chocolate fingers from her stash and slipped them into her bag.

The pink leather tassel on her car keys caught in her coat as she crossed the small sitting room, checked the thermostat was on the right setting and opened the pink half-glazed country front door. The 6am air was icy cold, the whole of the street dead quiet, most people still tucked up in the warm, the only sign of life Juliette's pink pansies catching in the wind in the basket above her head.

She got in the car and peered through the misty windscreen at the front, quickly turned on the ignition, blasted the window with air and pulled away from the street as smoothly as possible so as not to wake anyone up. Her creeping off to work was a long-established routine she'd been doing since the first days when she'd qualified, and it drove her crazy now when on her days off an inconsiderate person was noisy in the morning, getting their bins in or having a too-loud conversation at silly o'clock in the morning outside the window. Not that it mattered as much to her any longer now that she was tucked up in the bedroom all the way in the eaves of the cottage.

She drove out of Pretty Beach main, along to the bottom of Strawberry Hill, turned right onto the coast road and started the drive to the hospital. Radio 4 quietly played beside her and she wondered how Maggie would be when she got dropped off the next evening. Normally when she got back from being with Jeremy she was over-excited, out of routine and sometimes rude. It would take

Juliette a couple of hours to get her back to normal, occasionally a couple of days. At least Jeremy was still involved she thought as she drove along - her friend at work had been through a similar thing and her boys hadn't seen their dad for three years.

She sighed, took a sip of her hot chocolate and turned the radio up.

'Most of the country will experience some small snow flurries of some sort today or later on today, which is unusual for this time of year.' The weather lady said, and Juliette smiled to herself, whenever it snowed sales at A Christmas Sparkle would start to ping in through the app. She'd changed the notification on it to a Jingle Bells tune so that every time it went off she smiled. It always brightened her day and later on in the afternoon as everyone got home from work and had come in from the school run and got onto the Internet when she was just rounding off her shift at the hospital, the little vibrations would come in, pinging quietly away to themselves in her pocket and notifying her that she had sales. A high percentage of the profit from the sales would now be going straight into her savings account, for what she hoped would soon be a deposit on her very own little cottage.

She pulled into the staff car park at Newport Reef hospital and looked at the long walk over to the entrance and the flyover walkway glistening in the early morning frost. It did not look inviting; it was always freezing cold up there - whoever had designed it clearly didn't feel the cold. She put her car into park and wished she had enough money like some of the other staff to park in the multi-storey with the tunnel all the way into the reception of the hospital. Then again, she'd rather be watching the pennies and parking a mile away from the hospital than still be with Jeremy and starving to keep her weight down and spending most of her life trying to look and act the part.

She got out of the car, locked the door and just as she was making her way to the flyover her friend Milly in her cute little dark-green

Mini swung around the corner of the car park, slotted into a space and hopped out of the car.

'Morning lovely, how are you?' Juliette said, walking over to Milly and kissing her on the cheek.

'Good thanks,' she said, pulling her black puffer coat on and popping a fur-lined baseball cap on her head. 'Blimey, Juliette, who ordered this weather? It's absolutely freezing.'

'Good for me though, and especially if we get some snow later.' Juliette laughed and waited as Milly got her bag from the back of her car.

'Will we be getting all the little jingles from your phone like we did for Christmas in July?' Milly said, as she popped her bag on her shoulder and slammed the car door of the little Mini and clicked the remote.

'I do hope so! That was the plan when I ordered the snow,' Juliette chuckled, pulled out the packet of chocolate fingers from her bag, took off her glove and offered one to Milly as they walked across the car park in the freezing air.

'Don't mind if I do,' Milly said, taking two chocolate fingers and popping one into her mouth.

'So, the new anaesthetist starts tomorrow then. How very exciting for us. Have you seen the pic of him Juliette? Doris did make me laugh - she took one look at it and said she wouldn't mind putting him in her sandwich, even at her age.'

'Ha! That's hilarious. I haven't even looked, so no I haven't seen the pic, I've been far too busy, but anyway, ummm yeah, an anaesthetist - you know, not really my type.'

'Not your type! Any type would be good in my case right now. I have had an acute lack of types for, what seems like two years. Oh wait, it is two years. What is your type then?' Milly laughed, shoving the other chocolate finger into her mouth and her hands in her pockets as they started walking up the steps of the flyover.

'My type is nothing. My type is me keeping myself to myself, doing my job and getting out of here as quickly as possible. My type does not include, at any stage, having a man in my life ever again. I like my life without the complications and I'm liking it very much. Oh, and yes, I like eating whatever I want,' Juliette replied as the cold air at the top of the flyover swirled around them.

'Ahhh don't say that, you old mizog - we don't want you out of here as soon as possible - you know how much we love it when it's you, the best midwife around, we get on the wards, when we get to steal you away from Pretty Beach.'

'Hmm, well only a few more weeks and I won't be taking on any extra shifts here I can tell you that - I'm exhausted and in the next few weeks the shop is going to go nuts if it's anything like last year,' Juliette replied.

They walked down the steps on the other side of the flyover and proceeded through another small car park for the hospital executives, the hospital gardens, along a path beside a winding ring road and through the staff entrance at the back of the hospital.

Milly held her pass up to the pad and the doors automatically slid open in front of them.

'Okay, here we go, are you ready for the madness Sparkles?' Milly looked at Juliette and giggled, popping her lanyard around her neck and Milly continued, 'I tell you what I'm ready for, the very handsome new anaesthetist when he starts his shift later on this evening.'

Chapter 5

Juliette pulled her coat on and tied up the belt. The automatic staff door slid open and she stepped out into the cold evening. What a shift - thank goodness for Milly, she'd worked like clockwork between the women and they'd worked seamlessly together so that everything went smoothly. Neither of them had more than a few minutes break to get their lunch in and Juliette's feet were not only aching, they were cold too, and she hadn't had anything to eat for hours and could hear her tummy grumbling as she headed for the car. So much for guidelines, they hadn't reached her little part of the country yet.

She put her head down as she rushed through the hospital gardens, hurried across the flyover, stepped quickly down the other side and briskly walked over towards her car. Just as she was getting closer to her car, the keys in her hand, a very nice BMW went past, stopped right in front of her, reversed and went round again. She tutted as she waited for the driver to finish his manoeuvre, then she crossed over the aisle and squeezed in between an empty space between two cars. The car came back down the aisle and went round again. She was just about to click her remote when the car stopped beside her, wound down the window and called out.

'Excuse me! Wonder if you can help me at all?'

Oooh, he sounded nice.

She smiled at the man inside in the dark shirt, with short cropped hair with a floppy bit at the front and the news playing loudly in the background on the radio.

'Is this the staff car park?' The man asked with a confused look on his face.

'Yes it is, so you'll need the public multi-storey over there. It's expensive though.'

Juliette pointed over past the flyover and behind the hospital at the large multi-storey building.

'Or there are a few roads about a fifteen-minute walk away without any restrictions, but on a day like this I'm not sure that's a good idea,' she said, looking at the sky which was threatening snow, or rain, or both.

The man in the car leant across the dashboard and flashed a permit out the open window.

'Oh no, I'm staff. I'm new though - it just seemed a long way from the hospital and the last time I came I was not in my car - I got the ferry so I walked straight up the hill from the wharf.'

'Well yes, you're definitely in the right place then. It's better if you park under the lights over this side if you're going to get back to your car late - a bit creepy down here at night. The marshes over there get really cold and dark, but you can get a security guard to walk you back to your car, but they always take ages to come. I don't suppose by the looks of you you'd need escorting by security though,' she said, taking in his rather broad muscular chest and strong arms.

He smiled looking at the extremely attractive woman, her hair in a curled bouncy ponytail and packet of biscuits in her ungloved hand.

'Don't suppose you needed all that information. Anyway, good luck, I'm done for the day. In fact, I'm done for the week and I'm going home for some long-awaited peace,' she said, and laughed.

'Lucky you,' the lovely, handsome stranger said, and smiled back from the inside of his car, 'I'm Luke - might bump into you in the staff canteen one day then.'

He waved his hand, pushed the gear stick into first and drove slowly a few spaces along from where she'd parked. Juliette clicked the remote on her car, got in, and twirling the little heart charm on her necklace over and over, peered through the misted up window and watched the man in the BMW get out of his car, wrap a scarf around his neck over his dark blue shirt and head down through the car park towards the flyover. His long, thick legs striding along quickly as if they were eating up the ground, his flop of glossy brown hair at the front falling into his eyes.

She rummaged around in the console for a humbug, popped one into her mouth and could just about make out his silhouette as he jogged up the flyover steps two by two.

'Hmm,' she said to herself. 'Wouldn't mind bumping into you in the canteen, Luke whoever you are.'

Not that she went to the staff canteen that often. But maybe that could change.

Chapter 6

Juliette stood at the kitchen fridge in a thick, roll neck jumper and dark blue jeans, opened the little pink Tupperware pot labelled 'left-overs' and shovelled cold mashed potato into her mouth. She loved little moments like this, it signified freedom, the new freedom she relished every day; because in her old life she would never, ever, have eaten out of the fridge. Jeremy did not like eating out of the fridge, Jeremy did not like eating anywhere or any time other than at designated times in designated places, and now that she was free of Jeremy, well, she could do, eat, think and say precisely anything she wanted whenever she liked.

Maggie came pottering around the corner from the sitting room where she'd been playing a game on the tablet and having a drink.

'Okay, I'm going to go into the conservatory Maggie to get some wrapping up done for the shop. Come on, bring that in and you can watch it in there or you can help me with the wrapping,' Juliette said to Maggie as she finished squirting cream on the top of her hot chocolate and sprinkling mini chocolate buttons on the top.

Maggie went and got the tablet, Juliette picked up her hot chocolate and box of postal supplies from the dresser and they walked into the conservatory. Juliette hitched her jeans back up over her tummy, set Maggie up on the velvet sofa and sat down on the floor next to the pot belly stove with the hot chocolate and the orders from her shop that had come in overnight.

She opened the app on her phone which linked to the shopping cart on her website. Over thirty sales since she'd finished wrapping the last lot the night before, and as she scrolled all the way down the list she crossed her fingers that they were all in the UK and none of them were a tricky address. She scanned all the way down; excellent, only one was from overseas and she would deal with that when Maggie went to school - all the other ones she could happily sit and wrap while Maggie was playing on the tablet.

She leant over to the cupboard in the corner, pulled out the three wicker baskets with her supplies, one with the white plastic mailing sacks, one with all the little pretty bits of packaging and tissue paper and one with her printed marketing materials.

'Mummy, am I allergic to sweeties?' Maggie asked, looking up from her game.

Juliette sighed quietly to herself.

'No darling you are most definitely not. Sometimes they make you a teeny bit silly don't they? Remember before when you had too many and you had a lot of soft drink at the same time and you were very, err, busy?'

The tablet dinged from Maggie's lap.

'I shouldn't have too many things that have bright colours on them, that's right isn't it? But I'm not allergic, am I? Not like Maddy.'

'No, you're not, nothing like Maddy.'

Maggie seemed quite happy with that answer and Juliette got up from the floor, walked over to the table and pulled out the box where she had collated the orders ready to send. She carefully wrapped each order in layers of bubble wrap then covered them in white tissue paper, pulled each package together with butcher's string and carefully tied a tiny vintage gold bauble, a piece of white lace and tiny sprig of faux fir onto each of the packages.

She piled all the little white tissue paper covered packages up beside her as she slowly and methodically went through the list. It was quite an easy load of orders, mostly single vintage baubles and while it was sometimes tricky to get the bubble wrap on they were a winner in ROI and easy to pop in a mailing bag and drop off at Pretty Beach Post Office.

Maggie got down off the sofa and sat cross-legged on the rug in front of her.

'Do you want me to do the stamping?' Maggie asked, looking into the basket with the ribbon and stamps.

'I'd love you to do that for me, thank you.'

Maggie had seen Juliette wrapping parcels for her online shop A Christmas Sparkle which dealt in unique Christmas decor since just about the day she was born and knew the process nearly as well as Juliette did; it was a highly thought-out, exceedingly well-tuned process with not too much effort that made the products appear as a lovely gift someone had spent a lot of time on.

Juliette had got the idea to wrap her parcels as a gift when she'd first started buying and selling a few bits online. A top she'd ordered had come through the letterbox in an old, used, tatty brown envelope with a dried-up piece of breakfast cereal in the bottom - the top was stuffed in, creased up and the whole thing had been extremely disappointing. The next day another parcel had arrived very simply wrapped in pale blue tissue paper with tiny little stars, the item carefully folded and the fold stuck simply with a piece of washi tape - the contrast between the two experiences had been vast and so the packaging for her shop had been born.

She'd taken the idea of the tissue paper, changed it to white and then added in whatever bits and pieces she had to make the whole thing festive and as if a lot of effort had gone into it. There was even a section on her website showing the theme of wrapping for the month and a lot of her customers were excited just to buy something from her shop to see what little extra thing would be on the parcel itself. The way she looked at it, if someone was prepared to buy a vintage bauble for twenty pounds she was prepared to make a little bit of effort to make it look good.

As Maggie was carefully stamping a vintage, very pale gold stamp onto each of the parcels a message buzzed on Juliette's phone. She picked it up and saw Milly's name at the top.

Woah, the new anaesthetist! Everyone here's buzzing. Even Doris!

Haha. How's it all going? Busy?

Not too bad. When are you next in then? I know you said you don't have a type Sparkles but you need to get yourself in here, he's flipping gorgeous.

Milly sent through a whole load of emoticons, love hearts and happy faces.

Not in until next week - Pretty Beach community this week thank goodness.

Well, see you then, unless you're free for coffee. I'm off Thursday. Got to go - back to the new anaesthetist, hahaha.

Juliette finished wrapping all the parcels, popped them into the white mailing sacks, printed off the labels in the little office beside the kitchen and put the whole lot in her basket ready to take to the post office.

***

Juliette drove down Strawberry Hill, took a right and then a left to weave her car through the tiny little streets of Pretty Beach Old Town. It reminded her a little bit of the village in the Cotswolds she'd grown up in on this side of Pretty Beach. The one she'd rather forget.

She drove carefully through the lanes with the double yellow lines, over the cobbled back streets and past vast old Victorian villas with big double-width black doors and old-fashioned street lights.

She looked up at the curtain of huge white-gold lights crisscrossing the lanes - it was subtle, elegant and whoever was in charge of Christmas at the council had done a most excellent job. It was still a while yet until they would be turned on, but the installations were going well. On each of the old-fashioned street lights, huge baskets full of ivy and pansies spilt out, ready for the large gold baubles that would hang down towards the street below.

She drove slowly through making mental notes of what she could get pictures of for her stories on social media once Christmas arrived and the lights were turned on. Her friend Sallie had given her loads of tips and her following had climbed significantly since she'd started sharing bits and bobs of Pretty Beach, and more importantly so had her sales.

Juliette carried on driving slowly along Strawberry Hill Lane looking up at all the beautiful houses including Strawberry Hill house on the right. It was spectacular but in a state. Peeling plaster was falling off the walls and the window frames throughout were painted a horrible grim yellow. Not that she'd be complaining about the colour of the paintwork if she could live in a five-storey Victorian house by the sea.

She sat there looking up at it. Vast, beautiful and goodness would it rock Christmas.

She sighed and pulled away, and as she crawled along in the traffic her phone rang in her bag and she pressed the button on the steering wheel to answer as she drove through Pretty Beach towards the bay.

'Juliette, it's Jeremy.' As if she didn't know who it was - she'd been married to him for ten long years and he was currently looking after their daughter.

'Hi Jeremy.' She did her utmost to sound bright, cheerful even.

Deep breaths, positive thoughts, deep breaths, positive thoughts.

'I'm just clarifying the additive rule,' he stated, his voice alone irritating her.

'Do you mean that Maggie doesn't do well with too many sweets and soft drink Jeremy?'

'Yes. We're at the party and I've seen the cake is covered in jelly sweets and what with her food allergy I thought I'd better phone you. Concerned dad and all that.'

Jeremy was trying to make out that he was concerned, but in actual fact it was all just for show, she was sure of it. Maggie didn't have a food allergy as such and he knew it, Juliette had just worked out that if Maggie had too much sugar and too many artificial colours she would be running around for hours like crazy and Juliette wanted to avoid that, if at all possible, at all costs.

'That's fine Jeremy. She just can't have too much,' Juliette replied as brightly as she could muster, while she looked out the window at a young mum walking hand in hand with a child dressed in a pretty red velvet coat, cream tights and sweet little Mary Jane shoes.

'So she is allowed the cake?' Jeremy persisted.

'Yes, she can have the cake.'

'Okay just checking - always like to take care of my girl, you know that Juliette,' he said calmly, in a sickly-sweet tone.

Ha she thought to herself - he didn't care so much when it came to putting his hand in his pocket for her school uniform or ballet lessons. Then he always had to comment about how much it all cost.

She pressed end on the call, carried on through Pretty Beach, past Holly's bakery and White Cottage Flowers, and smiled as she pulled into Seapocket Lane. It was so pretty at any time of the year, but in the cold weather with people bustling around in coats and hats, it really was quite the perfect little small-town scene.

She drove slowly down the lane looking for a spot. Odd there weren't any spaces and she thought that someone must be having a get-together. On the right a man was getting out of a BMW, he looked vaguely familiar. Where did she know that face from? Oh yes.

She drove round again and reversed into a space at the top of the road, got out of her car, wrapped her coat tightly around her, went around to open the boot to get her midwifery bag out and nearly jumped out of her skin when a male voice from the pavement interrupted her thoughts.

'Hello again.'

She turned around. Yes that's where she recognised him from - the guy in the hospital car park. What was his name again? Luke. Luke with the broad, muscular chest, short floppy brown hair and deep brown eyes. That Luke.

'Oh hello.' She pretended to look confused as if she couldn't remember where she knew him from.

'Newport Reef - the car park. You gave me the tip about parking over by the lights.'

'Oh yes, yes of course. Sorry! Long day and all that,' she said, feigning that she suddenly recognised him when in fact as soon as she'd looked at him she'd remembered almost everything about him. Most especially the eyes. The eyes were unforgettable. And the chest, the chest was pretty nice too.

'I'm Luke, as I said before. Luke Burnette.' He held out his hand and waited for her to introduce herself.

But Juliette didn't reply because she was taking in the chest and the eyes and not able to say much at all. He moved his outheld hand closer, and it jolted her out of her thoughts.

'Oh sorry, yes. I'm Juliette.'

'Well, nice to meet you again, Juliette.'

He turned around and took a few steps down the pavement, heading back towards Pretty Beach laneway.

'It's very busy in the laneway today.' She said heaving her bag over her shoulder and pointing down to the end of the road and the start of the shops.

'I'm not going shopping, actually, I've just got home - that's my new house, the cottage right at the end of the road,' Luke said, gesturing to the house all the way down the end of the lane with the sold sign outside.

Juliette's eyes widened further. Luke, broad-chested Luke was moving into the lane, her lane.

'Well welcome to Pretty Beach, Luke. It's a fabulous place to live,' Juliette said and smiled, trying to look as casual as possible, and picking up her equipment, pressed the button to lock the boot of her car and walked down towards her cottage.

Juliette walked all the way along Seapocket Lane, rummaged around to find her keys in the inside pocket of her bag and turned into her cottage closing the gate behind her. She unlocked the door, closed it quietly behind her, kicked off her shoes at the same time and clicked the door shut against the cold.

She walked through the sitting room, down the little steps and through the middle room to the kitchen which was bathed in shimmering light from her lanterns. She plonked down her bag and case on the table and took off her coat.

So, she had a new neighbour, a very nice new neighbour going by the name of Luke.

Chapter 7

A few days later Juliette walked all the way down Seapocket Lane, looked down happily at the ruffles poking through the bottom of her pink coat and took a sip of her peppermint mocha as she gazed in through all the little windows of the cottages, wondering if she would ever have her own home again. Not that she was complaining, she'd struck gold renting where she was and the cottage was about a million times better than the poky little flat they'd been in. But she wanted to settle, to paint things and plant things and feel like things were hers again after the years since she'd left Jeremy when everything had been up in the air.

She strolled along past Pretty Beach Fire Station and made her way to the museum where the council offices were housed out the back. She walked into the stone-walled car park, down past the community hall where a playgroup was going on and into the council building.

There was not a single person in the waiting room except for a very large, very loud woman with dyed red hair who was waving a novel around her head and asking one of the staff behind the counter if she knew just who she was.

Juliette looked at the touch screen machine with the huge signs above it informing people to put in their details and take a ticket - she touched the screen, scanned her driving licence and a printed ticket with a bar code and number miraculously emerged from the machine and informed her that she had an approximate seven-minute wait.

She couldn't see how it was going to be a seven-minute wait - there was not a soul in the place and four staff sitting there seriously studying their computer screens not seeming to be doing anything much at all.

The loud, plump woman with the overly dyed red hair and glossy red lipstick some of it stuck onto her front teeth had started to raise her voice and proceeded to ask the young girl behind the counter if she had heard of her as she was a top author and very well known. The other three staff continued to stare at their computers and the woman announced to anyone who would listen that she was a very famous author and had sold more books than this young girl had had hot dinners, and she had added, she'd achieved all that fame before the young girl had even been born.

Juliette continued to study her ticket, biting her bottom lip to force herself not to get involved and the longer she stood there the more she realised that she'd also seen the woman and this whole scenario play out a few years before in the reception of Pretty Beach Surgery.

She hadn't recognised the woman at first because the woman had been a lot slimmer then and with jet black dyed hair - then she had been spouting on about not being able to get an appointment straight away and how when you were as famous as her it was just not good enough.

Juliette continued to watch it all play out until the young woman clearly pressed a button on the computer and Roy Johnson came striding out of the back office, took the woman off to the side and began to tell her calmly, quietly and in no uncertain terms that she was not welcome if she raised her voice to his staff.

Just as Juliette was enjoying the spectacle the screen informed her to move forward to the counter where she recognised Julie sitting behind in a dark blue Pretty Beach Council collared shirt topped with a bright pink string of chunky beads.

'Hi Juliette, how are you? Cold enough for you?'

'I'm good thanks, Julie. Yep, the weather's certainly turned.'

Juliette knew Julie from Pretty Beach and the surgery and they chatted as Julie keyed Juliette's details into the computer and started to work out quite what the mix up was with Juliette's council tax.

'How're you getting on in Seapocket Lane?' Julie asked.

'Fabulous, shame I'm almost certain I won't be able to afford to buy there though. But it's a whole lot better than that depressing flat we were in, so there is that.'

'You're getting a good deal then with Sallie are you, my lovely?'

'Yep, she's been initiated into the Pretty Beach way and I'm getting the benefit of it.' Juliette laughed as Julie continued to scroll through the computer.

'So you should, you're an asset to this town my lovely. Not many midwives like you around, I can tell you that.'

'Ah, don't be silly, just doing my job.'

'You're joking my lovely - I've been around here a long time and you are the best we've had, and don't you forget it.'

'Thank you, Julie, I'll take the compliment,' Juliette said, looking over the counter and smiling.

Julie put her hands into her peroxide blonde hair ruffled it out to puff it up a bit more and looked at Juliette directly, leaning over the counter, her electric blue eyeliner and fuschia lips deadly serious as she leant forward and lowered her voice.

'A little birdie may have told me that old Mr Jenkin might be going into a home and his old cottage could be coming up for sale in Mermaids.'

'Really? Oh, I didn't hear that at work.'

'Well, you wouldn't have done yet - my sister does his meals and she was in there the other day doing the fridge out and his daughter was down from London and on the phone to the home. According to Sandra, if they can get him in, they're going to sell the house as quickly as they can to get rid of it.'

'Interesting. I don't suppose I'll be able to afford it, though.'

'It's round the back there, in Mermaids, you know? A bit cheaper down behind the laneway, aren't they? Never understood why myself because the ones right down by the beach get all the noise in the summer from the tourists.'

'True, true, you're right they are a bit cheaper up there between the laneway and the hill.'

'Well there you go - not that it matters to me, my lovely. Quite happy with my new build on the estate, my nice central heating and double glazing and fifteen-minute walk into town, thank you very much.'

'You're funny - nothing like a bit of central heating though, I have to admit.'

'My lovely, I grew up in one of those fisherman's cottages - freezing cold in the winter it was, used to be ice on the inside of the windows in those days. You couldn't pay me all the tea in China to live in one of those again.' Julie leant back over to her computer, puffed up her hair and continued to click through Juliette's account.

She chatted as she was working out what had gone wrong with the council tax.

'My lovely, you should pop over and have a look, it's on Mermaid Lane.'

'I presume it will go up with Shane Pence then, you think?'

'I'd be very surprised at that... Shane Pence and Nicky Jenkin, let's just say there's not a lot of love lost there.'

'Oh, well, you learn something new every day, I never knew that.'

'Nope, not many people do, but when someone like Nicky Jenkin breaks your heart you don't forget it lightly.'

'Assume they'll put it on the market through someone in Newport Reef then.'

'Assume they will, that is unless someone puts a note under the door and says they're interested in the house and wants to buy it directly to save on all the fees.'

Julie passed a print out back over the counter to Juliette, pressed her fuschia lips together and nodded her head.

Juliette stuffed the print out into her handbag, said goodbye to Julie and walked out with a spring in her step at the thought of Mr Jenkin's house going for a low price and maybe being able to own her own home in Pretty Beach.

Chapter 8

Juliette did up Maggie's coat, put her basket full of parcels over her arm, took hold of Maggie's hand and stepped onto the pavement. The mild weather they'd thought it was when they had been getting ready in the cottage now seemed freezing as they stood in Seapocket Lane. Juliette pulled Maggie's hat out of her basket and put it on her head over her little blonde curls. She looked down at Maggie's double-layered pink corduroy skirt, thick grey tights and polka dot boots hoping that she would be warm enough.

They walked all the way along Seapocket Lane to the end, past Luke's sold house on the corner, looked down at the waves crashing onto the beach and turned right onto the laneway. Pretty Beach locals pottered along - a mum Juliette knew from school waved from the other side of the road, Pete from Seashells Cottages walked past and nodded hello and a woman in a lurid green jumper smiled as she hurried past with two loaves of French bread sticking out of a basket. White Cottage Flowers was just starting to look like the scene from the front of a greetings card with vintage ladders piled high with pots full of tiny little Winter plants wrapped in hessian and tied with white bows.

They continued along the laneway, Maggie holding tightly onto Juliette's hand in her sweet little pink mittens and passed Pretty Beach Fish and Chips, its roof completely covered in pastel blue icicle lights and Jessica the owner outside taking down the bunting ready for baubles.

'Ahh, isn't it all so pretty, Maggie?'

'Yes, mummy. Look! Look over there.' Maggie pointed to the bakery and a huge white crystal reindeer on the roof of the shop.

'Oh yes, it's beautiful. Father Christmas has a reindeer on the bakery roof. I can't wait until the turning on of the lights party!'

Maggie continued looking up at the reindeer as they strolled further along the laneway. Just as they got to the end, the lighthouse on the cliff glinting in the distance, they saw Sallie over the road, rugged up in a big coat and scarf over black skinny jeans, walking over the tiny bridge from the Boat House. Sallie waved, waited for a gap in the traffic and crossed over.

'Hello you two lovelies. How are you and where are you off to, the post office?'

'We're going to post the parcels and then we're going to the cafe for some hot chocolate,' Maggie replied.

'That sounds lovely. Have you seen Holly's reindeer on the roof over there Maggie? She's starting to get all her decorations ready.'

'We just walked past, I'll have to find out where she got that, it's so pretty.' Juliette replied.

'I know, I thought the same - cost a fortune if I know Holly. That's going to look gorgeous when we finally get the lights turned on and Pretty Beach is all ready for Christmas,' Sallie said.

'Fancy joining us for a hot chocolate then? As long as the queue isn't too long we should be finished at the post office and in Maisy's in about half an hour.'

'I'll take you up on that,' said Sallie as she pulled her gloves out of her pockets. 'See you in there then. Bye Maggie.'

Juliette and Maggie turned back and continued along the pavement, past the Boat House all the way to the end to Pretty Beach Post Office. Juliette sighed as she saw the line nearly out the door and saw the lovely poster on the noticeboard with a picture of the Boat House covered in snow announcing the Pretty Beach Christmas Dance.

'Good job we've got an account, I wouldn't want to be queuing up in that,' she said to Maggie. 'Right, now over there to the Drop and Go desk and you can put all the parcels over the counter.'

Just as they had finished with their parcels, Juliette had put her basket back over her arm and was looking at the back door ready to go, a voice called out.

'Helloooo, Juliette, excuse me, I think you dropped this!'

Juliette turned around and slap bang in front of her in a dark-grey cable-knit jumper, scarf and holding up a small pink mitten was the man from the hospital car park, the man who had bought a house down the end of her road, and the man she now knew as Luke.

'I saw it fall out of your pocket.'

'Oh, thank you. Goodness, we didn't want to lose that, did we?' she said to Maggie.

'So who have we got here then?' Luke asked, smiling down at Maggie.

'This is my daughter Maggie.'

'Nice to meet you Maggie,' he held out his hand seriously, 'I'm Luke.'

Maggie giggled, took his hand and he shook it gently.

'What are you two up to then? I saw you had rather a lot of parcels there and you were in the lucky queue - the one with no one in it!'

'We were posting our parcels of special things for mummy's Christmas ladies.'

'You have Christmas ladies? My goodness that sounds nice.'

Juliette smiled back, 'I have a little hobby, selling Christmas bits and bobs and at this time of year it starts to get busier and we had quite the haul of parcels to get down here.'

'I think I might need a few special things myself in my new house. I need a bit of help with decor. Never really was my strong point.'

Juliette looked up at Luke in the grey jumper, thought how much she wouldn't mind helping him with his decor, went towards the post office door and waved goodbye.

Chapter 9

Juliette had just taken off her coat, got Maggie set up at the table, made sure Maggie's mittens were safely tucked in her bag and was sitting down looking at the menu when Sallie strolled into Maisy's cafe and came and sat down.

'It's busy in Pretty Beach today. Everyone seems to be rushing around,' Sallie said, taking off her coat and putting it on the back of her chair.

'Yep, the queue for the post office was long. Thank goodness I've got the account or we would have been in the queue for ages,' Juliette said, taking off Maggie's coat.

She passed Sallie a menu and they sat there deciding what to have. Juliette settled on a slice of homemade chocolate cake, Sallie on a cinnamon muffin and Maggie a hot chocolate.

'So, from the number of parcels you had the shop's doing well, is it?' Sallie asked.

'It is - I've put a lot of work into it this year - the social media accounts, the website upgrade...' She trailed off.

'I suppose you'll be getting repeat customers now too.'

'Definitely - the customers know they're going to get a lovely parcel from me and good customer service if anything goes wrong, together with word of mouth marketing my repeat customer base has grown exponentially,' Juliette said as the cake and muffin arrived. 'I've been thinking of doing a special offer to my real regulars - like a Christmas treat from my shop. I would do it as an exclusive email to my newsletter list and have a limited number of pretty parcels available - each one with special bits and bobs in from my collection. Sort of like an Advent calendar.'

Sallie stirred her tea, 'Sounds like a good idea. Would you make enough money on it?'

'It wouldn't be like I'd won the lottery, but I've already got the products - then I'd bulk it out with lower-cost things that I've found that people love,' Juliette mused as she took another forkful of cake. 'The thing is, they love getting the parcels now - I even market it that way, so a one-off Christmas parcel with specially curated bits and bobs from the shop would work well and the effort involved wouldn't be too much.'

'Sounds heavenly, I'd love to receive one,' Sallie said, leaning over and helping to colour in a daisy Maggie was drawing in her notebook. 'Yup, especially if you popped in one of those Christmas scented candles you designed - I've never had anything smell as much like Christmas, though the Orangery gets close.'

'Hmm, they're quite heavy for the postage, but they sell like crazy and the feedback has been phenomenal on those.'

'It would smell as soon as the parcel arrived through the door - the ones you left me for the boathouse cottage were scenting the sitting room before I'd even opened the box.'

'You're right - they do fill the room, even before they're lit.'

'It's a great idea, Juliette, and if you do it as an exclusive it'll create a bit of urgency.'

'You know what? I think I will - I'll just have to work out how long it will take me if there are a lot of orders.'

'Well I'm happy to help out - once December comes around, we'll have to have an evening wrapping your lovely Christmas bits with Baileys and mince pies.'

'That makes it sound a whole lot more palatable, it's amazing how much quicker things get done when you're not on your own.'

'Tell me about it - when I did the first wedding at the marquee there was really just me and I was running around like a madwoman in the run-up to it. Just getting the chairs in position took hours, now here we are with the Christmas Dance all organised and ready to go and it really wasn't much effort at all, what with all the help.'

'I'll need to get product photos done pronto though, it's only a few weeks before people start their Christmas shopping,' Juliette said.

'Why don't you come and do them in the Orangery now some of the decorations are up early? It would make a lovely backdrop with all the lights.'

Juliette leant her hand on her chin, 'You know what, that really would be great - a scene not seen before and all that.'

'Yup.' Sallie replied, 'Good for your social media pages too.'

They both looked over as Maggie who had been sitting there quietly with her colouring book looked up from what she was doing, smiled and waved at someone.

Juliette and Sallie followed Maggie's eyes and looked up to see Luke from the house down the end of her road, Luke from the post office passing their table.

'Oh hi again, I've finally made it out of the post office in one piece! Thought I might never see the light of day again.' Luke, lovely Luke with the huge brown eyes and broad chest said, smiling at all three of them.

'You're better off in here and you've found the best cafe in Pretty Beach so you're doing well.' Juliette looked up at him and smiled while Sallie's eyes were nearly falling out of her head at the specimen in the grey jumper in front of her.

'I thought so, I came in here a few times when I came to view the house. All I need to do now is find a good pub and I'll be all set.'

'Sorry, this is my friend Sallie,' Juliette said gesturing over to Sallie.

Sallie held out her hand, the huge diamond on her finger catching the light from above as Luke shook it firmly.

'Nice to meet you Luke. You've just moved into Pretty Beach have you?' Sallie asked gazing up at Luke.

'Yes, down the road here, Seapocket Lane,' Luke replied.

'Well, there are a lot worse spots around. You need to go to The Pretty Smugglers if you're looking for a pub - cosy with a fire and does the best selection of handcrafted beers you'll find.'

'Sounds just what I'm looking for. I'll look out for it. Anyway, I'll let you get back to it, enjoy your tea,' Luke said, gave a little wave to Maggie and proceeded to the other side of the cafe and lined up at the counter.

'Oh. My. Goodness! Who is that?' Sallie whispered over Maggie's head.

Juliette checked that Luke was well out of earshot and replied, 'My new neighbour - going by the name of Luke.'

'Goodness. Luke is a very nice addition to Pretty Beach. Do we know much about Luke? Do we know if Luke has a wife? A family?'

'I've no idea.' Juliette tried to remain nonchalant as Sallie asked more questions.

'Interesting, very interesting,' Sallie replied. 'I wonder what Holly knows about this situation,' Sallie said, smiling.

'I've no idea. Not for me Sallie - as I said before, after the you-know-what and the other thing, I'm out of the game.'

The other thing where she'd been so head over heels in love with Bella's father when she was eighteen that she hadn't cared about contraception. Unfortunately, he hadn't felt quite as over the moon when she'd told him about the baby, and he'd gone off to university. Juliette had been left with her heart smashed to smithereens and eighteen years and one marriage later she had still not fully recovered. Throw in the situation with Jeremy and she wasn't willing to let herself go anywhere near anyone quite possibly ever again.

'Hmm, yes. I do see your point. - that was quite the crash course in why not to get involved with anyone for the rest of your life,' Sallie agreed, whispering quietly so as not to let Maggie hear.

'But I don't know, Juliette, I'd get back in the game if old Luke there with the very nice chest and I must say, extremely, errm, pleasant bottom was the prize,' Sallie said and started to giggle as they both sat there looking over at Luke.

Juliette pretended it was all of little consequence to her as she sat there next to Sallie, but a little bit at the back of her mind was silently nodding and agreeing that Luke was a very nice prize indeed.

Chapter 10

Juliette stood in the doorway of the bedroom on the first floor of the cottage and walked over towards the wide sash window on the far wall. It was all very tired in this room, that was all that could be said really. Sallie had done a good job of ridding the place of the previous tenants, pulling out carpets, putting in new bathrooms and painting most of the rooms but this room had not been decorated because of problems with the walls. As Juliette looked around it now, she was very thankful that everywhere else had been done. It would have been a very different kettle of fish to move into the cottage if it was all in the same state as this room still was.

When they'd first moved in Maggie had gone into the small room on the other side of the corridor with its soft grey panelling, but it was small, at the front of the house and not looking out to the sea and Juliette wanted to get her in the bigger room.

She stood there in her painting clothes faced with what was quite a lot of potential in the large room with the sea views, but what was also quite a lot of work. The first thing she would need to do would be to get rid of the awful grey and yellow wallpaper on the feature wall, lighten up the dark grey floorboards, paint the tall scuffed and peeling Victorian skirting boards and door surrounds.

Determined to break the back of it and with Maggie out on a play date, she got a bucket and sponge and started to methodically wipe the walls down with a soapy solution crossing her fingers the wallpaper would fall off easily. An hour later, Pretty Beach radio playing in the background and a family-sized pack of Minstrels by her side and Juliette had stripped the feature wall, cleared up all the fallen wallpaper and silently asked herself why she had thought doing all this on her day off was a good idea.

Next, after scraping off all of the remaining bits of wallpaper, she moved onto the skirting boards with a small block and sandpaper.

On her hands and knees, she sanded all the way round, rubbing away years of wear and knocks and bumps from another family at another time.

By lunchtime the woodwork was ready to be primed, the walls were dry and she stood at the window looking out over the Orangery roof at the bottom of the garden, and at the little fishing boats bobbing up and down. She watched the ferry chug past over towards Pearl Beach and rays of sunshine glinted off the water. Her phone started buzzing in her pocket.

'Hey, mum. How are you?' Bella asked.

'Good, what are you up to?'

'Assignments coming out of my ears and shifts at the pub and not a lot else. I wish I had more exciting news to deliver, but I don't,' Bella said, sighing.

'Ha, well I've been stripping wallpaper and crawling around on my hands and knees sanding down skirting boards, so I don't know what's worse.'

'Sounds fun! Not. Well, you'll love it when it's done. All pretty and girlie for Maggie. I'm really missing Maggie. Let me have a look at the wallpaper you bought.'

'Hang on. It's still downstairs.' Juliette replied, walking across the bedroom.

Juliette turned the phone onto video, stepped carefully down the steep stairs and pattered across the middle room to the kitchen at the back.

The bag of wallpaper was sitting on the pink table in the kitchen, and she took it out of the bag, pulled off the wrapper and held it up to the camera showing Bella the tiny little dusky pink flowers on a white background.

'That's so pretty. Maggie's going to love it! She loves pink bits just as much as you do,' Bella said into the screen of the phone.

'I know. I'm thinking of doing the skirting boards in this pink-white and the same to the floor,' Juliette said holding up a can of paint.

'Oh my. Pale pink floorboards - that sounds divine. What about Sallie, what did she say about it all? Is she okay with you painting them?'

'She said do whatever I like once she saw how I've done the sitting room etcetera, so I've been lucky - most landlords never let you touch anything.' Juliette replied, smiling into the phone at Bella who was sitting on the bed in her room.

'Wow, that cottage is like everything you want to buy in a house,' Bella said.

'I know, but I won't be able to afford Seapocket Lane.'

Juliette finished the call to Bella, went back upstairs and spent the rest of the afternoon grappling with the removable wallpaper. By four, marvelling at the ease of it, she'd papered the whole of the wall behind the bed and it was now covered in the beautiful dusky pink flowery paper.

Next was to put up the beautiful white linen ruffled lampshade she'd bought online when they knew they were going to be moving into the cottage. She dragged a stepladder over, grabbed the oversized light fitting, and balancing on the top step of the ladder, fixed the linen ruffle shade over the bare bulb.

She stood back and looked at her work - it was already looking a million times better. The other walls were in a plain matte white and coordinated beautifully with the wallpaper and the shade.

She cleared up the offcuts of the wallpaper, put the lid back on the paint and closed the window. Up next was the floor and then it would nearly be ready for Maggie's beautiful wrought-iron white bed to be brought in and she'd have to somehow work out how to fix the pale pink fabric canopy above it.

***

Juliette finished off sweeping the old wide floorboards with the broom to get rid of any remaining dust. The floorboards were in excellent condition, they'd obviously been covered in carpet or rugs since the day they were fitted, so all she had needed to do was lightly sand them down and put on the floor primer.

It was her first time painting floorboards - Jeremy liked glossy, modern floor tiles and had them fitted in their house and she'd hated them. Every time the underfloor heating had come on she'd looked down at the floor and wished for the thick old floorboards she'd gazed longingly at in country homes. She'd always loved the look of stripped and painted floorboards and they were one of the main must-haves on her wish list for a cottage... and here she was with just what she wanted and about to paint them pale pink.

After slowly painting on the primer, she stood there looking down at the floorboards; the primer had done exactly what it said on the tin and seemed to have worked. She'd read all sorts online about tannins bleeding through, and she didn't know if it was luck or what, but so far so good. She'd asked Sallie what she thought and she'd said she'd painted all sorts over the years, never with any problems.

A few hours later, once the primer had dried, she opened the can of floor paint and crossed her fingers that the colour she'd had mixed actually matched the vision in her head. She stirred it through with an old screwdriver, and examined it closely. It was just as she'd asked for - the palest, almost white pink. She'd seen something like it online years ago and fallen in love with it and it had been in the back of her mind ever since... when she'd seen the bedroom in the cottage the pink floorboard idea had come flooding back.

Crouching down on the floor Juliette began to paint the pink over the primer and painstakingly one by one painted each of the floorboards carefully going around the old fireplace. Slowly as she moved backwards towards the door it began to take shape - the soft pink worked beautifully with the strong white of the old fireplace surround and skirting boards.

The floor finished the room off, bounced around the light and contrasted with the white walls. It picked up the tiny bits of pink in the wallpaper and with the huge white soft ruffled lampshade the whole room had become softer and more feminine. Slowly her dream for Maggie's room was starting to take place.

She groaned as she stood up, her knees creaking - crawling around on the floor was not good for her back or anything else these days and doing everything on her own took a long time and a lot of dedication.

She walked over the tiny little hallway with the jute carpet and into the smaller box room with the timber built-in wardrobes and took out a pale pink paisley eiderdown she'd found in the back of a charity shop in Seafolly. She walked back over the landing and held it up against the wall and the pink floor.

It was just as she thought, the pale pink pulled the colours out of the eiderdown beautifully - she would have the eiderdown carefully folded at the end of the bed and Maggie could pull it up when she was cold.

She mentally went through her list, all she needed now before Maggie moved into the bigger room were curtains and something to put in the grate of the fire. Then Juliette would need to finish painting her bedside table and bring up the huge wicker toy box she'd temporarily stored in the Summer House at the end of the garden.

Carefully folding the eiderdown up and putting it back in the cupboard she looked out the window at a couple whose birth she had been at about a month before out walking with their tiny little baby in a pram. Just as she turned back a car caught her eye, a very nice navy-blue car, the same navy-blue car that had been in the hospital car park. She stood behind the curtain and peeked to the left as the car reversed into one of the last spots in Seapocket Lane.

She watched as Luke Burnette got out of the car, reached in and took his bag off the back seat, closed the door, pressed the alarm and walked along down the lane towards his new house.

Wow, she thought, I could get used to seeing him walking down my road, very used to it indeed.

Chapter 11

A few days later, Juliette Sparkles had finished clearing up the breakfast dishes, neatly stacked the dishwasher, sprayed the sides down in the kitchen with raspberry scented spray, straightened up the dusty pink checked display tea towels on the oven and mopped the kitchen floor.

She'd put on Maggie's coat, they'd walked outside and she had hold of Maggie's gloved hand and they'd walked down Seapocket Lane on the way to drop off her parcels for A Christmas Sparkle. Then they were going to take a swift detour to Mr Jenkin's house to deliver a note through the letterbox that she was in the market to buy a house as a serious buyer with her finances ready to go - finances that weren't huge, but were there.

They walked down the laneway, popped into the bakery to nab the last of the batch of Holly's vanilla buns and Holly made Maggie a hot chocolate topping it with brightly coloured sprinkles.

Maggie had been quite enchanted by the sprinkles and the reindeer on top of Holly's roof and Holly had taken them through the shop, out through the back to show Maggie it from behind and let her have a go at changing the flashing lights to all the different sequences and all the different colours.

'We're not meant to be turning on the lights yet until the official lighting up ceremony but I'll let you have a little go,' Holly said to Maggie.

Maggie stood there with the remote control flicking the switch, standing back and watching the lights above turn to blue, then red and green.

'It's a lovely one, Holly - some of them can look quite tacky unless you spend a lot of money,' Juliette noted.

'It wasn't a budget buy I can tell you that, but I thought I'd give the shop a present this year and people haven't stopped talking about it, even though we're not yet officially turning them on. In fact I think I may have even started a new Pretty Beach tradition.'

'You'll have to get all the shops in the laneway to follow suit.'

'I don't know about that. Anyway, what are you two lovelies up to today?' Holly asked as she pottered around in the back room of the bakery.

'Did you hear about Mr Jenkin? I'm not sure why I'm asking actually, you know everything that goes on in Pretty Beach,' Juliette replied, asking Holly if she knew anything more about Mr Jenkin the old man in Mermaids Julie at the council had told Juliette was going into a home.

'Yep, I certainly did - going into the home at Seafolly Beach as far as I know. I remember when he used to come in here after a night of fishing and now look at him. Sad really, he was good to me when we first got here from Vietnam,' Holly said, sadly.

'I know, it is sad when it gets to this stage. So Julie at the council's sister Sandra heard that the daughter is going to put the house up for sale.'

'Ha, it won't be with Shane Pence then, I can tell you that for certain,' Holly said.

'Julie said exactly the same!'

'She's going through an estate agent at Seafolly.'

'How do you know?'

'Ahhh, I have my feelers out, Juliette,' Holly said laughing.

Juliette popped a piece of one of the vanilla buns in her mouth and helped Maggie change the colours over on the remote control as Maggie stood in the doorway looking up at the roof.

'I was going to put a note through the door to say that I'm an interested buyer - see if they'd be interested in selling that way, but if it's already going on the market maybe I won't bother.'

Holly sucked in through her teeth and looked at Juliette earnestly.

'Don't know about that and even if they did, that daughter of his, sheesh, she's a one. Rory knows her. I tell you what, why don't I get him to have a word with her? I know he bumps into her quite often. His flat is near her huge house in town.'

'Every little helps I suppose, but, to be honest Holly, I don't think I'll have a hope of affording it. It's just that Julie mentioned that her sister said it's in quite a state and they just want to get rid of it and so the price might reflect that.'

'She's certainly right there. The last time I delivered some bread, I let myself in and I nearly cried. That daughter of his should be ashamed of herself, living up there in luxury in her huge house in town. The whole place stunk of wee and damp and goodness knows what. I spent an hour in there myself cleaning up the kitchen. Getting it for a good price though, I very much doubt that if Nicky is involved - she wouldn't give anyone anything without a fight.'

'I guess I've got nothing to lose though really,' Juliette said, quietly.

'No you haven't, but I wouldn't get your hopes up and I wouldn't be going into any kind of negotiations with Nicky Jenkin - she is one not very nice person, always found that so strange what with her lovely, kind parents and all.'

'Gosh Holly, I've never heard you say anything like that before!'

'I know. Well there was the thing with Shane Pence, and then how she let her dad end up in that state, and then there was how she treated Nel at school, quite the little bully she was there it turned out... yeah not a very nice one. You'd be doing well to give her a wide berth as they say.'

'Well thanks for the heads-up, I'll keep that in mind.'

**

Juliette held tightly onto Maggie's hand as they wound their way behind Pretty Beach laneway, through the one-way streets, past posters on lampposts for the Pretty Beach Christmas Dance, which was earlier than usual because the village hall roof was being repaired, and to the area of Pretty Beach commonly referred to as Mermaids. They came to the left fork in the road to Mermaid Lane and walked two-thirds of the way along the long line of three-storey, terraced houses with neat gardens, all painted in the pastel colours of Pretty Beach.

'That's a lovely house.' Maggie piped up holding onto her hot chocolate and pointing to one in the middle painted a dusty blue with white bay windows and a white bee hive in the front garden.

'It is darling,' Juliette sighed wistfully.

Just as they were approaching Mr Jenkin's house she noticed a For Sale sign on the other side of the road further down at the end. She hadn't seen it come up on the internet so it must have only just been put on the market - what with the Christmas shop, and her extra shifts, looking for a house had gone a little bit down her priorities list, maybe she had missed the notification for it.

They stopped in the middle of the pavement and she got her phone out of her pocket, opened up the We Move website, typed Pretty Beach into the search bar and hit go. It came up straight away, 34 Mermaid Lane. She scrolled through the pictures and heaved a big, disappointed sigh - 34 Mermaid Lane was out of her budget, just far enough out of her budget that even if they were willing to take an offer, which would be highly unlikely in Pretty Beach, she wouldn't be able to afford it.

Juliette felt a tear well up in the back of her eyes, put her phone back in the pocket of her pink wrap coat and pulled herself together.

Is this better than always being on a diet and living with Jeremy? she asked herself in her head.

Yes, she replied in her mind. *Yes, it most definitely is.*

'Come on Maggie, let's walk down the end here, then we'll go back down and past the Boat House, along the jetty, have a look and

see if we can see any fish then we'll go home and make some chocolate cake and video call Bella, what do you think of that idea?'

Maggie nodded and they walked further along Mermaid Lane
until they got to Mr Jenkin's house - it was the eyesore on the street
and compared to all the pretty houses painted in their pastel ice-
cream colours it looked very much like it needed some love.

The timber, pale blue door had last seen a fresh coat of paint a
very long time ago, and in the little round window to the side, broken glass had been fixed up with brown tape. The tiny lawn surrounded by black railings was more weed than grass and an old wheelbarrow thick with stinging nettles sat in the corner under the window.

Juliette reached into her bag to take out the little white envelope
where she'd written a note with her phone number and details saying
that she was interested in the house.

Just as they walked up the path, a red Volvo pulled up outside
the house and a tall, thin woman with a razor-sharp platinum bob
and a bright red blazer with gold buttons got out, slammed the door,
clicked the remote alarm and called out.

'Excuse me, can I help you?' Her shrill voice tore through the
peace and quiet of Mermaid Lane.

'I'm interested in the house - we heard it was for sale didn't we
Maggie?' Juliette said.

The woman in the bright red jacket looked Juliette up and down
taking in her pale pink coat, her curled hair and pom pom covered
scarf, completely ignored Maggie and pointed one of her long, red
talons at Juliette.

'You are, are you? We've not decided yet, but it will be going up
for sale with Seafolly Homes if it does go up for sale. I might just
keep it and do it up for holiday rental though. We heard that this old
dump could fetch a bit now that Pretty Beach is more accessible. Not
that we need the money, of course. But we could throw some money

at it and make some more.' The woman said her lip curling in distaste at the tall, terraced house in Mermaid Lane.

'If you're interested in this then you must be one of two things and to be quite honest I don't know which really, either completely mad wanting to live in a place like Pretty Beach or desperate. It's not exactly happening around here, is it?'

Peace, peace, peace, Juliette repeated to herself over and over as this angular woman looked down her nose at her and continued jabbing at her with the long fingers.

'As I said, we might keep the little dump - the best thing I ever did was move out of this place,' the woman said, nodding her head up and down and holding her hand out in front of her examining the long, red shiny fingernails.

'Right, okay,' Juliette said, taking in the pointy nose, overpowering perfume and immaculate hair.

'We can take your number - I can get my assistant to give you a call when we decide I suppose, I mean who likes paying bills from an estate agent?' she said holding out her hand to Juliette.

'Okay, thanks, that would be great,' Juliette said, offering the envelope with her details inside to the hideous woman.

'I'm thinking that on this side of the road, obviously the side with the sun, with the long garden out the back and the sea views from the upstairs rooms and the outhouse at the back that it will be quite a bit more than number 34 over the road.'

Juliette felt her heart sink as the woman with the red jacket, red lips and impeccable hair started talking into her phone, held out her hand, took the envelope from Juliette, signalled to them that she was finished with them and pushed on past.

Juliette looked on as the woman stalked down the path and sighed heavily to herself, all her high hopes that she might be able to afford a place on Mermaid Lane dashed in precisely sixty seconds by a woman in a red suit.

Chapter 12

The next day, Juliette pulled into the car park of Waterlock House prep school, parked her car, opened the door for Maggie, put Maggie's straw boater carefully on her head and backpack on her back and they strolled into the school. The huge old house stood majestically behind them and the chapel bells rang indicating that school would be starting soon.

'Morning Maggie,' Miss Henshaw, Maggie's unbelievably young, unbelievably pretty teacher who made Juliette feel four hundred years old said as they approached the inner gate and Maggie kissed Juliette goodbye.

'Thanks Miss Henshaw,' Juliette said smiling. 'Stay warm today - there's an icy wind on the way according to the weather forecast.'

Miss Henshaw smiled back and Juliette walked back across the grounds carefully avoiding the school mums, and especially Feony Gaterham. Feony liked to think she was the alpha mum of the school, but really was a desperate try-hard on every committee going because it made her appear popular. Feony took great pleasure in making it her business to know the reading levels of the children who weren't hers, what went in the lunchboxes of other children and most importantly where they lived. When she'd found out that Juliette lived in a flat in Pretty Beach, she'd gone silent, coughed a little and had almost walked away. The only reason she still had the time of day for Juliette was because Juliette had gone up in her estimation when she'd found out firstly, who Juliette had been married to, and secondly, that Bella had sailed into Oxford and had achieved the best results at Waterlock House in its history.

Juliette had seen it all before with school mums like Feony when Bella was young and so steered herself onto the other side of the path, waved a faux cheery hello and hurried back to her car; getting stuck with Feony Gaterham was the last thing she wanted to do on any morning, but this morning she certainly was not in the mood. She got back to her car and headed over to her small storage space in Seafolly Beach she used to store her Christmas stock. She found a space, made sure she had the tag for the door and walked into the bright orange and blue industrial unit.

'Hey, Michael! Cold enough for you?' Juliette said as she walked into the brightly-lit lobby area.

Juliette had got to know Michael, the storage unit manager, over the years as she'd come in and out with boxes of Christmas products she'd ordered from around the world and in the busy periods she would drop in daily to pick out her orders, so they'd become quite firm friends.

'Juliette, I've got my thermals on this morning, so it must be cold. I said to my wife, the thermals are going on for the year! I thought of you in this weather and thought *well there's one good thing when it gets like this, Christmas sales will be up!*' He laughed and offered her a chocolate from a tin of Roses.

'Ha! Well, you'd be right. I've had loads of orders already, we've been packing and dropping them at the post office as fast as we can. Bit early to have the Roses out already! Ooh yes please though, I'd love a chocolate,' she said, dipping her hand into the tin of Roses, rummaging around and helping herself to two strawberry cremes.

'Need any help in there this morning then?' Michael asked.

'I think I'll be fine - I'll let you know, thanks,' Juliette replied, as she started to pull off her pom pom covered scarf.

'Rightio, see you on your way out - give me a shout if you want any help with the boxes.'

Juliette sucked on the chocolate, waved the fob over the keypad and the door slid open. She walked all the way along the narrow harshly-lit corridor to the small blocks at the end, opened the door to her unit, turned on the light and walked in.

As she walked around the room the ice-cold concrete floor and metal shelving racks made the cold weather outside seem warm. She opened the app on her phone and walked along picking out the orders; some for the replica vintage baubles she'd bought from overseas, some from the one-off range of vintage decorations she'd been collecting for years and some from the rustic collection she sold alongside her own things. Fifteen minutes later and she had all the orders collected and she'd also gathered a stash of the most popular products she predicted would sell in the next few days.

She walked back out carrying the huge plastic box, looked out over the top of it, said goodbye to Michael, made her way back to her car and pressed the button on the remote to open the boot. She popped the boxes in and drove back to Pretty Beach.

She drove all the way along Seapocket Lane, turned at the end and pulled up outside the double gates of the Orangery, the building at the end of her garden, also owned by her friend Sallie. Juliette got out of her car and pushed open the gate to the Orangery. Approaching the huge, arched door, she could see Sallie sitting at one of the tables, her laptop open, pen in hand and what looked like a large planner at her side. Sallie was concentrating hard, hadn't heard Juliette approach and seemed deep in thought, so Juliette tapped on the door gently. Sallie looked up and saw it was Juliette, got up from the table, pulled down the handle on the door and heaved it open.

Warm air and the scent of fir, citrus and botanicals hit Juliette's nose as Sallie kissed her on the cheek and closed the door behind her.

'Looking good, isn't it?' Sallie said as she gestured around to the decorations.

'That's an understatement. It looks stunning...' Juliette said, gazing at the decorations Sallie had already put up and wondering what they would look like as a backdrop for her new Christmas parcels idea.

Juliette had spent the last few days thinking about it, musing what her best and most loyal customers would want to receive as a special parcel exclusively sourced, chosen and wrapped by her, and more importantly, how much they would pay.

Juliette had gone over and over the idea in her head and couldn't really see a reason as to why not to do it - she had all the stock already, had loyal customers who loved anything she offered and it was the time of year where many women treated themselves.

She'd come to the conclusion that there would be a few different parcels which would arrive a few weeks apart and each filled with a combination of one-off vintage finds, her exclusive Christmas scents, the tiny little lip balms she handmade and the pom pom Christmas garlands she made in her spare time.

She'd already made up a few sample packages for photos, and today she was hoping bar any complication from either any of her ladies about to give birth or childcare, that she'd get them all photographed, up on her website and with any luck selling by the end of the day.

Juliette walked in, a basket over her arm with the parcels she'd already prepared and put the basket on the table next to Sallie.

'Cup of tea?' Sallie asked.

'Gosh, yes, I'd love one. It was all a bit of a rush this morning getting Maggie to school then I went straight to get stuff for the shop and I'm desperate for a cup of tea. All I've had is a handful of Roses.'

'You know Christmas is coming when you have Roses for breakfast!' Sallie said, chuckling.

Sallie went and made a pot of tea and then coming back in with a tray with two mugs, the teapot and a tray of shortbread, helped Juliette arrange the parcels on the white tablecloth with the Christmas lights as the background. They stood back, sipping on the tea and looked at the beautiful little pile of white gifts wrapped with pale gold ribbon, sprinkled with gold stars and the pretty lights glistening in the background behind it all.

'So, what did you decide on with what is going into the parcels?' Sallie asked.

'I knew I wanted each piece to have elements in common that my Christmas lovers would use and adore. Each parcel will be unique with some things that are one-of-a-kind. Some of the little clay decorations will be total one-offs and I'll add a few of those to each parcel. Other things will be bits I have collected over the years just because I thought they were wonderful and the last little thing I'm going to put in will be a few specialities from Pretty Beach - like Holly's shortbread and the tea from Maisy's and the dried botanicals in White Cottage Flowers.'

'Oh, that's such a great idea. Each parcel will be a delight to open and if they share what they get in your Facebook group, everyone will have something different, but with the same thing in common. Genius,' Sallie said, nodding her head in agreement.

'Yep, that's the plan.'

'It's great Juliette. I really like it,' Sallie concluded.

Juliette carried on fiddling with a piece of holly to get it exactly in the right place and replied, 'It's great for marketing and lovely to give my customers something really special but in terms of financially it will be the hand-selection thing which will mean I can charge more money for it.'

'Yeah, like you've curated a gift from your own private collection,' Sallie replied, touching the exquisitely packaged parcels on the table in front of them.

Juliette started to take images on her phone as Sallie stood to the side, moving things here and there to get just the right shot.

'Oh, how could I have forgotten to mention it? It turns out that Ben knows of your new neighbour.'

Juliette was concentrating on the image in the camera of her phone and pretended to be only mildly interested, when in actual fact, her ears had pricked up instantly.

'Oh really?'

'Yep - so you know the new GP?'

'I wish I didn't,' Juliette replied, moving a vintage bauble, zooming the camera in further and taking a few more shots.

'Well, he knew Luke through one of those stuffy old-school clubs in town. I can't remember the name of it, somewhere in Soho I think and that's how Luke came to hear about Pretty Beach.'

'Right - so he just came down here, plucked a house out of the air and bought it?'

'Seems that way. Anyway, yes, so Ben's younger brother, the one with all the children, well it turns out that Luke and him played water polo together years and years ago. Not close friends nowadays, but they know each other through water polo.'

'Interesting - so how does Ben know all this then?' Juliette replied, feigning that she was more interested in taking pictures of the parcels than she was in hearing more information on Luke.

'Ben's brother saw on Facebook that Luke had moved to Pretty Beach, thought it was a bit of a coincidence and sent Luke a message and Luke replied back that yes he'd moved down here because of the train as he was over living in town and wanted to rent it out up there and live down here.'

'It's a small world isn't it?'

'A very small world. I won't be complaining if there are more like Luke in Pretty Beach though.' Sallie said, and laughed as she opened up one of the white tissue paper packages and Juliette stood on the table and took shots of it all from above.

'I guess so.'

'You guess so. You sound quite nonplussed.'

'I am really - way too much on my plate to think about the man who just moved down the end of my road Sals,' Juliette said, while in her mind was thinking about hot-footing it back to her cottage and looking up online about men who played water polo.

Chapter 13

With Maggie at Jeremy's and not on call until the next day, Juliette had plenty of time to get the food ready for the evening. She hesitated to call it a dinner party, she couldn't stand the thought of 'entertaining' and all the connotations that came with that. It reminded her of her days when her wifely duties had included entertaining; which had actually meant Jeremy showing off to people at work, mostly local politicians and his old cronies at the yacht club that he had the requisite blonde, slim, tanned, perfectly capable, perfectly acceptable wife on his arm to tend to his every whim.

When Jeremy gave dinner parties he'd liked the food to be perfect, for there to be plenty of fancy courses and he preferred it if Juliette cooked it all from scratch. He liked her to make it all happen faultlessly, but that she didn't eat too much of it and that she went to a spin class the next day.

She stood at the little worktop in the cottage, looking out the window and chopped up leeks, grated some cheese and cut up potatoes for a creamy fish and leek pie; these days she was so far away from those times of fancy dinner party meals... nowadays she loved hearty, homemade comfort food and nothing better than inviting a few friends over for a cosy supper with wine, lots of food and to finish it all off with a nice box of chocolates by the fire.

Once the potatoes finished in the instant pot, she added copious amounts of butter, lots of sea salt, a lug of cream, mashed them up and ladled it all thickly onto the creamy fish and prawn mixture in the old-fashioned pie dish she'd inherited from one of the nurses at work.

Juliette's phone vibrated in her pocket as she was getting the pie ready to put in the oven. She answered it and her friend Daisy popped up on the screen.

'Hey, how are you?' Daisy asked.

'I'm good, just pottering around making a fish pie and a few other bits for Sallie and Ben coming over for supper tonight.'

'You mean you're making fish pie without me?' Daisy said, smiling into the screen.

'I certainly am - I mean if you wouldn't keep jetting off around the world and came down and visited me a bit more often I wouldn't have to be making fish pie that you wouldn't be eating. What have you been up to anyway?'

'Now you're asking.'

'Oh no, what? What are your latest woes?' Juliette replied.

'Nothing, nothing at all, it's just that I've been thinking...'

'Nooooooo, that's the first of our worries. Don't think Daisy, it doesn't really suit you that well does it?' Juliette said, laughing and scooping the leftover mashed potato out of the bowl and popping it into her mouth.

'I've been thinking Sparkles, that I am going to come down for Christmas, in fact, I might come for a weekend before that too,' Daisy said.

Juliette leant back on the kitchen counter and stopped scraping the spatula around the dish of mashed potato, moved closer and looked into the phone screen.

'Exciting!' Juliette said.

'Will you have room, will Bella be back?'

'Bella will be back, but there's enough room certainly - it's not like that awful flat we were stuck in.'

'Give me another tour then, you know what my memory is like!'

Juliette turned on the oven, put the fish pie in, turned the screen around on the phone and started to walk around the cottage.

'There's the little conservatory here and then this small room is an office with the sofa bed, so you'll be toasty in there if you want to come and Bella is back at the same time.'

Juliette walked out of the kitchen through the tiny middle room with the window out to the terrace and into the sitting room at the front.

'It's small, Daisy - small and cosy, ha!'

'Wow, you've made it lovely - you're allowed all your little floral bits now, I see,' Daisy replied, commenting on all the pretty floral lamps she wasn't allowed in her old house with Jeremy.

'Yup, I'm in pink and ditsy overload at the moment. Right, then we go up here to the first floor - what will be Maggie's bedroom, the box room and a bathroom. This big room was the only one not decorated because there was a problem with the plaster so it had awful paper I removed and I painted the floorboards a very pale pink,' Juliette said, walking around with the phone showing Daisy all the rooms.

'Then up here to the room in the attic - there's a really small bathroom, but it's all for me!'

Juliette held onto the bannister and climbed the steep stairs, out of breath by the time she reached the top.

She moved the phone around the room.

'My goodness, those stairs seem steep,' Daisy said.

'They're certainly making me fitter!'

'Sparkles, it looks delightful and you've made it really homely and cute.'

'Just how I want it - it's like I've been rebirthed in pink and florals.'

Juliette continued to walk down the stairs as she held onto the old timber bannister with one hand and held the phone out in front of her with the other.

'So why the sudden decision to come down at Christmas?'

'I dunno - work is all sorted and scheduled, my writing will tank a bit over the festive season and to be quite honest I'm sick of work and I've got loads of holiday to use up... and then, of course, there's what happened with Matt.'

'Yeah, I'm guessing that wasn't the best Christmas present you were ever going to get,' Juliette said.

'Nup, but then again, he was never going to leave her for me, was he?'

'No Daisy, he wasn't - but you needed to find that out for yourself to be honest. We were all trying to tell you that for years. I even bought you that book about why he wasn't that into you.'

'Sparkles, it took me ten years!'

'Yeah, you don't need to tell me that - it was a long ten years. I did try to intervene...'

'I know you did. Yeah, so anyway, there's that and then there's the new train - it used to be such a pain in the behind to get home, but now as long as you don't mind the extortionate price of the ticket then you're whisked all the way through the countryside and to the loveliest little seaside town in just over an hour. It's so different from when I was young,' Daisy explained.

'Tell me about it, you just need a mortgage for the ticket.' Juliette laughed, and walked back through the middle room to the kitchen, opened up the oven and checked on the fish pie.

'You're welcome whenever you like - we've not arranged yet where Maggie will be so it will be go with the flow. I might be on for the Christmas babies too - but you know how that works out.'

'Alrighty, Sparkles, I'm gonna do it, I'll see you at Christmas and maybe before. Okay, I'm out of here. Enjoy the dinner, have a bit of fish pie for me.'

Juliette waved to Daisy, closed her phone, checked on the fish pie again and started laying the small, round, pale pink table, opening up the dresser drawer and rummaging through her vast collection of napkins, tablemats and coasters. Each was neatly stacked and sorted by colour and theme. She pulled out white wicker mats with tiny silver dots, matched them with vintage linen napkins with tiny hand-embroidered flowers in the corner and slowly and methodically went around the table folding the napkins on top of the mats.

An hour later and after a shower, a sit with her book in the cosy chair in the conservatory and a little nip of Campari and lemonade to start the evening off she pottered around lighting candles, put frankincense and chamomile in the diffusers and turned on the lanterns by the window.

She heard the old ship's bell ring by the front door, opened up the door to Sallie wrapped in a huge coat, pom pom hat and scarf and a potted plant, wrapped in white paper with a huge bow on the front.

'Come in! Where's Ben?' Juliette said, as she answered the door.

'He's just gone to the off-licence - some new special edition craft beer they've got in he wanted to try. I said to him, well you're on your own, I'm heading straight to Juliette's and getting out of this cold.'

'Yes come in!' Juliette said, ushering Sallie into the warm.

'No Maggie?'

'She's at Jeremy's,' Juliette said, smiling.

'Ooh you've the night off then.'

'I certainly have and I'm intending on making the most of it.'

'Here you go - I thought of you when I saw these little plants and I got the girls in Felicity's to change the bow to a pink one - thought it would be a bit more appropriate and you could use it in your photos,' Sallie said, touching the ribbon on the front of the pot.

'It's perfect, thank you, I love it,' Juliette said, taking the little plant from Sallie, touching the leaves and smelling the gorgeous scent.

'I love that dress,' Sallie said, feeling the fabric of Juliette's deep green tea dress with puffy sleeves and tiny little leaves all over it.

'I'd look like a cross between a bag lady and a whale in that,' Sallie joked.

'A size eight whale, would that be Sallie?' Juliette said, giggling.

'Ha, you know what I mean, I just can't seem to pull off dresses very well, even though I lust after them,' Sallie replied, taking off her black coat and pushing the stack of sparkly bangles up her arm.

'I do know what you mean - like those awful bandage dresses I used to wear when I was with Jeremy,' Juliette replied, and physically shuddered at the thought of it. 'Never did get on with those, it felt like I'd been poured into a drainpipe half the time. Now I float around in my frills, I'm four sizes bigger and about a trillion times more relaxed and not thinking about eating the table for the best part of my day.'

Sallie laughed, they walked into the kitchen and Sallie sat down at the pretty pink table dressed in white and silver with two vanilla-scented candles lit in the middle.

'It smells delicious whatever it is you're cooking - I could smell it from halfway down the laneway and then when we turned into Seapocket Lane I could really smell the garlic and lovely cooking smells wafting down the road.'

'Creamy fish pie and molten chocolate cake, and a few little nibbles to start - with that little lot I didn't think we'd be wanting more than that. Now what can I get you to drink?'

Sallie pointed over to Juliette's half-finished Campari on the worktop.

'I'll have whatever you're having, Ben I guess will be raring to try the limited-edition beer he's been after.'

'How's it going with the organising of the Christmas Dance? It's so early this year, the posters look fab though.'

'All done and dusted, I didn't really have to do much. Nel's sorted out all the prizes and the marquee is all ready. Who would have thought I would be so laid back about an event? But with Lochie and Phia running the show and everything set up, there's not a lot to do except make sure the DJ turns up,' Sallie said.

'Ahh, that's good to be so organised.'

'You still don't think you can make it?' Sallie asked.

'I don't think so this year. I'm so busy and I don't know, I've got something on almost constantly that week and that's on top of work and the shop,' Juliette replied as she poured out another two glasses of Campari. Ben arrived, kissed Juliette on the cheek, told her she looked gorgeous and with a can of his craft beer and a cold glass from the fridge plonked himself down at the table next to Sallie.

'Guess who I just bumped into in the off-licence?' Ben asked.

Sallie and Juliette both looked at him, shaking their heads.

'Your new neighbour. I was standing there looking at all the new craft beers Jeddo has got in and he was on the other side looking at the wine,' Ben said, pushing up his sleeves in the heat of the little kitchen.

Juliette pretended not to realise who Ben meant and frowned, taking a sip of her Campari, pouring Ben's beer into the glass and sitting down at the table.

'Oooooh, you mean, Luke. Luke Burnette,' Sallie said, giggling.

'I do - seems like a nice chap. Knows my brother from his water polo days. We had a bit of a chat standing in the off-licence. He has his mum and her husband here for the weekend and was getting wine for his mum and laughing because she'll only drink a certain brand of Chardonnay.'

They all laughed and Ben told them how Luke had said he couldn't wait until his visitors went home again.

'So, have you seen him at all then?' Sallie asked Juliette.

'Seen who?'

'Pretty Beach's best new bachelor - he lives about ten doors down the lane, I thought you would have bumped into him,' Sallie said.

'No, I haven't, not since the post office last week and I'm not interested in Pretty Beach's newest bachelor, thank you Sals.' Juliette said, appearing as if she was not in the slightest bit interested in either the conversation or Luke.

Sallie laughed and drained her glass.

'Hmm, we'll be keeping an eye on you Sparkles.'

Chapter 14

A week or so later, Juliette heard the knocking on the front door as she finished off putting Maggie's neatly ironed clothes, underwear, dressing gown and four pairs of pyjamas into Maggie's little pink suitcase on wheels.

'Right Maggie, here we go, daddy's here. Do you want me to put Delilah in?'

'No thank you, I'll leave her on my bed.'

Maggie ran to the door to Jeremy who stood on the doormat on the porch peering around the doorway and looking in. Juliette wasn't going to let him in, even though she knew he was desperate to have a really good nose around. He'd been quite miffed when she'd moved into the cottage - she knew exactly what he was like and he would have been secretly quite happy that she was stuck in a flat while he'd moved into the new-build house his family owned in Newport Reef. If he'd pushed it she would have had to let him in, but he'd been surprisingly well-behaved for the last few months and after the initial time when they'd first moved in and Maggie had wanted to show him her bedroom he'd kept his distance. She had even thought, (and hoped), that he might have someone on the scene.

'All in there?' Jeremy asked, indicating towards Maggie's bag and stepping back out onto the doorstep.

'Yep, everything's in there, including the present for the party - have you remembered the other stuff?' Juliette said, opening her eyes a bit wider over the top of Maggie's head.

'All done and ready to go, ironed it all this morning and layered the bed,' Jeremy said nodding.

There was one thing about Jeremy that she couldn't knock - he was organised and efficient and had never done anything other than get on with it with Maggie's little problem of wetting the bed.

They now had a system down pat which included making the bed up in layers of sheets and pads and spare pyjamas ready, so that if and when it happened there was as little fuss as possible. The first night it had happened had been when Juliette and Jeremy had first split up and Maggie had been to stay over at his new house and he'd woken up to her crying and a soaking wet bed. The first Juliette had heard of it was later on the next morning after he had gone out, bought another set of pretty pink linen and sorted it out without any drama. He'd always been a control freak, and he was a bit of a show-off about doing all the nice things with Maggie, but Juliette would hold her hands up and say that when Maggie was with him he was certainly doing his share.

'Great, see you tomorrow then, Maggie.' Juliette leant down to Maggie, kissed her and took a big sniff of her pretty blonde curls and smiled as Jeremy put Maggie's pink girly backpack on his back. She looked at him and smiled - he was still stunningly good-looking with his mop of blonde hair the same colour as Maggie's and amazing blue eyes but she felt not a single thing for him and wondered if she ever really had. He irritated the heck out of her, but at least he turned up when required and was a good dad, she'd give him that.

Juliette closed the door, waved to Maggie out the window and felt a little pang of sadness as Jeremy drove away. It was a shame it hadn't worked out with him. He wasn't that bad.

She walked into the conservatory, finished off wrapping the last of her orders for A Christmas Sparkle, popped them into mailing sacks with the correct printed labels and put them in the wicker basket all ready for the post office the next morning.

She opened the fridge, took out a bottle of chocolate milkshake, poured it into a long tall glass, topped it with syrup and carried the glass carefully into the sitting room. She sat down, turned on Netflix and put her feet up as she clicked play on a sitcom about a tiny little village in Scotland.

A message popped up from Sallie on her phone.

What you up to Sparkles? I'm thinking of going over to the Smugglers for their Friday Night Special - I think it's steak and chips this week.

I've just sat down, not sure I'm up for it - it's been a busy week.

No probs, totally understand. I might stroll over there anyway - can't be bothered to cook and I've just blitzed the place from top to bottom. Don't want to mess the kitchen up. Haha.

I've just done the same! I've sprayed the whole place with disinfectant and cleaned it all to within an inch of its life. You know what, sod it. You're on. How long?

I was going to have a long soak in the bath and then head over there about seven.

Deal. See you there.

Juliette finished off watching her show and polished off the milkshake and then carefully climbed up the steep stairs to the bathroom on the top floor, opened the shower door, had a long, hot shower, double-conditioned her hair and was considering what to wear to the pub. She loved wearing dresses and she loved her new curves so much that she'd treated herself to a few lovely ditsy tea dresses that made her feel gorgeous. Sometimes when she put them on she did a double-take at the new her and pranced around, flicking the material around in her hands and dancing around her room.

She opened up the wardrobe door, chose a dark berry tea dress with tiny white flowers and ruffled arms, pulled on thick black tights and started to wind up rollers into her hair.

She looked in the mirror at the finished result. She was hardly recognisable from a few years before; Jeremy had liked her hair blonde and she'd spent every six weeks in the hairdressers with a headful of foils. Jeremy also liked her to be slim so that she could squeeze herself into the kind of clothes he'd liked to see her in, so she'd spent her life constantly counting calories and running for miles on the beach every morning just so that she could eat lunch.

Now she indulged her love for food, tea dresses, floaty floral tops and cute cropped cardigans and as she'd slowly transformed from her too-thin, too-blonde former self her self-esteem had shot up. She was much happier, more relaxed and it showed and now she turned even more heads whenever she stepped into a room.

She walked down the steep stairs of the cottage, grabbed her small going out clutch bag, put her thick pink wrap coat on over the dress and stepped into her boots.

As she walked out onto Seapocket Lane, Pretty Beach was quiet, a few Christmas lights had started to come on outside all the cottages and the fresh sea air after her long week was more than welcome.

***

The multi-coloured lights all the way around the Smugglers pub lit it up from afar and Juliette could see its brightly coloured sign swaying in the cold winter evening as she approached from way down the laneway.

As she walked along in a world of her own, the queue for Pretty Beach Fish and Chips was out the door and the beautiful crystal reindeer on top of Holly's bakery twinkled in the dark night, even though the official turning on of the lights wasn't for a few weeks.

She got to the Smugglers, pushed open the old, timber door with the round handle and the noise, smell and familiar feel of the best pub in Pretty Beach made her shoulders drop and put a smile on her face. She weaved in and out of the tightly packed tables through people standing in groups with pints of beer and glasses of wine, said hello here and there and slowly made her way up to the bar. She took out her clutch bag and phone, read a text from Jeremy that he and Maggie had got fish and chips and were now all rugged up and watching a film and waited her turn at the bar.

A text flashed up from Sallie.

Running late. Sorry Ben called, I'll be there in five.

Juliette sent back a thumbs up and as James the barman came over she ordered herself and Sallie a drink. He came back a minute later, with a glass of wine for Sallie and a small gin and tonic for her.

'What've you been up to then? Apart from delivering babies,' James asked, as he put the drinks down on the bar and keyed in her order.

'Not a lot of time for not a lot else,' Juliette said and laughed, 'What about you?'

'I think I'm about the same my love, not that I've been delivering any babies - it's been packed in here every night and not showing any sign of slowing down. We've had so many very early work parties already the place has been rocking - I can't imagine how busy we will be when it actually gets closer to Christmas. Not that I'm complaining, come January and it'll only be the locals in Pretty Beach until the warm weather.'

'You're not wrong - it's always a quiet month. Quite looking forward to it, to be honest - it's the first year I'll be able to enjoy Christmas and then take a bit of time off from working every day under the sun in the New Year.'

'Yeah, me too - and then we gear up for Summer and it all starts again,' he replied and pointed over to a laminated flyer on the side of the bar. 'Well at least we've got the Pretty Beach Christmas Dance to look forward to - it's never let me down yet, always a fun night. And for the first time ever it's in the Boat House marquee even though it's much earlier than usual which feels a bit strange. It's going to be lovely down there by the water.' James said.

'Actually, I'm not going this year James - it's my weekend for Maggie and I don't really have a babysitter so I've decided I'll give it a miss this year.'

'Oh right, that's a shame. Any news on the house-hunting?'

'Not a sausage. I presume you know Mr Jenkin's place might be coming up, but it'll probably be out of my price bracket. Anyway, see you later,' Juliette said, and picked up the drinks, walked around the bar and spied the only free table right down in the corner next to the fire.

She walked over, put the drinks down, put them onto a couple of beer mats and sat down. She sat there gazing around the pub, looking at all the jolly Pretty Beach locals chatting about their weeks. She spied Roy Johnson from the council in his regular spot sitting up at the bar with his own glass tankard and the husband of one of the nurses she knew at the hospital in Newport Reef looking remarkably friendly with a girl in a very short, very sparkly skirt.

Five minutes later she watched Sallie weaving the same way through the throngs of people in the pub and Sallie joined her at the table. They sat with their drinks, perusing the bar menu and trying to decide whether or not to have the special steak and chips or the beef and ale pie.

'I think I'll go for the ale pie, Sallie - it's lovely eating pie when it's so cold outside, and I'm dreadful at pastry so, well, I can't even tell you when I last made my own pastry, it's been that long,' Juliette said, looking at Sallie over the top of the menu.

'I'm okay at pastry, but can never be bothered with it and I always have a packet of frozen in the freezer anyway, so I'm in the same boat.'

Juliette nodded and continued looking down at the menu.

'We really should make it in here one lunchtime for the Locals Only specials - I hear it's a great deal. How about we get one of each and decide when they arrive?' Sallie suggested.

'Suits me perfectly,' Juliette replied, closing her menu.

Sallie went up to the bar, ordered the food and more drinks and came back to the table with a little basket lined with red fabric holding two sets of knives and forks, a tiny white salt and pepper pot set and a bottle of vinegar.

The food arrived, they ended up both having a bit of each and they'd both had a couple more drinks when Sallie had a text from Nina and Holly who both said they were on their way.

'Quite the jolly little impromptu night out we'll all have then,' Juliette said - the drinks were slipping down nicely.

Half an hour later and Nina and Holly had scrounged chairs from other tables and all four of them were sitting in the corner of the small, packed pub talking about Ottilie's upcoming naming ceremony, and Holly had them in stitches telling them all about her mum, Xian's, on and off romance with her boyfriend Drew. Apparently, they were worse than teenagers and definitely more romantic.

Nina, Sallie's friend who lived in the fisherman's cottages coughed and wheezed and fumbled around for her puffer.

'That's really not sounding good,' Juliette said thinking that Nina's asthma was sounding worse. 'Have you booked in for another appointment?'

'I certainly have. It just seems worse in the cold weather. All good.' Nina dismissed the conversation and Sallie who had polished off a good few drinks got up to get another round.

'Same again for everyone?' They all replied in the affirmative and after squeezing her way to the bar and doing two runs back and forth with the drinks she finally plonked herself back down at the table.

'Well, that was interesting!' Sallie said as she passed the drinks around. They all looked at her questioningly. 'Guess who I chatted to whilst waiting to be served at the bar?'

'We've no idea, Sals, do tell,' Nina said, laughing and taking a sip of her wine.

'The newest, most eligible bachelor in Pretty Beach, that's who. I mean, seeing as I apparently bagged Pretty Beach's best free man this one must be the next one in line if you ask me. He's absolutely, well

I don't quite know what to say, he's absolutely… delectable,' she giggled, looking over towards the bar.

'What was his name again Juliette?' she asked, widening her eyes and raising her eyebrows at the same time, laughing.

Holly leant forward, looked left to right, lowered her voice and said, 'Luke Burnette is his name.'

'What? How do you know? Holly! How come you know everything in this town?' Sallie roared with laughter, slamming her water glass down on the table.

Holly tapped the side of the nose, 'Ha! I did tell you Sallie when you first arrived here that nothing gets past me and that I know all that goes on in this fair town.'

'You certainly did, but he's not been here that long, I mean that was quick, even for you, how did you find out the information that fast?'

'I have my ways, Sallie, I have my ways,' Holly replied and they all sat back giggling and laughing and Holly tried to raise her eyebrows.

Just as Sallie was removing some of the empty glasses to a side table, Luke Burnette was manoeuvring around the fireplace. He bumped into their table and knocked into Juliette's shoulder as she was taking her glass from the table. Juliette's drink surged forward, the whole contents of the glass pouring onto the table and a pool of it landed on her dress. Juliette let out a tiny squeal as she tried to save the glass and the wine rapidly ran across the table and into her lap. She jumped up from her chair and it fell over as she pushed it back.

'Ahhh, sorry, I knew I shouldn't have tried to carry too many drinks back to the other side of the pub. This was bound to happen. Oh, and it's you, my new neighbour too. God, so sorry.'

Luke put the drinks he was carrying down on the table, leant over to the mantelpiece where a stack of paper napkins were lined up against some beer mats, grabbed a handful and turned back around to the table of women who were now all quietly gaping up at him.

'Here, let me,' he said, leaning over Juliette and dabbing at her dress with the wad of napkins.

Juliette leant back and her eyes widened at Luke Burnette's muscly arm dabbing at the bottom of the skirt of her dress. She bristled, pushed his arm away and a half laughing, half serious, she didn't really know what it was, sound came out of her throat.

'Umm, I'm fine thank you.'

'Oh yes, you don't want some stranger dabbing you with a paper napkin and ruining your night. Sorry. Yes, yes, I can see that,' Luke said looking Juliette straight in the eye.

Juliette looked back at Luke, Luke with the broad chest and quite frankly delicious looking eyes and did a funny little shake of her head and a giggle, and thought to herself,

Oh no Luke Burnette you didn't ruin my night, you didn't ruin my night at all.

Chapter 15

Juliette Sparkles leant against the board behind the desk, her hands cupped around a mug of hot chocolate, and peered into the bottom of a box of chocolates choosing which one to have next. She stood there with the hot chocolate and leafed through the files and tutted as she glanced at the headings on a magazine lying on the side extolling the virtues of the latest diet and something that was called 'midlife chic' - what a load of hogwash.

She stood there sipping on the hot chocolate to give her a bit of energy and chatted with Doris about the goings-on at the hospital, about how Doris had had to take her forty-year-old daughter to emergency with a suspected case of sepsis in her ear from a dodgy tattoo and how she'd decided that she was going to put off her retirement for a few more years because she wanted to buy a caravan further down the coast.

Milly walked along the corridor, approached the desk, leant over, took a chocolate and joined in with the conversation.

'If you're getting a caravan down the coast, Doris, I'm coming to stay for a week to get away from this crazy place,' Milly said, unwrapping a chocolate and popping it in her mouth.

'You'll be welcome, the more the merrier.'

'Talking of houses, has anything come up?' Doris asked as Juliette sipped on her hot chocolate.

'Not really, there's an old cottage in Mermaid Lane, you might know him actually, Mr Jenkin, anyway he's going into a home and the house is a pit and so I'm hoping it will go for a low price, but I'm not holding my breath, to be honest. You know what Pretty Beach is like, there's no such thing as a bargain unless it's nearly falling down, which actually that is.'

'Oh yes - my friend Sandra does the meals on wheels in Pretty Beach, she mentioned old Mr Jenkin was going into a home. He's lived in Pretty beach all his life - my mum used to know him if I re-member rightly. Something about the daughter, yes that's right, she did the dirty on someone and left him at the top of the aisle.'

'Really! I didn't know that part of the story, but I did meet the daughter. And I have heard about her and it doesn't sound very nice. You're the second person who has told me that about her.'

'Yeah, all about the money I think it was. She was meant to be marrying Shane that was it and then bang left him for some proper-ty developer at work and they went off to London and have hardly been back since, even when Mrs Jenkin got sick,' Doris said, rifling through the box of chocolates.

'Oh well, she's not someone I think I'd like to deal with then. I guess I need to get Christmas out the way anyway and the longer I hold on the more I can save. I'm not even thinking about it, at least I'm not in that horrid little flat now.'

Juliette chose another chocolate and looked at the files on top of the filing cabinet and a name badge and pass that were lying on top of them.

'What's this?' Juliette said, holding up a badge that looked as if it had been left on the side by mistake.

'It's the new anaesthetist's - there was a delay with badges when he started and that's just come through, I opened it up and then left it there to remind me when he comes in,' Doris replied, as the phone started ringing.

Juliette felt her heart beating hard, she gripped onto the edge of the filing cabinet and tried to remain calm and sound not interested.

'Right, well we don't want that then, a new member of staff los-ing their pass straight away.'

She put the file back on the top of the cabinet and pretended to continue looking in the tin of chocolates.

So, she thought to herself, *I might have to add myself a few more shifts at Newport Reef.*

***

Five hours later and Juliette had not had a break, was busting to go to the loo, had had texts to confirm that Maggie had been safely picked up from school from Jeremy, and one from Bella telling her that she'd topped another assessment.

The shift had flown past and she was hungry, tired and ready to go home. It had been busy with lots of babies, lots of problems and a couple of agency staff who didn't seem to care enough and were, in her opinion, more interested in their breaks and what they were and were not paid to do rather than in working efficiently.

It was pointless, though, to worry about it - over the years, even as she'd got more senior, she had learnt to put her head down, do the best she could do, not worry about anyone else and got on with it and didn't think she would ever see much change, particularly not in her time at work.

Juliette walked slowly through the ward, down past the main area, put her phone on charge in the staff room and started getting her things together from her locker. She'd changed out of her uniform, taken off her clogs, put on her coat and put her bag over her shoulder and was on her way to the lifts when Doris called out to her.

'So, when are we seeing you next?'

'I'm not sure, I haven't checked my shifts yet, I wasn't going to do more but I might do now, the money would be nice and Maggie's going to loads of Christmas events with Jeremy so I'll have some time.'

'Rightio, good work, love it when you're here,' Doris replied.

'Oops, just realised I've left my phone in my locker. I took it out to put it on the charger for a bit while I was getting changed and didn't go straight back to get it.'

Juliette walked back through the staff room, squeezed around the coffee table and around the fridge to her locker, unplugged her phone and put it in her pocket. Just as she was walking back out to the main area, had waved to Doris and was turning to leave through the staff entrance on the right she rounded the corner and Doris called out.

'Hang on Juliette. I've someone for you to meet'

Juliette turned back around and walked over towards the desk and standing there in front of her dressed in black jeans and a grey cable-knit jumper was the man from the car park, the man whose name was on the badge, the man who lived down her road, the man who had knocked her drink all over her at the pub.

'Juliette, this is the new anaesthetist, the one whose badge we were talking about all those hours ago when you were drinking your hot chocolate. This is Luke Burnette. Luke, our senior midwife.'

Juliette looked at Luke, a huge smile had spread out across his face.

'Ahhh, so you're the scary midwife they've all been telling me about - the one who knows more about birth than anyone else.'

Juliette looked back at Luke, Luke with the broad chest, chiselled jaw and dreamy chocolate brown eyes.

'That would be me then, yes Luke.'

Chapter 16

As Juliette walked around the brightly lit supermarket she remembered why she'd never liked shopping after a late shift, and as she aimlessly went up and down the deserted aisles, she'd asked herself why she'd done it. As if she didn't know - she'd fancied a chocolate doughnut after her dinner and so instead of taking the coast road to Pretty Beach, she had found herself detouring along the bypass so she could go to the supermarket. Once she'd parked in the empty car park and had got inside she had thought that if she was going in anyway she might as well get a trolley and do a small shop.

She'd walked around the supermarket, added too many treats to her trolley, piled it all into the back of her car and then as she drove back towards Pretty Beach was annoyed with herself that she had to put it all away before she could sit down. She hated that feeling after the shopping - dragging it all in, unloading it all and then the nagging little voice in the back of her head reminding her that she really should empty out and clean the fridge before she put it all away.

She pulled into Seapocket Lane drizzle hitting the windscreen and found a spot right outside the cottage, parked up and got out. She squeezed in between the bonnet of Ali over the road's car and her boot and held three bags in one hand, her handbag over her shoulder, four bags in the other and somehow managed to press the button to close the boot.

The shopping bags full of food weighed her down as she struggled across the pavement, jammed open the little gate with her foot and stepped up onto the pathway. She got to the front door, slipped off her boots on the front step and struggling with her keys, one of the shopping bags came crashing down on top of the step and a jar of Marmite fell to the floor. Then, like it was in slow motion she watched the large bottle of Baileys she'd treated herself to roll all the way down the path, proceed through the gate and smash down onto the pavement below.

She looked down at the Marmite on the path, sighed, put the rest of the bags down on the step, turned around, walked down the path and looked out at the smashed bottle on the pavement. The Baileys caught the light from the streetlamp and had seeped into a puddle by the drain. Fragments of glass from the broken bottle spilled onto the step and pavement. She looked at it all thinking that it would need a proper clean up with a dustpan and brush and overwhelmed by the long shift, her achy legs, tired eyes and the thought of all the shopping having to be put away she felt for the wall behind her and slowly lowered herself all the way down and sat down on the pavement. She watched the creamy white Baileys seeping all over the tarmac making its way down to the gutter and a tear ran down her left cheek. She brushed the tear off with the cuff of her coat and sat there staring at it all.

She sat there in her socks, her feet on the cold pavement and looked up at the sky, her breath forming clouds in the cold air. Sitting there surveying it all, she wondered if there was any Baileys left in the cupboard and thought about how many pounds worth of the lovely creamy liqueur were slowly trickling down the pavement and into the drain.

She brought her knees up in front of her, put her chin on her hands, saw that she'd stepped in some Marmite smeared all over her socks and looked glumly down at the pavement as big fat tears rolled down her cheeks.

All of a sudden everything was too much; the move into the new house, the long hours at work, the looking after Maggie, the keeping on top of the shop... and looking at the Baileys label on the floor she started to sob, huge ugly heaving crying into her hands.

'Errr hello, umm, you ok?'

She was jolted from the crying into her hands by a man's voice. The voice of Luke Burnette no less.

'Oh yes, sorry, I'm okay.' And to her horror, a faint shuddery sobbing sound escaped from her lips. 'Oh dear, sorry I'm fine.'

'Have to say you don't actually look fine. It's not very often on my way home from the pub I see a woman in a huge pink coat, fluffy polka dot socks and a bobble hat perched on the pavement in the middle of winter sitting in a pool of Baileys.

She looked around her, a smile forming through the tears.

'No, no I suppose you don't, I must be quite the sight!'

'Can I ask what you are doing then? Baileys all over the floor - it's rather late for a party for one, and rather cold.'

'It's a long story really - a very long day at the hospital, you know what those shifts are like and I fancied a chocolate doughnut so I took the bypass to the supermarket and then I thought I might as well do some shopping for Maggie's lunchbox and then when I was driving along after the shopping I wished I hadn't done it because now I have to put it all away and... I'm just so tired.' Juliette said and then mortifyingly heard another sobbing sound escape from her mouth.

'And so you came outside into the freezing cold night to drown your sorrows on the step?'

Juliette wiped her cheek, sniffed and hugged her knees.

'It was so cold and I couldn't face coming back out to the car, so I tried to carry too much, took my shoes off at the door and then the Marmite dropped.'

'So, then you took the Baileys down here for a quick nip?' Luke said, touching her on the leg.

She laughed through her hands.

'The Baileys fell out of the shopping bag, rolled all the way down the path - I'd propped the gate open with my foot and it got all the way to the end, dropped onto the pavement with a smash and slowly started to seep all over the place.'

'Right, so you then sat down on the step for a little rest to watch your drink run down into the drain.'

'I sat down and thought I might never get up,' Juliette said, her feet freezing, her teeth starting to ever-so-slightly chatter as the cold from the pavement and step started to permeate up through her bones.

Luke, who certainly didn't seem to feel the cold wearing only the same cable-knit jumper she'd seen him in before, gently took her by the elbow and started to help her up.

'Tell you what, why don't we get you inside, I'll clear this up and I think you'd better get those socks off and some dry ones on.'

Luke helped Juliette up from the step, Juliette brushed off her coat, looked down at her wet feet and replied, 'No, look, honestly, don't worry Luke, I'm fine.'

'Yeah, nah, sorry, but I'm not taking no for an answer. It's half-past-eleven on a Saturday night, you're sitting on the step on your own in the middle of the road with wet feet smeared with Marmite and an open front door - I'm seeing you inside.'

Luke turned around and led Juliette up the path, swiftly grabbed all the shopping bags from the front step, pushed open the door and stepped inside.

'Wow, this is cosy - my new place, needs, how shall I put it, some love like this, it's lovely!'

'Thanks, I like pastels and decorating and cosy houses.'

'Right, well you've made a great job of it compared to my place. So where are these going?' Luke asked, holding up the green shopping bags and looking over towards the door on the left. Juliette followed behind him.

'It's fine you can just leave them there. Honestly, I'm okay.'

'Nah, I'll take these in for you. Why don't you go and change your socks while I put these into the kitchen and then I'll leave you to it? I can clear up the outside on my way out.' Luke said, striding through towards the middle room. Juliette sighed and not having the energy to say much at all nodded, pointed to the kitchen through the tiny little middle room and replied.

'I'll just go up and change then.'

'No worries.'

Juliette held onto the bannister and pulled herself up the stairs.

Great, she thought to herself. *My new, extremely good-looking neighbour, who also just so happens to be a work colleague, who I'm not interested in anyway so why am I having this thought, has just found me sitting on the pavement in the rain, in tears, surrounded by Baileys and looking like I've the mental capacity of a Twiglet.*

She went up the second set of stairs, said a silent thank you for the lovely central heating, opened up her bedroom door, took off her socks, coat and clothes, threw them on the pink velvet chair in the corner, opened her wardrobe and pulled out pale blue wide-legged soft jogging bottoms and a matching sweatshirt, clean socks and her pale blue slippers and walked into the bathroom, went to the loo and as she turned the tap to wash her hands looked up at the mirror and gasped.

Big thick streaks of black mascara ran down her face, the horse-shoe-shaped birthmark on her left cheek she usually covered up poked through the mascara and her hair had gathered into clumps and sat flat to her head. He must have thought she was crazy, sitting in the rain with black streams running either side of her face.

She opened the vanity cupboard, pulled out some cleanser, blobbed it all over her face and rubbed it in, ran a flannel under hot water and slowly wiped every last bit of makeup and mascara from her face. She grabbed one of Maggie's pink velvet scrunchies, gathered up her hair and knotted the whole lot on top of her head then washed her hands and face.

She padded slowly back down the stairs, ready to get rid of Luke, make something to eat, have a shower and get into bed. She walked back into the kitchen, the shopping bags emptied and neatly folded up on the table and Luke standing at the door to the conservatory looking at the Christmas tree in the corner.

'Oh, wow, thank you,' Juliette said as she walked in, seeing that he had got all the shopping out.

'I stacked it there for you and put the cold stuff in the fridge - thought that might help a bit, and I've cleared up outside.'

'Thanks, that's so kind of you, but you really didn't need to.'

'No dramas Juliette - I have to say it's the first time in my life I've come upon someone on the way home from the pub looking quite as sad as you did.'

'Just tired and hungry, really. Obviously, you'll know what it's like in the hospital sometimes - I didn't even get a break and stuffed a stale old sandwich in when I had a quick five minutes and that was hours ago.'

'Yeah, I know what that's like,' Luke said.

'I must have looked like a drowned rat, a drowned rat with black streaks down my cheeks.' Juliette said, laughing.

'You were quite the picture, I should have taken a photo, but I thought that might send you over the edge,' Luke replied, smiling kindly.

'Why don't you sit down Luke, I was going to have a Baileys but I guess I'll have something else now...' she trailed off.

'Look, I know we've only just met really, but you do look in quite the sorry state. I know what it's like on that late shift sometimes - you come in and end up falling into bed exhausted and hungry and then it takes you the whole next day to recover because you didn't end up eating properly for 24 hours. Why don't I make you a cup of tea?'

Juliette looked at this Luke with the loveliest deep brown eyes standing in front of her and seeming to actually read her thoughts - she did need to eat and she was exhausted. She went to say no, and then she looked at the earnest, kind look on his face and decided to throw caution to the wind and say yes. What would it hurt?

'You know what, you're on.'

Luke, making himself right at home, walked over to the sink, took the kettle from its base, filled it with water, flicked on the switch and emptied the teapot into the sink.

As the kettle boiled and he poured the boiling water into the teapot, Juliette walked over and turned around to Luke who had put the tea in the pot and was now sitting back at the pale pink table, his long legs stretched out in front of him.

'Actually Luke, I'm going to follow my original plan. I'm going to have a drink and a chocolate doughnut. Do you fancy joining me in that?'

'Hmm, that's quite the question - I'm not sure how well a chocolate doughnut goes with the two pints of craft ale I've just had in the pub.'

She laughed back, opened the fridge and examined its contents, pulling out little pink boxes and peering inside.

'Maybe you're right, maybe I'd be better off with something a bit more substantial than a chocolate doughnut too. I tell you what, stuff the tea, how about a cheese and ham toasted sandwich? That's after-the-pub food at its best, is it not? I'll even throw in some very finely sliced red onion if you like.' Juliette laughed, as she pulled out a pink container with red onions in it, grabbed a packet of cheddar from the cheese drawer and took out a paper-wrapped package of ham.

'It looks like I'm in for a Saturday evening cheese toastie with my new neighbour then,' Luke said as Juliette pottered around the tiny kitchen, sliced up the cheese and onion, put it all together in a sandwich and took two craft beers out of the fridge.

Juliette finished cutting the sandwiches, topped the side of the plates with salt and vinegar crisps, poured the beers into glasses, slid Luke's over the table to him and led him into the conservatory. As she opened the door, lovely warm air hit them, the scent of her Christmas candles filled the room and the sparkly lights of the Christmas tree tucked in the corner filled the room with a golden glow.

'This is lovely,' Luke said, taking a seat on one of the velvet sofas, putting his sandwich and beer down on the little coffee table and looking around. 'My cottage has a similar conservatory at the back, but I must say it's nothing on this.'

Juliette flicked on the button on the side of the pot belly fire sitting between the two sofas. 'Never underestimate the power of a fairy light Luke,' she replied, 'it makes everything cosy. My tree is up early for my shop photos.'

They sat in the little conservatory, ate the toasted sandwiches, chatted about the hospital, what it was like living in Seapocket Lane, his new house and the best pubs in Pretty Beach which he'd also worked out was the Smugglers. He had also worked out that the tiny little pup at the end of their road was quite nice to stroll to, have a couple of quiet drinks at the bar and stroll home.

At just after half-past midnight he got up from the sofa, picked up the plates and glasses and went out to the kitchen.

'I'll be off then - it's been most unexpected this stop for a very nice sandwich. I didn't foresee saving someone in a pool of Baileys on my way home this evening, but I've had worse journeys home from the pub for sure,' Luke said, chuckling.

Juliette saw him to the door, he wrapped his scarf around his neck, put on his boots and she opened the door and he stepped out onto the moonlit pathway and turned around to her, touching the side of her arm.

'By the way, will I be seeing you at the Pretty Beach Christmas Dance? Everyone has been telling me about it since the day I moved in - that it's early this year and in the Boat House marquee for the first time.'

Juliette smiled, raised her eyebrows and nodded that yes she was going to the dance and she said goodbye to him as he walked down the path.

She hadn't bought a ticket for the dance, hadn't wanted to go, hadn't wanted to spend the money, hadn't wanted the fuss of getting ready or to find someone to look after Maggie... now she was very much going to go.

Chapter 17

Juliette had survived the incident with the Baileys and a few days later walked into the Marina Club, signed in, undid her coat, put her scarf into her bag, walked up to the bar, ordered herself a lemonade and joined Holly and Sallie at the table over by the window.

'Hey Sallie, I don't suppose there are any tickets left for the Christmas Dance, are there?'

'Depends who it's for,' Sallie said, and laughed as Juliette sat down at the table.

'Well, it's for me actually.'

'Oh right, I thought you said you couldn't make it because of Maggie?'

'I know, but Jeremy wanted to change his weekend and I thought, oh that's perfect, I'll be able to go to the dance now,' Juliette said, hoping it didn't sound like she was making it up. She'd totally called Jeremy up, made up a story about how much Maggie loved their Saturday nights together and asked him if he could change the weekday night over that weekend.

'All the tickets are sold out, but that doesn't mean there's not any space for you.' Sallie chuckled and took a sip of her drink, 'I mean when I'm providing the venue, I guess I can squeeze another guest in.'

'Speaking of which, we need to get thinking about how we're going to set up the auction prizes. What with the competition and my trip I've put it on the backburner, which I know I shouldn't have done, but oh well...' Sallie said.

Holly leant forward on the table and opened up the fundraiser document on her phone.

'According to this there's not much to do - seems like Nel is all over it. That girl has some contacts in Pretty Beach. She never fails to be able to squeeze things out of people. We've got a day at the spa in Seafolly Beach, a yearly flower subscription from White Cottage Flowers, Jessica has donated a monthly meal for two at the fish and chip shop, the Smugglers have offered a very generous supply of vouchers and the list goes on...'

'All sounds very good,' Juliette said as she folded her arms and leant back in her chair. 'I'm just trying to think if I could donate anything.'

Holly patted her on the arm, 'I'm thinking you do enough for Pretty Beach as it is and I'm thinking you have enough on your plate looking after those beautiful girls of yours and you're already covering Gina's days at the surgery. I think it'd be a good idea, if you get dressed up, kick back and enjoy the evening.'

Sallie joined in, 'Same here, Sparkles - everything is under control with taskmaster Nel and to be honest there's not a lot to do with the marquee apart from switching on the lights and making sure the alcohol and food are in which is also all sorted out. It's part of the reason I've put it to the bottom of the list - it's the good thing about having the Orangery now - I don't have to worry about the marquee being ready, or a quick turnaround.'

Nel came flying into the door of the club, walked up to the bar, bought a large wine and had already taken a sip before she sat down.

'What have I missed ladies?' Nel asked.

'Absolutely nothing - though we were just talking about you and the brilliant job you've been doing with the donations for the dance,' Holly said.

'A lot of people in Pretty Beach and its surrounds owed me favours - that's all I'm saying on the matter,' Nel said, plonking herself down and chuckling. She flicked her baby blonde hair over her shoulder. 'Let's talk about more interesting things, what is everyone wearing? I've seen a dress in Newport, it's a skin-tight gold bandage dress, and makes the most of these little babies,' she said and looked down at her boobs. 'I stood there looking at it and thought there we go, there's my Christmas dress for this year.'

Juliette chuckled, 'You make me laugh Nel, I tell you who won't be wearing a bandage dress now or anytime soon.'

Nel laughed back with her, 'Ahhh, you used to though, didn't you?'

'I certainly did, but those days are long gone.'

'I'll be lucky if I can prise myself out of my black jeans,' Sallie replied, 'but I do have my eye on a silk dress I saw online, it's super expensive though, well super expensive for me - not quite your designer stuff Holly, so we'll see.'

Juliette sat back in her chair and thought about what she would wear - but it wasn't what she was wearing that was in the back of her mind, more like who would be there.

'So, I'll be good to come then, even without a ticket?' Juliette asked.

'Don't be ridiculous, Sparkles, of course you're coming!' Sallie said, getting up to go back up to the bar for another round of drinks, 'it's going to be a really fun night, I'm so pleased you're coming now - so pleased you had a change of heart.'

Juliette smiled to herself and tried to believe her own little fib that it was Jeremy's plans which had given her the change of heart.

Chapter 18

Juliette opened the front door, 'Morning Steve. I thought I might see you today, I got an email yesterday to say my order was on the way.'

'Morning gorgeous. Right, you've been busy, I've got four parcels for you here.' Steve the postman said, pulling the parcels out of his bag, giving them to Juliette and holding out the little machine for her to sign.

'Lovely new dresses for the dance, Steve - I thought I'd treat myself to something really special.'

'You and a lot of the other ladies in Pretty Beach, I've been delivering these parcels all week and I've just dropped two at the Boat House, and I'm including my wife in that. I was doing the credit card balancing the other day and looked at the entry from the boutique in Seafolly and I was like ouch. After twenty years of marriage though, I knew better than to say anything. It'd better be a good night, the amount that dress set me back,' Steve said and stood back down on the step.

Juliette laughed as she passed him back the little machine and held the parcels under her arm, Maggie at her side. Steve turned around and walked up the pathway, looked over his shoulder and waved to Maggie.

'I'll see you on the night then. Have a good day, my lovelies.'

Maggie waved to Steve as he continued along Seapocket Lane with his parcels and Juliette closed the door.

'Right Maggie, now there are a few dresses in here for me to try on, remember I told you I'm going to the dance when you're going to the cinema? But I've also got you a special little Christmas dress. Let's see if it's going to fit.'

Juliette pulled a tiny little pink velvet dress out of one of the parcels, flicked it to get out the creases and held it up against Maggie and then popped it on over her head.

'I feel like a princess in this - it's so pretty. I can wear it with my sparkly shoes.'

Juliette laughed and smiled to herself, oh to be young again and feel like a princess - she started to open the plastic satchels and look at the dresses she'd ordered for herself. Maybe at this dance, she would feel like a princess too.

***

Juliette tucked Maggie into bed, switched on Maggie's tiny little mushroom night light, gave her a kiss, gently closed the door and went to her bedroom. The five dresses she had ordered for the Christmas dance were hanging on the outside of her wardrobe.

She looked at the dresses, touching the fabric, thinking how differently she felt now about clothes to how she had just a few short years ago. Then she was always thinking about whether or not they would make her look smaller, thinking about the size written on the label, and monitoring before a big event what she could eat and how long she had to ensure she had a flat stomach. Whenever she'd attended any social occasion with Jeremy she'd spent the days before eating very little, and attending appointments for hair, nails and face.

Now when she got ready to go out she had none of that stress, none of those thoughts and she took great pleasure in planning the few hours before with a long bath, lots of nice treats and a few little tipples before she even got on her way.

She pulled the first dress off the hanger - a pale pink empire line with puffed sleeves and pulled it over her head and looked in the mirror. It was nice, pretty even, but the shade of pink looked different in real life than it had on the website and the cut of the fabric clung to all the wrong bits. It missed her tiny waist and clung to all the lumps and bumps and cut into the tops of her arms.

The second dress was more fitted, dark green velvet with a cut-off sleeve and square neckline, she struggled to get it over her head and burst out laughing as she stood there looking in the mirror - the sleeves made her look ginormous, the square neckline did nothing for her now ample boobs and the length finishing halfway down her legs made her look short, dumpy and not feel very attractive at all.

The next two dresses weren't a lot better - she hadn't seen this coming, since she'd left Jeremy she adored getting dressed in her pretty, frilly clothes, loved her more natural hair and softer makeup and had looked through the website choosing things she thought she would love, she hadn't thought they would make her look like an over-fussy frump.

She sighed as she took the last of the dresses off the hanger thinking it would be joining the other ones thrown on the chair in the corner and be winging its way back to the online store it'd come from.

She held up the dress in front of her, walked over to the lamp on her dressing table for more light and examined it - black had been her last choice, but there was rarely a woman who didn't look passable in a little black dress so she started to undo it and hoped for the best.

The silky fabric wrapped around at the front and did up high on the waist with a small, delicate frill going all the way down to the hem. Similar to the green dress, the arms puffed out at the shoulder but the soft, shiny fabric fell away all the way to a wide gathered cuff at the wrist. A huge, silky bow tied it up at the side and it was edged delicately at the front and bottom with black velvet ribbon.

She opened up the little ties on the inside of the dress, put her arms into the sleeves, did up the fabric-covered buttons at the wrist and fastened the inside ties and wrapped the front over tying the bow to the right-hand side.

She looked up in the mirror and beamed, she felt amazing. The dress skimmed over her beautiful new curves, the gathered fabric at the wrists flattered her arms and the full bias-cut fabric of the skirt fell to just the right spot and floated around. She pulled her hair up and moved to the front and then the back, turning this way and that to see how the dress looked from different angles. It was a beautiful dress, a beautiful dress for the new Juliette.

She picked up the bottom and just like Maggie had done when they had opened her little pink velvet dress that morning she twirled.

Juliette hadn't twirled for a very, very long time.

Chapter 19

Juliette finished packing the paperwork into its case and slowly started to load her bags into the back of her car parked in the driveway. She stepped back into the house and through to the sitting room where the baby and one of her lovely new mummies sat with her partner.

'Rightio, well done again. I'll be off now,' Juliette said.

'We can't thank you two enough,' Jake, the husband said, as her and Sarah the other midwife stood at the sitting-room door ready to leave.

Juliette and Sarah stepped out onto the driveway.

'What are you up to then?' Sarah asked, as she put her bags in the boot of her car.

'Popping home and going for a walk - then getting a nap in after that.'

'Same, minus the walk, I'm going to the dry cleaners to pick up my dress for the dance and then having a sleep. What are you wearing to the dance? Have you treated yourself to a new outfit?'

'Well I wouldn't have done as a rule, but I've found a very nice little black dress - not sure what shoes I'm wearing yet though so we'll see.'

'Okie dokie, well enjoy the rest of your day - make sure you put your feet up Jools after that, that was a long one!' Sarah said.

'Will do - see you tomorrow.'

Juliette went home, showered, answered the text from Sallie telling her that she had finally made it home and was ready for their walk. Ten minutes later and she headed down to the beach and their meeting point by the playpark. The waves crashed in and out on the beach bringing in a fresh sea breeze.

'Hey, how are you?' she said to Sallie, kissing her on the cheek.

'Good, busy, but good, getting all the details organised for the Christmas wedding.'

'Me too, busy, busy, busy - I guess it's better than being quiet. I'd be moaning if there were no sales in my little shop.'

'Ha, same here. Right, where shall we walk today?'

'Don't mind, where do you fancy?' Juliette replied, bending down to tie up her shoelace.

'Sounds a bit ungrateful, but I'm sort of sick of the beach walk,' Sallie said, putting her hand up to shade her eyes as she looked out to sea.

'Oh, how lucky we are to be able to say that - I feel the same though.'

'How about we go through the dunes, all the way over to Strawberry Hill and then through the old High Street? That'll give us something to look at, I've not walked up that street for a while.'

'Perfect.'

***

Juliette and Sallie emerged from the dunes, kicked the sand off their boots, walked past the bus stop and restaurants and stood at the bottom of the street outside the pub on the corner.

'Up through the shops or over to the lane and up the hill?' Juliette asked.

'I wouldn't mind a wander through the shops and then we'll make our way home around the back.'

They started walking up the old High Street, past the little cake shop, the tourist gift shops, and the old-fashioned sweet shop with jars of sweets lined up on shelves in the window. They stopped and peered in the window of Seaside Elegance, a fancy high-end boutique Juliette hadn't been in since she'd left Jeremy. Sallie screwed up her nose as they looked at a dress on a mannequin in the window.

'You need a mortgage to even walk in this place - I saw a silky shirt there last summer that was nearly as much as my phone!' Sallie whispered, giggling. 'Really not my cup of tea - I'd rather be poking around in the hospice shop.'

'Ahh, yes, me too, and now I can - I wasn't allowed to before,' Juliette said, pushing her tortoiseshell glasses up her nose so she'd could see properly over the cobbled road.

'What do you mean you weren't allowed to?' Sallie looked at her with a frown.

'Well, not actually not allowed to, as in it wasn't forbidden, but it was just frowned upon to be seen anywhere like that.'

'You're kidding me? Stuff that for a game of soldiers. Cripes he sounds awful. So it was frowned upon to be in a charity shop? I spend most of my waking hours in them.'

Juliette sighed, 'No he wasn't awful, it wasn't as if I wasn't allowed - it's tricky to explain, he's not a bad person - just very wrapped up in appearances and portraying things in a certain way.'

'Well come on then, now you can,' Sallie said, and grabbed Juliette's arm, leading the way over the tiny cobbled street. They stood outside the Heart of Pretty Beach hospice shop, its little string of bright green bunting flapping above the doorway in the wind and looked in the window at the display of bright red clothes, old china and crystal glasses. Sallie pushed open the door, a little bell tinkled above them and an old lady with white set hair and an electric blue wool skirt and brown shoes welcomed them.

'Morning lovelies, in you come out of that cold. We've got a special offer on today just to let you know - all black things are half price,' her voice sing-songed out at them.

'All black things?' Sallie asked.

'Yep, you name it, if it's black it's half price.' The old lady lowered her voice, 'Actually, for you two, I'll throw in red too seeing as that's the theme in the window,' the lady said, straightening some clothes on a rack. Juliette and Sallie giggled and started to look around the shop.

Sallie made a beeline to the back of the shop and the crockery as Juliette picked up things, looked at the prices on the bottoms and then made her way to the toys and left Sallie looking through a basket full of napkins. Juliette made her way back to the front of the shop and just as she was looking at a carousel full of handbags a pair of shoes right up on the top shelf caught her eye.

She walked over to the shelves, reached up to the top and pulled down a pair of sparkly nude heels, covered in glitter, with a cascade of crystals over a dainty ankle strap. They were beautiful and had obviously not come from China. She couldn't believe her luck when she saw on the bottom the size was hers, a size three.

Sallie walked over with an armful of vintage silver platters, a big pile of white napkins and a big smile on her face.

'Ooh, they're gorgeous,' Sallie said looking at the shoes.

'I know. They look tiny though, I'm a three, but these look really narrow.'

Sallie touched one of the straps and turned the shoe over. 'I knew it, I knew they looked gorgeous - they're from you know who, the guy in London, all the royals wear them. I looked at them for my wedding,' she whispered. 'They're about nine hundred pounds.'

'Really? Well, they're not in here - look.' Juliette turned over the other shoe and the price label which read six pounds.

'Oh my, come on, run for your life,' Sallie said, widening her eyes.

Juliette put the shoes down on the floor, pulled off her boot and slipped her foot into the shoe, did up the thick satin bow at the side and walked over to the mirror.

The shoes sparkled and glittered and made her feet look pretty and elongated her leg, even her ankle seemed to take on a new life of its own. Whoever this celebrity shoe guy was Sallie was talking about, he certainly knew what he was doing.

The old lady, her arms folded over her ample bosom, looked over the top of the glass counter and down at the floor where Juliette was turning her foot this way and that in the mirror.

'They're marvellous, look at them catching the light like that. Got a special occasion have you? Are they for the Christmas Dance?'

'Actually yes, I've got the dance and I have a new dress but no shoes,' Juliette replied smiling at the old lady behind the counter.

'You're about the tenth person this morning to try those on and you're the only one they've fit. Tell you what my lovely, I know they're not black or red, but I'll do them for half price. I think they were made for you.'

Chapter 20

Juliette stood in front of the bathroom mirror with an old towel around her shoulders, sectioned her hair with clips and started to paint hair dye onto the roots of her hair.

Approaching forty and the ferocious march of the grey hairs had taken her round the neck, clenched her in tight and held on for the ride. The battle was real and there was no way the greys were going to win. She'd done away with the monthly trips to the hairdresser for her highlight upkeep when she'd been the perfect politician's wife blonde, but she wasn't prepared to relinquish power to the greys, ever.

She'd become quite the expert in Operation Rid Greys as well. Her friend Milly at work whose mum owned a hairdresser in Bristol dyed her hair for her a few times a year and in between she topped it up at the roots and it all worked quite nicely - the greys were kept at bay without too much fuss.

As she stood there concentrating on her hair Juliette realised that she hadn't really thought a lot more about preparing for the dance since chatting about it with Sallie. She'd certainly not made any of the kinds of preparations for it as she would have been compelled to do when she was married to Jeremy; because when she was married to Jeremy primping, fussing and perfecting was part of her weekly routine and the weekly social occasions she'd had to attend. How she'd looked and acted were very much a part of his profile and it was a part of her life she absolutely did not miss.

So, since Jeremy had bitten the dust and on the rare night she didn't have Maggie and she was actually going out-out she relished the ritual of getting ready for a night out and freshly coloured hair was part of it. It wasn't about looking a certain way, plastering herself in make up or hiding behind a mask, it was more the enjoyment of the pampering - preparing for fun, and most of all celebrating being her with all her imperfections, rather than trying to hide them.

She sat on the toilet with a book and waited the required time for her hair, washed it off, put on the accompanying treatment, wrapped the whole lot up in a turban towel and hopped in the bath.

With her small makeup mirror and tweezers she went over her eyebrows, found a hair on her chin that had escaped previous scrutiny and putting the mirror and compact down on the side of the bath suddenly sat straight up, the bubbly water splashing out over the sides.

What is happening to me? A voice inside her head asked. *What is this strange feeling I'm feeling? Am I actually looking forward to going out? Am I putting in all of this effort because of the tiny little bit of suggestion that Luke will be there?*

She laid back down in the water and sloshed the warm bubbles over and over her shoulders.

Oh my God, I am! I am interested. I am very, very interested. What is happening to me?

She leant over the bath, pulled open the door to the little cupboard, took out her favourite rose body oil, poured it into her hands and rubbed it up and down her arms.

I'm thinking about a man who lives at the end of my road, who I know pretty much nothing about and I'm wondering whether or not he will be there tomorrow night.

She reached around the back and smoothed more of the oil onto her shoulders.

And I don't know one, if this Luke Burnette would be interested in looking twice at me and two, and more importantly, if he is available.

She laid there thinking about the availability thing a bit more - even though Milly and Doris at work had done as much digging as feasibly possible on Luke's status the only evidence that they had at the moment was that he didn't have any children, that he'd moved to

Pretty Beach from a quite-nice-thank-you-very-much suburb in west London and that he had played national water polo in his younger days. The water polo clearly evident in the width of his shoulders.

Juliette mused it all while turning the tap on at the end of the bath with her foot and topping up the bath with hot water. What man in his late thirties came without baggage, though? She already knew the answer to that - pretty much none of them.

She'd not even thought about a man since she'd been with Jeremy and as she lay in the bath thinking about what complications Luke might have she thought to herself, *who am I kidding, I'm the one with the baggage.*

She lay there analysing it and admitted that she had not truly had feelings about a man since she had found out she was pregnant with Bella - and that had been over eighteen years before.

Yes, there had been Jeremy, but that whole thing had been a mistake, and somewhere in the very deep, very dark, recesses of her mind she had a smidgen of guilt about everything with Jeremy. Yes, she'd played the game from the outside, but her heart had never been really in it, she'd never really been into him. And he was certainly a royal pain in the behind and a control freak to excessive levels, but he wasn't all bad. The problem was that she'd never really had her whole heart into him in the first place and that had never really been fair on him.

In fact, she couldn't even really remember what being into someone was like anymore. Until now. And she knew exactly when it was that she had last felt like this about someone. Precisely eighteen years ago when she'd been so very much into Jack, Bella's dad, that she'd even thought that she wouldn't mind having his baby and they were so in love, or so she thought, that it would be quite nice to have his baby when she was so young.

When she was really into Jack she'd lived, breathed and thought about him twenty-four hours a day - she was that into him that she found herself at nearly nineteen with a baby. The trouble was, he hadn't been into her in quite the same way and when she'd told him breathlessly over the moon that she was pregnant, he had upped and left and she'd felt like all her emotions had evaporated with him.

And she hadn't felt anything like it since, until standing in a cold, dark car park in Newport Reef with a half-eaten packet of biscuits in her hand and talking to a man in a car, her heart had very much started to race and definitely missed a beat.

She lay there in the hot water thinking about her feelings and emotions. Looking back on it now she realised that for years she'd been in some sort of emotional abyss including when she'd met Jeremy. Then Maggie had arrived and she'd put her head down, packed her emotions neatly away in the back of her mind and endeavoured to be a first-class wife, a top mummy and always striving to keep all the balls up in the air, all of the time.

Juliette dipped down under the warm water, letting every little part of her skin soak up the warmth and thought about how the two men in her life had both turned out to be completely wrong and she'd ended up coming out the other side scarred but with two beautiful girls.

Furthermore, with her emotions so tightly under wraps and locked far, far away in the depths of beyond, she'd truly believed that she would never even look at someone again. Until now.

Chapter 21

Juliette looked at the Boat House in the distance as she walked along the laneway. The spotlights all around it lit up the very tops of the trees, and the beam from the lighthouse glinted in the distance as the ocean crashed onto the beach behind.

She stopped on the pavement just before crossing over the road, pulled the drawstring velvet bag from her arm, opened it up and re-applied a layer of berry lipstick. She blotted it with a piece of tissue paper, tried to check that it wasn't bleeding halfway down her chin in the camera of her phone and curled her hair around to the front.

Not bad, not bad at all she thought, looking at the image looking back at her from the phone camera and thinking about just how different the reflection was from a few years ago when her blonde hair made her skin look pallid and dull and her gaunt cheeks had given her a look as if she was constantly on the brink of being ill - which she was.

She crossed the bridge over the little stream to the Boat House and walked across the pebbles. She could hear the music and chatter over the sound of the waves crashing on the beach and the masses of fairy lights twinkled prettily on the approach to the Boat House marquee giving the whole thing a magical feel. Huge spotlights lit up the tops of the trees and large oversized gold baubles hung from the branches and inside the little cottage to the right a Christmas tree's lights glowed in the dark night. She had to give it to Sallie, she was a master of styling.

Juliette walked along the path, down the right-hand side of the marquee, past the seaplanes alongside and as her eyes swept over the jetty on the right she thought she felt a tiny little flutter of butterflies in her stomach. *What were they? Were they butterflies for Luke Burnette?*

What on earth was she thinking? It had started again, her mind wandering to him. There had been nothing to suggest he was interested in her, and from what she'd gathered and according to the Pretty Beach fountain of knowledge, Holly, he lived alone and there was nothing much to report. Which was a tad different to Juliette - if there was one thing Juliette specialised in it was baggage... she had quite the history behind her and quite the life experience to boot.

Carefully stepping along the driveway, the pebbles crunched under her super-sparkly heels. It went through her mind that there was no way he would be interested. She couldn't even believe that she was even letting her mind peruse such frivolity. But nowadays, the new Juliette behaved in very different ways to the old one. The new Juliette was more prepared to go for it, more prepared to take a chance. It was as if her feelings, her heart and her ability to let herself go had been locked up for so long that now that she had her own money, her own house and could make her own decisions she was ready to play.

The eighteen years since Bella had been born and all the heartache that had come with that, the years of trying to please everyone else, trying to behave a certain way, trying to be the world's best young mum, trying to look a certain way as a politician's wife, trying to succeed at everything she did and always trying to fit in - all of that had meant that Juliette Sparkles had been so tightly wound and she was now more than ready to let go.

All those pent-up emotions and feelings had finally bitten the dust when she'd moved out of the flat and here she was walking into a party, on her own, single, loving the freedom and even letting her mind wander to such giddy things as the new man in her street. The man who just so happened to look like a walking talking jeans ad and from what she had gathered so far was available, nice and from the way he looked at her, maybe was as interested in her as she was in him.

She walked into the back of the marquee and looked down at her glittery shoes - Jeremy hadn't liked glitter but she loved them and she loved even more that she'd found them in the hospice shop. Jeremy hadn't liked second-hand things and didn't like her to be seen going into charity shops, in case someone saw her and it harmed his image. She flicked the side of one of the shoes up towards her, wiggled it so it twinkled and shined up at her and thought how happy she was to be rid of Jeremy and his blooming image.

She pulled back the door to the backroom of the marquee where all the auctions were laid out, put her bag and coat down on a chair and started to go through the checklist as per Nel's instructions; Nel had messaged her to ask for a fresh pair of eyes to read over them all and as far as she could tell everything was correct and ready to go.

Juliette walked through to the main room, the ceiling covered in fairy lights, gold Christmas decorations hung from the roof and the floor seemed to sparkle more than her shoes. She tottered across the dance floor, the dress floating around her, to Sallie who was standing at the side talking to Ben.

'Hi! Let me get you a drink,' Sallie said as she grabbed a glass of sparkling bubbles from Ollie who was walking past with a tray.

'Thank you, I could do with a good drink. Everything sorted here with you?'

'Yep, all we need to do now is have a few drinks and enjoy ourselves - Ben and Nel are doing the auction and Ollie and Lochie are in charge of everything else.'

'Fabulous, right I'm going to go and have a little sit down over there then,' Juliette said pointing to a side table. 'Do a bit of people watching and look at all the gorgeous dresses.'

'I'll join you in a while, by the way, how are the shoes?' Sallie asked looking down at the silver, sparkly heels.

'They're a joy - just goes to show money can buy you comfort.'

'They look adorable too and so does that dress. In fact Juliette, you're positively glowing tonight. I think you need to grab yourself Pretty Beach's newest most eligible bachelor.'

'Not for me thanks, I've had enough men to do me until I'm old and retired.'

'Never say never, Sparkles.'

Juliette sat down at the side table, the party had been in full swing for a while and people were beginning to dance. She sat there thoroughly enjoying the comings and goings, watching people in their little groups all dressed up in their finery. She took another drink as they went past, and feeling the bubbles relax her tensed up muscles, sat back on the chair, answered a text from Jeremy informing her that Maggie was ok and just as she was about to get up and go to the loo the auction started so she stayed where she was.

Ben had the microphone, got everyone going and Nel paraded in front of him in her skin-tight gold dress, the highest heels Juliette had ever seen and her long, blonde hair beautifully curled and hanging down her back. Juliette smiled as Nel wiggled and performed and Ben played to all the people standing on the dance floor bidding for all sorts of things they probably didn't need.

Half an hour later and having raised lots of money, Ben handed the microphone back to the DJ, Juliette went to the loo and looking here and there about the place she had come to the conclusion that her new neighbour Luke was very much not going to show.

I don't like him anyway, she told herself as she headed to the toilets at the back of the marquee. Just as she got to the door, she saw the queue and remembered what Sallie had said about using the cottage loo. So she walked all the way across the pebbles to the boathouse cottage, pushed open the unlocked door and went into the tiny loo in there instead.

She looked in the mirror, put on a layer of her lipstick, topped up the thick line of black on her eyelids and taking the mini bottle of perfume from her bag sprayed it into the air in front of her and walked through, giggling.

The bubbles had gone to her head just enough to make her feel nice - it had been years since she'd really had a drink while she was out at a function. Jeremy had never liked it if she was seen in public drinking, it didn't go with his political image and since she'd been on her own she'd always been really conscious that she needed to keep her wits about her for her girls so it had been years since she'd had a drink whilst out having fun. Tonight was a bit different with Bella now in Oxford and Maggie overnight at Jeremy's place.

Yes, she thought, as she headed back to the marquee, stuff whether or not Luke Burnette had turned up, she was going to have a nice time. She might even get herself a takeaway on the way home.

She meandered through the marquee, looking up at the beautiful hanging fabric and Sallie's fabulous decorations. Trailing greenery and baubles hung down from the ceiling and huge vintage chandeliers twinkled with little faux candles.

She walked up to the bar and leant over the top to Ollie.

'Lovely Juliette, what can I get you?' Ollie asked.

'I don't suppose you have a margarita?'

'I'm not meant to be doing them tonight, but for Pretty Beach's best midwife, I'll do it.'

Ollie got to work on the margarita, topped a glass with salt, threw in some ice and poured the drink carefully into the glass from the shaker.

He passed it over and Juliette took a sip.

'Wow, that's lethal. Lethal and absolutely delicious.'

'Just call me Tom Cruise.' Ollie laughed and passed her a little jug in which he'd poured the remainder of the cocktail.

'I'm surprised you even know about that film at your age Ollie.'

'Ha - I've based my whole barman persona around it.'

Juliette laughed and crossed back over the dance floor. The marquee was now very busy, hot and as the effects of alcohol kicked in more and more people were on the dance floor. She sat down, sipped the margarita, and topped up her glass with the leftovers. As she sat there people-watching all of a sudden the main music went off, and she presumed there was going to be another announcement. Then some music started in the background and Sallie came marching up to the table.

'Houston. We have a problem'

'Oh no, what?'

'The short version is that the DJ's girlfriend started dancing with one of the guests, an old friend she'd known from college. Then she disappeared and disappeared for quite a while.'

'Oh no, has something happened to her?' Juliette replied.

'Something has happened alright. She disappeared out the back of the marquee with the guy she knew from college and let's just say they weren't looking at the sea down on the beach.'

'Really? It's freezing out there to be on the beach doing that.'

'I know. So the DJ took one look at them, you know, pumping, and well, he's gone.'

'What do you mean he's gone?'

'He's gone home. Abandoned all his equipment and left.'

'And now you have no DJ?'

'And now we have no DJ.'

'We're going around asking everyone and anyone if they know how to work the system - it's like a huge great computer. We can't even work out how to play anything.'

'Absolutely no idea, can't help, sorry, I do babies not turntables,' Juliette said, giggling.

Sallie continued to walk around the marquee asking various people if they knew how to work the equipment. Juliette sat back into her chair and was thoroughly enjoying the drama and the fact that she had a night off to enjoy herself.

She watched as Sallie moved from table to table, and thought to herself it was a shame the lovely new resident of Pretty Beach hadn't managed to make an appearance at the dance. She wondered if he'd got caught up at work as it had happened to her enough times.

She poured some more of the margarita into her glass and then all of a sudden, there he was. Standing right at the other end of the marquee. She hadn't seen him before, or when she had been to the loo because from where she was one of the podiums had stood right in the line of her view. Now as Sallie had approached his table, he'd got up, walked forward to speak to Sallie and she now had a full, and very lovely view of the whole of him.

She sat up in her chair, took a large lug of the margarita and rummaged around in her bag for her lipstick.

Holly came strolling over from the other side of the marquee as Juliette was popping the lipstick on her lips, Xian shuffling along beside her.

'Evening! What are you doing all the way over here in the corner sitting on your own?' Holly asked.

'I don't know, really. I got myself a drink, took a pew and have been here ever since,' Juliette replied, smiling.

'Can we join you then?' Holly asked, pointing to the empty chairs.

'Of course!'

Holly and Xian sat down. Xian got out her flask full of her special drink, offered one to Juliette, who said she might try one later and started to look at shares on her tablet.

'What's been going on with you?' Holly asked Juliette.

'I wish I had some really interesting gossip to tell you Holly. I know you like that, but I've been working and looking after Maggie and doing not a lot else.' Juliette replied.

They both looked at the dance floor and watched Sallie walk right across the middle, followed by Luke. Luke in a navy-blue shirt, jeans and the very nice bottom.

Holly sat up and rested her chin on her hand.

'This looks interesting. It seems as if Pretty Beach's new bachelor knows how to work the equipment.'

'It certainly does,' Juliette said, tipping her glass up and finishing the rest of her drink.

'He works in the same department as you, doesn't he?' Holly asked.

'Sometimes, but he's on the other rotation to me, so I haven't actually worked with him yet.'

Holly nodded her head and Xian went back to her shares. Juliette shifted in her seat and went to get up.

'I'm looking a bit empty. What can I get you, Holly? I persuaded Ollie to make me a margarita, even though it wasn't really on the menu tonight.'

'Gosh, I haven't had one in years. I think I'll join you in one of those.'

'I'll get him to make us a jug, then.' Juliette said, and took her little velvet bag off the table and went to walk all the way down the other end of the marquee to the bar.

A few minutes later, she walked down the side of the marquee, back down to the side table to the left of the DJ's table where Holly and Xian were sitting. Balancing the two glasses and a glass jug in her hands, she looked across at the DJ equipment and Luke. Luke who looked right back at her, caught her eye and held it for just that little bit longer that made her take a sharp intake of breath.

Chapter 22

Juliette sat at the table with Xian, Holly and now Sallie's mother-in-law Susan who was down from the city for the weekend. They all sat there chatting, reminiscing about Sallie and Ben's wedding and how Xian should try and mass produce her special drinks. They watched Ben twirl Sallie on the dance floor, and Nel who was giggling and gyrating in the tight, gold dress with one of the other bus drivers from work.

Ollie came up to the table with another tray of bubbles, handed one to Susan and raised his eyes to Juliette, asking her silently if she would like another margarita.

She stood up and told him that she shouldn't really but what the heck and she was sharing it with Holly. He came back five minutes later with another small jug and two fresh glasses and poured it into the glasses, leaving the rest on the table for them.

'Cheers Juliette. Here's to a successful Pretty Beach fundraiser, lots of Christmas fun this year and a bit of time off from work,' Holly said, over the music.

'I'll drink to that!' Juliette responded, and they clinked their cocktail glasses together.

'I think you need some time off Juliette, I mean it's been what a good few months since you moved into the cottage? Every time I see you, you're either on your way to or from work, or you are piled high with parcels for the post office.'

'I'm having some much-needed time off over and after the Christmas break, actually, and I cannot wait,' Juliette replied, swirling the cocktail around the glass.

The lovely dance with all the Pretty Beach locals dressed up, the aura inside the marquee and the potent cocktails had made her relax. She felt soft around the edges, and a feeling she had quite forgotten which she could only describe now as giggly. It had been a very long time since Juliette Sparkles had really fully giggled and now they were coming every few minutes.

Sallie led Ben back to the table, announcing to them all that she'd had enough, was hot and was going to help herself to a glass of water.

'Take your mum for a spin around the dance floor,' Sallie said to Ben, laughing.

Ben's mum shook her head fervently and grasped onto her glass.

'Come on Juliette, why don't you dance with Ben? He loves a boogie when he's had a few drinks. Strange man!' Sallie said, chuckling and patting her hand on the back of Juliette's chair.

Ben laughed and held out his hand to Juliette, 'Come on Sparkles, I'm taking you and those shoes for a spin.' Juliette took Ben's hand and he pulled her up out of her chair. Her beautiful sparkly shoes caught the light as she strolled behind him to the dance floor and as they laughed and he twirled her around, the frills of her dress floated out behind her and she threw her head back and laughed.

Xian looked up from her tablet and nodded over towards Juliette.

'She's an absolute stunner that one. Plus, she's a heart of gold. I'm surprised she's not been snapped up already - it's been a good few years since she left the husband.'

'I was just thinking the same. She's beautiful this evening, absolutely glowing. She used to look so skinny and drawn all the time, and she had that bright blonde hair. It's amazing to see the transformation,' Holly commented, topping up her margarita with a lug of champagne from Susan's bottle.

'If I remember rightly she helped out when Tana was in the hospice too. I remember Ben saying something to me about the local midwife who was sometimes the nurse at the surgery,' Susan added, taking a sip of her drink and watching as Ben spun Juliette around the floor and Juliette laughed happily, tottering on the high sparkly heels.

Just as they were coming back over towards the table, Juliette laughing and Ben grinning at all the ladies on the table, Luke appeared from behind the deck, smiled at them all and offered his hand to Juliette.

Juliette half shook her head as if to say no, and pushed her curls back over her shoulder when Xian poked her in the side, widened her eyes and whispered for her to get herself out there.

'Oh, umm, oh, ok,' Juliette said, taking Luke's hand, looking a bit embarrassed.

Luke led her to the middle of the dance floor and grasped her hand, the other hand on her hip.

'I thought I might see you here tonight, so I was looking for the pool of Baileys outside but when I didn't find it I thought you must be inside, you know, having a regular drink at a table,' Luke said, with a smile.

'Luke, I'm so embarrassed about that, I thought about it afterwards. I must have looked quite the sight, sitting on the pavement in your new road, without any shoes with a smashed bottle of alcohol beside me on the ground.'

'You're not wrong about that. You certainly did look a bit concerning actually - the broken bottle and everything.'

'Yes, it must have looked a bit weird. I promise you I don't go around smashing bottles on public pavements as a rule.'

Luke pulled her more tightly towards him and she smelt his dark, musky scent and swallowed. As he led her slowly around the floor she felt almost mesmerised, the thousands of lights, the softness of the dress floating around her, the relaxed feeling from the drinks and this Luke whose woody, dark smell she could quite easily get lost in and not surface again for a very long time.

'I should hope you don't,' Luke said and moved his hand ever-so slightly down towards the small of her back.

Chapter 23

Juliette waited on the pebbles with the last few stragglers outside the Boat House marquee as Sallie and Ben finished off switching everything off and closing it all up.

Nel, with a black glittery wrap over her tight, gold dress was wriggling around trying to take off her heels and put her flats on, and Sallie was looking in her bag for her phone.

'Okay, so you're walking down the laneway and then home that way? Do you want to hop in the car? Rory is picking us up outside in a minute,' Holly asked Juliette.

'Actually, thanks for the offer, but I'm going to walk.'

'Do you want me to walk with you?' Ben asked.

'No, thanks, I'll be fine.'

'If you're sure? It won't take me a second to walk you home,' Ben replied.

'I'm all good. It's lit all the way there through the laneway, and there are so many people walking home from the dance and the pubs will be closing so it'll be quite busy. Plus, I may just stop and get myself a little takeaway on the way home,' Juliette said, pointing out to the laneway which was full of bright lights, and packed with cars and people.

Ben looked dubious but nodded his head.

Juliette kissed them all goodbye, walked down to the end of the Boat House driveway, over the little bridge with Holly and Xian and said goodbye to them as they climbed into Rory's car.

The laneway was brightly lit with streetlights and Christmas lights and various people walking back from the pub and spilling out of the restaurants. Juliette clipped along behind two girls in party dresses and no coats and took out her phone as it pinged in her bag.

Mum, I've just seen the pics of you at the dance on social media! My goodness, you look so beautiful!

Thank you, darling Bella. I'm just on the way home now.

Did you have a fun night?

I most certainly did. I've chatted with everyone and I don't have to get up for a shift all weekend.

Maggie is with Jeremy???

Yes, so I've even got a lay-in. I've already planned I'm having choco-late waffles and a big pot of tea in bed in the morning.

Sounds fabulous. You deserve it. I'll speak to you tomorrow then.

Will do darling. Night.

Juliette carried on along the laneway, right to the end, passed a couple canoodling under a lamppost and headed towards the Pretty Beach curry house. She pushed open the door, every single table was taken with customers since the pubs had closed, the aroma of glorious spices and Indian food hit her and the warm air felt lovely on her face after the cold wind as she'd walked along the laneway. She turned towards the counter, picked up a takeaway menu and sat down on one of the red velvet, gilt-edged chairs by the door.

She chose her food, then looked up and there standing right in front of her at the ordering desk was Luke, she hadn't seen him come in while she had been head down looking at the menu.

She got up and stood behind him to order her food, not sure what to say, he beat her to it.

'Hi, fancy seeing you here!' he said, chuckling.

'I know. I suddenly realised I was starving and, you know, didn't want to end up on the pavement in a heap again so thought I would get myself some sustenance. There's nothing quite like a curry on the way home after a night out is there?' Juliette said.

'I thought exactly the same. Though I love any food after the pub, it has to be said. Your cheese toastie was just right.'

'Hmm, true.' Juliette replied.

Ali, owner of Ashiana's curry house, dressed in his usual suit and tie, strode around from the middle of the restaurant, ordering his staff this way and that and moved around the gold desk as Juliette was about to give her order to his son behind the till.

'Good evening, Juliette. How are you?' Ali enquired with a big smile as he straightened up a bunch of menus.

'I'm very well, thanks, Ali. How are you?'

'I'm good - busy this evening after the dance!'

'I thought you would be but couldn't resist a curry on my way home.'

'I've actually got the small table right in the corner at the back just coming available. Would you like it?' Ali asked, indicating that a couple had just got up to leave and looking at Luke who was standing beside Juliette and assuming that they were together.

'This is Luke Burnette, he's just moved into the end of Seapocket Lane too.' Juliette said, stumbling over her words. Not sure whether it was the copious amounts of alcohol making her stumble or the fact that it was now awkward seeing as Ali had gestured for them both to sit down.

'Ahh, welcome to Pretty Beach, Mr Burnette,' Ali replied, politely and held out his hand.

'Ali lives over the road from me, well and you really, in the big house with the fir trees,' Juliette said, turning to Luke.

Luke stuck out his hand to Ali, who shook it and smiled.

'So, are you staying then? It's nice and warm in here or we can put your orders in for takeaway right away,' Ali asked.

Luke turned to Juliette, who was standing looking from Ali to him and not saying anything.

'Not sure about you Juliette, but I'm up for sitting in for my curry. I'd love it if you'd like to join me.'

Juliette went to say no, it all seemed way too structured for her to actually sit down at a table with him. Then she caught a glimpse of the sparkly shoes and remembered that the new Juliette, the relaxed one who didn't have to be wary about how she behaved and what people thought could do completely and utterly whatever she liked.

***

Ali led them all the way through the red and gold carpeted restaurant, Indian music trilling in the background, every table packed with people. She nodded hello to someone she knew from Pretty Beach Surgery and gathered up the skirt of her ruffled dress to squeeze past an adjacent table to the seat in the corner.

She sat down and Luke took the other chair, Ali handed them the thick, black plastic embossed folders and lit two little tealights in the food warmer in the middle of the table.

'Poppadoms for two?' Ali asked.

'Yes please,' Juliette replied as Luke nodded in agreement and Ali swiftly navigated himself around the table and went out towards the kitchen.

'So, Juliette, how was the dance?'

'Fabulous. I actually really enjoyed myself. It's been a long time since I've been out and relaxed.'

'Oh, why's that?'

Juliette instantly regretted that she'd said anything like that at all. She had no intention of telling this Luke the complicated intricacies of her last ten years but all of a sudden heard herself doing just that.

'Let me put it this way - I've spent the last ten years watching what I say, watching what I eat and watching how I act and tonight, well tonight I didn't do any of that. Tonight I did exactly what I wanted to do and it felt absolutely glorious,' Juliette heard herself say, and grimaced inside at the way she'd elongated glorious and had even picked up her water glass as she'd said it and clinked it on the side of his.

Luke leant forward as she said it, elbows on the table and as she clinked his glass replied, 'Juliette, I will very much drink to that.'

Ali came back ten minutes later to take their order. Juliette and Luke had chatted about all sorts of things about Pretty Beach - how lovely it was in the warmer weather, how the locals were a rare breed but woe betide you if you didn't behave properly and about how Seapocket Lane was a lovely place to live.

'Just to let you know, we've a few portions of the LO house curry left, if you'd like that,' Ali said, leaning down towards them and lowering his voice.

Luke looked up confused and frowned.

'LO stands for Locals Only, you'll find it all over Pretty Beach. It's a strange and very lovely little tradition and if anyone offers you anything Locals Only you say yes,' Juliette explained, giggling.

Luke shifted his long legs under the table, raised his eyebrows and started nodding his head enthusiastically and looking up as Ali shut his menu.

'I'll take the Locals Only curry - sounds like the best offer I've had for a very long time,' Luke said, smiling.

Ali smiled back at them both, took their menus and headed off towards the computer to put in their orders.

'It seems as if there are quite the few traditions and customs in this little town I'll need to get my head around,' Luke said.

'For sure,' Juliette replied, taking a huge swig of her drink and thinking that she really shouldn't drink any more alcohol.

'When I was in the cafe the other day in the queue for a coffee, I got to the front of the line, ordered my coffee and when I went to pay, it had already been paid for! I was like what happened there?' Juliette nodded as Luke continued, 'Someone in the front of the queue had paid for my drink! I was astounded.'

'Oh yes, that's a Christmas thing. You do little random things for people all around Pretty Beach and as the Christmas months start to arrive it'll happen all the time.'

'Really! So, you do anonymous kind acts?'

'Yup, random acts of kindness the Pretty Beach way - but don't you think for a second that they're anonymous.' Juliette smiled, pursing her lips and nodding to herself.

'What do you mean they're not anonymous? Thought that was the whole point of it.'

'Well everyone thinks they're anonymous, but they're actually not. The little ears of Pretty Beach will be listening and whoever bought you that coffee will be noted.' Juliette started giggling.

'You're sure?'

'Oh yes, Luke, yes I am very much sure. You do nice things in Pretty Beach and nice things will happen to you. Mark my words the fact that you jumped in to help out at the dance right away tonight will be all around Pretty Beach already. If it's something they consider of some significance you'll have made the community page too.'

'Yikes. I need to up my game.'

'You may well have to, Luke, you may well do.'

Chapter 24

Juliette gathered up the bottom of her dress to squeeze around the tiny table and smiled at the sight of the shoes. The beautiful, glittery shoes were almost like a direct comparison to her life - before she was dull, grim and always worrying whether she was doing the right thing and always concerned about looking a particular way. Now the shoes, the ruffles and the softness of her new curves sparkled, nearly as much as she did.

She followed Luke through the red and gold wallpapered walls of Pretty Beach curry house, said goodbye to Ali as he opened the door to them and she wasn't sure if she was imagining it or not, but she was convinced that as she walked past Ali might have given her the tiniest bit of a wink.

Juliette had known Ali for years and now that she lived in Seapocket Lane she received even more special little parcels of food delivery than she had before when she'd lived in the flat. The best thing about it was Ali and the restaurant were one side of the cooking skills of the family, the little deliveries weren't the restaurant food, but the real home-cooked southern Indian dishes Ali's wife made with recipes that had originated from her mother. It was melt in the mouth good and Juliette had several carefully labelled home-cooked curries stacked in the freezer for nights when everything was too much effort and she guarded them with her life as did anyone else in Pretty Beach who was lucky enough to get a delivery.

As Ali closed the door behind her she looked back and wondered what he had meant with the ever so tiny wink of his eye - could other people see that Luke Burnette was doing something to her which was making her feel and act in a very different way?

She fell into step with Luke, lovely Luke who again was without a coat and it seemed was never cold. She pulled her scarf out of the pocket of her coat and wrapped it around her neck.

'Cold?' Luke enquired as they walked along in the pools of light from the Christmas lights crisscrossed all the way above the laneway.

'Are you not? It's really going to be a chilly night by the looks of it. I saw on the weather forecast that it's going to dip down tonight to below freezing. Just thanking my lucky stars I'm not on call.'

'Oh yeah, I know that feeling - having to go out in the early hours when everyone else is tucked up in bed in the warm.'

They got to the top of Seapocket Lane and Luke's cottage and Juliette stopped.

'I'll see you down to the end of your house. It's late now and not a lot of people around.'

She went to say no and then left it and they strode down the pavement looking at all the pretty lights outside the houses, and the bright colours from a string of lights on a fir tree at Ali's house standing out in the dark night.

'What are your plans for Christmas then?' Luke said as they walked along the pavement.

'I'm not sure yet, we've quite a while to go... and I have to wait and see what Maggie's dad wants to do.'

'Maggie's dad is in charge then is he?' Luke asked.

'Not really, it's just easier if I let him think he is,' Juliette said, giggling and tucking a piece of stray hair behind her ear.

Her eyes wandered up the street - a few houses along the whole roof was a mass of multi-coloured lights and beside it a tall tree twinkled in a net of white gold lights even though the official Pretty Beach lighting ceremony had not yet occurred.

The whole of the evening had finally caught up with Juliette, she was tired, her feet had suddenly started to hurt and the Indian had meant she was ready to curl up in bed.

'What about you? Any plans for Christmas, or are you working? Going to stay with family or anything?' she asked Luke.

'Oh no, no, no. My parents split up about twenty years ago. My mother's new husband is as boring as anything and my dad, well let's just say he ran off with the village airhead, shall we? Whenever I see him it's like pulling teeth all having to sit around and pretend that we like each other. How a top consultant in the city can go off with someone with literally no brain always baffles me and always will.'

'Oooh tricky.'

'Yep and this year I've got two great excuses. One, I'm pretending I'm doing up my new house and two, my friend has invited me to go to his cabin in Sweden after Christmas, or his house in Spain and I think I'm actually going to take him up on the offer. My brother and his wife will be here for Christmas Eve and Christmas Day and then I'll probably head off a few days later.'

'Sweden, that sounds delightful. As does Spain for that matter.'

'I'll never get there if I don't just make a commitment at some point, I didn't have a break this year what with moving and everything. The Swedish place is a farm with cabins dotted here and there, the place in Spain is more a holiday home.'

'Sounds right up my street - I could do with a holiday home in Sweden or Spain!'

'Let me find the name of the Swedish place,' Luke said and took out his phone and scrolled down to some pictures of a tiny red cabin, topped with snow, a Christmas tree outside the front door and a chair on the porch.

'Wow, that's real snow! It looks sooooo Christmassy. I've always wanted to go to Sweden. I mean I love Ikea and the meatballs,' Juliette said, laughing. 'On the other hand, Spain, sun and relaxing sounds borderline nicer than snow at the moment.'

'Yeah, Spain does sound nice and warm, come to think of it I could do with some sun. I just need to get my act together and have a look at the flights.'

She gave him back the phone, they reached Juliette's gate, the tiny windows of the cottage looking warm and inviting with the little Lucia candle in the window and the lights all the way around the front door twinkling.

'I'll leave you here then,' Luke said, and touched her in the small of her back.

She went to turn away, it felt like bolts of electricity were running between them. At first when she'd felt it when she was dancing with him she'd wondered what it was and then she'd remembered it was the same as when she was eighteen and Jack, alpha male of the school had started paying attention to her and she had felt the same then.

He moved towards her and she all of a sudden pulled back, the tiniest little moment gone.

'Oh, sorry.'

'No, my fault. Oh God, look, sorry Luke. It's just well...'

'Not a problem.'

He took her hand and squeezed it and she got a whiff of the musky dark scent.

'See you then Juliette, thank you for a wonderful evening. It's been quite a long time since I've enjoyed an evening with a beautiful woman.'

From over the road at Ali's house, a red curtain twitched ever so slightly back into place.

Chapter 25

Juliette walked up to the pale pink door of the cottage in Seapocket Lane after dropping Maggie off for a sleepover. The last thing she felt like doing was going out but the surgery Christmas party was always fun and she knew that once she got there she'd enjoy herself. Plus it was in the Italian restaurant in Seafolly Bay and the taxis were all booked and paid for so there was no brain power required for her at all. All she really needed to do was turn up.

She went slowly up to the top floor, had a shower and put her dressing gown on and carefully wound her hair into large Velcro rollers. Once it was all set on the top of her head she sprayed it with product, put her slippers on and padded back down the stairs, opened the fridge and took out some brie and sliced off a thick hunk of sourdough.

She poured herself a very small glass of sparkling water, replied to a text from Bella and checked her schedule for her visits the next day.

Just as she was finishing off tucking into the brie there was a loud thumping on the front door. She almost jumped out of her skin and dropped the knife and the brie onto the plate. Slipping her feet into her pink fluffy slippers she walked through the middle room and over to the left behind the sofa so whoever it was couldn't see there was anyone inside but she could see out.

The thumping went again. And then it turned into a more frantic knocking. Then she heard a male voice, Luke's male voice. 'Crap! Now what shall I do?'

'Luke?' Juliette called out.

'Yeah, it's me. Look I need you, Juliette,' he called through the letterbox.

'What on earth?'

She opened the door and stood there in the huge pink Velcro rollers, the fluffy slippers and her dressing gown over the top of her bra and knickers. Luke was turned the other way, looking down the road.

'Ashley next door!'

'Luke, what?'

'She's gone into labour. I heard her shouting from the bathroom. Her phone's dead and no one is there.'

'Okay.'

'Juliette, it's coming, like head out coming!'

Considering Luke was a highly accomplished medical professional he had switched to member of the public mode.

Juliette turned around, took her keys off the hook and handed them to him. 'Get my gear out of the back of the car,' she instructed.

Juliette flew past Luke in the pink slippers, rollers in her hair and with the dressing gown flying about behind her she started down the path.

'Have you called an ambulance?' she shouted over her shoulder.

'Yes, on the way.'

Luke slammed the front door shut, looked down the road for her car, ran over to it and pulled out her bags as Juliette ran down the lane in her slippers until she got to the door of the house next door to Luke's.

She knocked on the door quickly and calmly and called out - assuming Ashley was still in the bathroom she went up the stairs.

She announced her arrival, who she was and gently opened the door to see the young mum on all fours on the floor panting. Juliette could tell the baby was coming, and Ashley started pushing.

'There's been no pain! I thought I had indigestion for a few hours and now this!' Ashley panted and yelled.

'We're all good here. I've got you,' Juliette said calmly and crouched down on the floor of the bathroom.

***

The ambulance crew had left, Ashley's husband was meeting them at the hospital and Juliette and Luke had locked up their house and gone next door. Juliette still in her dressing gown, rollers and slippers stood in Luke's kitchen with a large glass of iced water.

'That was all a bit of a surprise, how did you hear her?' Juliette asked Luke as he took a beer out of the fridge and popped off the lid.

'I was just putting my bike in the back shed and heard groaning.'

'What, from the bathroom window out the back?'

'Yeah, and I called up from the garden and she yelled back that the baby was coming and that her phone was out of battery and she was alone! I'd seen your sitting room lights on when I went past on my bike so thought you were in.'

'Good job I was, though that baby was coming whoever was there.'

'I phoned the ambulance and then ran like lightning around to you, well, and the rest you know.'

'What a turn up for the books, eh? I didn't expect that on a Wednesday night before drinks.'

Luke crossed the kitchen and touched Juliette gently on the arm.

'Juliette, you were absolutely outstanding.'

Juliette looked up at Luke, the huge velcro rollers still in her hair, took a deep breath in and felt like someone had just placed a red hot poker on her arm.

Chapter 26

Juliette stood at the bar of the old pub by the canal in Pearl Beach waiting to be served. She was out with the other midwives from work for drinks, not to be confused with their Christmas party which wasn't actually until January when everyone was less busy and, more importantly for most of them, a whole lot less expensive.

It was certainly busy in the Pearl Beach Ship Inn; admittedly it was a tiny little pub, right on the canal but even so, every table was full and lots of locals were standing around chatting and drinking as last orders were called.

'What can I get for you, my lovely?' the barmaid asked.

'Red wine and a house white please.'

Two minutes later and Juliette walked back to the table with the two drinks, one for her and one for her friend Milly.

'Any news on the boyfriend front then, Milly?' Juliette asked, as she sat down next to Milly.

'Ha, I wish Jools. Nothing. Not a sausage. I can't even get to meet anyone online. I think I'm doomed.'

'You're thirty-five! You're not doomed!'

'I know, but my clock's ticking and every man I meet seems to have a tonne of baggage or ghosts me after two dates.'

Juliette fell about laughing.

'There are many, exceedingly many reasons to be on your own,' Juliette said, twiddling the stem of her wine glass in her fingers.

'True,' Milly said, nodding and sipping her wine.

'You've got your own home, your own car and you do very nicely on funding your own lifestyle,' Juliette stated. 'You should be very proud of yourself.'

'I do. That's true, I need to think about that a lot more I guess,' Milly said, sighing.

'Absolutely you do - you're young, you've got a good career, can do whatever you like within reason and you've a nice little pension pot going there with that flat in Seafolly.'

'You're making my life sound fabulous, Jools!' Milly exclaimed.

'Well, trust me, if you've been where I have you'd be appreciating it a whole lot more. Pregnant at eighteen and your parents disowning you and ending up giving birth in a bedsit is not quite the start in life I wanted. Then add on a marriage where I was underneath all the trappings of a very comfortable life, but actually quite miserable.'

'Crikey, that must have been hard on your own with Bella.'

'Yeah, it sounds it now, but looking back I don't know, I think I just put my head down and got on with it.'

'Hmmm. I mean how on earth did you cope on your own at eighteen with a baby?'

'It was hard, so very hard. Everyone knocks benefits, but thankfully I had that and then as soon as some childcare was available I started out with the midwifery. I was the youngest in my cohort, with a three-year-old, no partner and hardly any help.'

'How did you get the studying done?'

'I just made it work.'

'Right.'

'I don't know, I was super focused, got on with it when she went to bed, went to bed late and then started the whole merry-go-round the next day. I was so lucky with the placements - I met Daisy, she lived downstairs from me, she was lodging and she was cooking at night which left her free in the days. I paid her hardly anything but she loved Bella so much. I don't know, it just all seemed to work out ok.'

'It takes a village, right?'

'Ha! Not in my case - my parents disowned me and the love of my life did a runner.'

'Errrrr yah, that's not quite so good,' Milly replied.

'Oh well, it all worked out in the wash.'

Milly suddenly leant forward in her chair.

'You're not going to believe who is over there in the corner.'

'Who?'

'Luke, as in anaesthetist Luke.'

Juliette twisted her hair and pretended to look disinterested.

'Luke Burnette and he's headed right our way. What? Even better! He's with Max Holten the anaesthetist from Berts. I wonder how they know each other then?'

'No idea.'

'Good evening Juliette, Milly, how are you all?' Max Holten anaesthetist, charming, handsome and very nicely tucked up and married with two equally as handsome little boys.

'Hey Max, haven't seen you for ages.' Juliette stood up and kissed him on the cheek.

'You've met Luke?' Max asked, gesturing his hand to Luke who was holding an empty pint glass by his side.

'Oh yes, we have.'

'That's right, sorry, the brain is a bit mushy at the moment, sorry you were at the Pretty Beach Christmas Dance with him weren't you?'

Milly kicked Juliette under the table and Luke stepped in.

'Nice to see you again. Hi Milly, having a nice evening?'

'I am, but, I'm on the way home, we've all just booked an Uber and Juliette's waiting for the next ferry over to Pretty Beach.'

'Not got room in there for one more, have you? I'm getting the last train back if I'm in time.' Max asked.

'Hold on let me check.' Milly nudged one of the other girls on the table who opened the app and had a look at what car they had coming.

'Yep, we do.'

'What about you Luke, how are you getting home?' Milly asked.

'I'm waiting for that same ferry,' Luke said, frantically clicking on the app to cancel the car he'd just booked to take him to Pretty Beach.

'Oh, what a coincidence! You can go home with Jools, even better that you both live on the same street!'

Juliette nudged Milly, then Milly and the three other midwives got up to go, said goodbye and kissed Juliette and went out to their waiting car.

So now I'm on my own with Luke, what a shame. Juliette thought to herself as she watched them hop into the car.

Chapter 27

Juliette pushed the door open to the pub toilets and took a deep breath in. She hadn't seen it coming when she'd forced herself to go to the work drinks that she would be travelling home with none other than Luke. Luke who she was doing an admirable job of pretending she was cool with when inside her heart was racing.

She went to the loo, washed her hands and looked in the mirror. She'd curled her hair before she'd come out and it had lasted well so that was good. She topped up her makeup, rummaged around in the depths of her bag, found a little vial of perfume from the bottom, spritzed it on her wrists, dabbed it behind her ears and then giggling to herself popped some in her cleavage.

What, are you doing Juliette? You're thinking that the very nice, very handsome doctor is going to be going near your cleavage? She thought, putting the perfume back in the bag and curling her hair around her finger and pulling it around to the front.

She pulled open the door of the loos and looked over at Luke who was leaning on the bar, waiting for her and scrolling through his phone. Leaning on the bar with his extremely broad chest and flop of hair falling into his eyes.

'Eighteen minutes until the ferry arrives, so we better get going,' Luke said, looking up from his phone. He put the phone in his jeans pocket and led her to the exit, opened the pub door and a gust of wind hit them.

'Do you not have a coat, Luke?' Juliette asked.

'Yeah, I can never be bothered bundling up in a coat and then I always forget I've got one on the way out, so I no longer bother. I just make do with a scarf,' he said, winding his thick, grey cashmere scarf over the navy-blue wool jumper, over the broad chest.

'It's going to be cold on the ferry though with no coat I guess,' Luke said. 'It's not the cold I'll be concerned about tonight with these winds - it's the choppiness.'

'Yep, it's going to be bumpy out there by the looks of it.'

'I love it though being able to get a ferry here and there. It's one of the reasons I chose Pretty Beach actually - there's not many better ways to commute to work I believe. It sure beats a smelly old underground train!'

'Yep, I love the ferry, it's like part of the Pretty Beach furniture. Chugging in and out, the horn sounding every now and then, I love that sound when I get home from somewhere.'

'I know what you mean. I've already got used to it. It's like a comforting sound that you're home.'

They strolled along, chatting about work, about the Christmas party being in January which he found strange and then started to talk about how he was getting on in his new house.

They sat on the bench waiting for the ferry to come in, the wind howling around the jetty, huge waves crashing onto the shore and the Pretty Beach lighthouse shining far out in the distance.

Juliette tucked her scarf further into her coat, turned up her collar, fished her gloves out of her bag and folded her arms against the wind. A lone biker freewheeled down the jetty as the ferry chugged in and an old couple, holding hands in big coats, hats and gloves stood up from the other side of the bench and lined up as the ferry pulled in clunking and knocking against the wharf.

Juliette and Luke tapped their travel cards and walked onto the ferry and went and sat up the top right at the front.

'Hey folks, Captain Jones here.' A voice announced from the speaker.

'Uh oh,' Juliette said, taking off her gloves.

Luke looked at her with a frown.

'If we're getting an announcement, that means it's going to be a fun ride in the Middles.'

'What do you mean?'

'Well, they give you a bit of a warning if it's going to be rough and when they mean rough they mean nearly capsizing,' Juliette said, chuckling.

'You're joking!'

'I'm certainly not joking, Luke - you'll need to hold on as we go through.'

Captain Jones continued, 'Yeah, big weather out here tonight - going to be a bit choppy there through the Middles - stay in your seats all.'

The ferry pulled away and started to heave backwards and forwards, Juliette gripped onto the railing as the ferry dipped up and down, the swell bashing against the boat and waves breaking onto the deck right at the front.

'Wow, it's like the real-life version of a theme park ride.' Luke exclaimed.

'It is!' Juliette said as they slid from one side of their seats to the other. The ferry suddenly heaved left and Juliette lost her grip, slid along the seat to the end and Luke's strong arm just about saved her from falling onto the floor. He pulled her back up onto the seat and she laughed, loving the feeling of his hand on her waist, sparks going between them.

'Ha, thanks, I nearly went off the end there!'

Not long later and they were on dry land, walking up from Pretty Beach jetty. They walked up the road in the icy wind. Outside the little fisherman's cottages a gate banged in the wind and as they turned the corner onto Seapocket Lane, Ali's lights flashed in the fir trees.

'Do you have to get back for the babysitter?' Luke asked.

'No thank goodness, Maggie's at her dad's,' Juliette replied sounding casual, wanting to actually scream out, *hooray Maggie is at her dad's!*

'Nightcap? I've got Baileys and it's intact and still in the bottle.'

Juliette started giggling, 'You know what, Luke, I will pop in for a nightcap, though, really I'd quite like to have a nosey at your house,' she said, whilst thinking that yes she did want to have a nose around his house, but that his house wasn't the only thing on her mind.

She followed him down the path to his cottage, he opened the front door and they stepped in.

'Oh that's better, it's lovely and warm in here. You must have been freezing sitting on the ferry in just that jumper,' Juliette said, standing in the little entrance hallway to Luke's cottage.

Luke pulled off his scarf and hung it on the coat hook by the door and took her coat and hung it on the end of the bannister.

A narrow staircase came down into the hallway and four stripped pine doors led off to other rooms. He held one door open into a small square sitting room with two dark grey sofas, a brass lamp in the corner, a small coffee table and not a lot else. No pictures, no books and no photographs.

'Not quite into decorating unfortunately and I haven't had time to unpack anything. Not that I've really got anything - so it's all a bit bare. Shall we sit here, or do you want to come through to the kitchen?'

'I'd love to sit in the kitchen, it's my favourite room in the house.'

'Well, that's handy because it's the warmest room in this house.'

Luke opened the door in the corner of the sitting room to a cor-ridor with another set of tiny stairs, and a walk-through room with a tiled floor and a desk under the stairwell. He opened the door to the kitchen. The whole of the back of the cottage had been knocked out and opened up into a conservatory with a glass roof.

'Wow! It's like a Tardis through here.' Juliette said.

'Not a bad setup, is it? I was concerned about the heat, but apparently it's some new-fangled double glazing, underfloor heating and it's really not been too bad. In fact, I'm now concerned about how hot it's going to be in the summer.'

'Right, what can I get you? I can offer you a Baileys, a whisky, limoncello - homemade actually, or I can make us an Irish coffee,' he asked.

'The last option sounds perfect. It's been years since I've had an Irish coffee,' Juliette replied with a smile.

Luke made the coffee, poured cream onto the top and brought it over and placed it on the table. Juliette took a sip, the cream sticking to her top lip, the hot sweet coffee making her taste buds happy.

'Delicious, thank you.'

Luke clinked his coffee glass onto hers.

'Cheers Juliette, it's nice getting to know you.'

'Same to you, Luke, same to you,' she said, feeling a little bit of that same sensation again somewhere in the depths of herself.

The sweet coffee, ride on the ferry and easy conversation made Juliette smile to herself as she sat there taking sips of her drink and gazing at the vision in front of her.

'Juliette?' she heard Luke say, as she sat there daydreaming, the fresh air from the walk, the drinks in the pub and the loveliness that was Luke making her drift off into a world of her own.

'Ooops, right, sorry, yes. Well Luke, it's been lovely but I've got a full day tomorrow and then I'm straight to pick up Maggie so I really need to get myself home, showered and into bed.'

'Yeah, me too. A few pints and I'm done for.'

'I'll walk you to your house,' Luke said, as he picked up the coffee cups and put them in the sink.

'I'm fine, thanks, there's really no need.' Juliette said, as she got up from the table and started walking through the cottage.

'There's no way I'm letting you walk on your own.'

'You can watch from the pavement, you'll just be able to see down to my cottage at the end.' Juliette replied, trying to sound nonchalant, but really hoping he would very much walk her to her door and imagining him ripping off her clothes once they got there.

She opened the door to the entrance hall and just after she'd put her coat on and was tucking her scarf around her neck while he stood holding onto the bannister she turned around. Luke was very close and as he went to reach forward and open the front door she could smell that same dark, musky scent that almost made her go weak at the knees. She was sure that Luke Burnette, and possibly the whole of Seapocket Lane could hear her heart banging in her chest and the trombones playing in her head.

She looked up at him as she was about to step out the door and he bent down and touched his hand on her waist and then he kissed her gently and she stepped forward, drawing them closer together and kissing him back.

She stood there in the little hallway, clutching onto her bag with one hand and put her other hand on the top of his leg, blinking up at him. Far away in the distance, the sound of the Pretty Beach ferry sounded in her ears and she wondered if, in fact, she was in a dream.

Chapter 28

What do you do when you've kissed someone and you were nearly forty? That was the question Juliette continued to repeat over and over in her head. *What did she do now?* She had no idea how to play the dating game and indeed she wasn't even sure what game she was playing. What she did know was that the trombones that had played in her head at Luke's door were now positively booming and banging in elation.

Juliette opened her front door, slipped off her shoes and walked through the sitting room. She opened the fridge still in her coat and took out a block of cheddar, lifted the lid on the pale pink bread bin and got out a loaf of bread. She took off her coat, washed her hands and stood at the counter cutting slices of cheese whilst two slices of bread were in the toaster.

She turned the grill on in the oven, laid the slices of cheese onto the toast and finely sliced slivers of onion on top of the cheese, shook on some Worcestershire sauce and shoved the whole lot under the grill.

Waiting for the cheese on toast she poured herself a long, tall glass of lemonade and stood leaning back against the counter of the kitchen thinking about Luke and what had just happened.

Should she have left? Should she have stayed? She could quite easily have followed him up to his bedroom and spent the night with him having wild, abandoned sex with this man who she pretty much knew hardly anything about.

She pulled out the toast from under the grill, piled it onto a plate, picked up the lemonade and pushed open the door to the lovely little warm conservatory and sat down on the sofa.

No, she definitely should not have stayed. Anyone would have given her the same advice, and casual sex wasn't something she was interested in or wanted. But goodness it was tempting, there were stirrings, stirrings in places she didn't know could any longer be stirred, and trombones had thundered about in her ears.

She finished off her cheese on toast. Stirrings, maybe she'd look that up on the Internet. Well at least she had something interesting to tell Daisy when she called. Daisy would be jumping up and down and not believe it and Daisy would know what to do about stirrings.

Daisy had been in a relationship with a married doctor on and off for ten years and in between had had all sorts of very unsuitable relationships and would definitely have an opinion about what had happened with Luke.

Juliette's phone pinged as she put her plate on the coffee table.

Mum, how are you, I've just got back from work, how were the work drinks?

They were lovely actually. I got the ferry home with one of the new doctors.

Oh what? Really!

Yes.

What's he like then? Mum I have never heard you mention anyone like ever!!!!!!!

Don't be silly Bella I was just telling you I got on the ferry with someone.

No way, you NEVER say stuff like that. OMG!

Yes, way. Anyway how are you?

You are not going to believe what I did? I'm so embarrassed.

Oh no what?

Well you know what I'm like I was sitting up reading about the industrial revolution and writing an assignment all afternoon and then I suddenly realised I had twenty minutes to get to the pub for my shift and I was still in my nightie!

Juliette waited for the next instalment.

So I ran into the shower, picked up my jeans from the bathroom floor, grabbed a jumper and my coat and ran down the road.

And...

And when I opened the door to the pub and started walking across the carpet I felt something behind me and I looked behind and last night's tights and knickers were dragging along behind me out of the leg of the jeans!

Hahahahahahahahaha Bella, so you. Too busy learning and reading.

Mum I was just so embarrassed!

Don't worry darling, we've all done similar silly things. That is a good one though. So what did you do?

I just carried on walking towards the bar dragging the tights and knickers with me then gathered them up and stuffed them in my coat pocket.

No one said anything?

Nope, but I could feel everyone looking at me.

Well you've given me a laugh anyway.

Back to the man on the ferry. Who?????

Bella it's nothing I was just letting you know.

I don't believe that for a second. Oh my god mum, you like someone!!!!

Chapter 29

Juliette had arrived back from dropping Maggie at Jeremy's, taking a load of parcels to the post office and was walking along Seapocket Lane on the phone to Daisy arranging what they were going to do when Daisy came down for the weekend. Just as she had said goodbye and was putting her phone back into her bag, she saw Luke's front door open and a black leather sports bag land on the front step.

From where she was down the lane he wouldn't be able to see her and she absolutely wanted to see him. She quickened her step and saw an arm and then a reusable supermarket bag also placed on the front step. *Crikey* she thought to herself, *I'm going to need to run if I want to bump into him by his car.* She started the teeniest of runs on the slippery pavement and started to laugh at herself.

She hadn't run since she'd left Jeremy - in those days she'd wasted many hours of her life on the back of a treadmill running for her life. And she'd wasted way too much brain power on analysing calories, positively calculated how many calories the flavoured water she drank was and here she was attempting to run down the road to chase after a very handsome man and not making a very good job of it. It was as if every single part of her body was jiggling - her tummy, the backs of her arms and she could feel her bottom touching the backs of her legs. *Oh, what would Jeremy have thought about this?* She loved it.

Out of breath, a layer of perspiration running down her back she slowed to a walk and placed her bag nonchalantly over her arm. She slowed right down as she stepped along the pavement hoping to time Luke walking down his path to the gate and into his car with her walking past. She felt so hot she pulled her scarf away from her collar and undid the buttons on her coat letting the air in to cool her down.

The same what were becoming familiar feelings stirred as she saw him open the front door fully, shut it behind him and pick up the black leather holdall. *Oh no she wasn't going to make it* she realised - his strides were a lot quicker than she had anticipated. She looked up and down trying to see if she could see his BMW. Luckily, it was halfway down the road, if she jogged down the left side of the road without him seeing her she could cross over just as he was getting to his car.

She jogged over the road and started to run along, sweat ran down her back and her hair at the front started to stick to her forehead. She ducked down a bit hoping he wouldn't see her and hurried along. She glanced back, yes, he was fiddling with the handle on the shopping bag, she couldn't quite see but he looked as if he was putting a bottle of water in it.

She turned back about to run along a bit further and then cross and nearly bumped straight into Ali, who dressed in his suit and tie, was clearly on his way to the restaurant.

'Oops, not looking where you're going, Juliette?' Ali said with a chuckle and put his arm out to steady her.

'Oh, ah, sorry Ali.'

'Are you okay, Juliette? You look a bit... flustered.' Ali said taking in Juliette's now bright red cheeks, open coat and the sweat on her forehead.

'I'm fine,' Juliette puffed.

Ali stood in Juliette's way and glancing to the right over Ali's shoulder she could see that Luke was well out of his gate and halfway to his car.

'Do you want me to get you a drink of water or something?'

'No, no, no I'm fine Ali, really, I'm errrr, just late for an appointment.'

'Are you sure? You look ever-so hot. Do you want to sit down on the wall for a bit?'

'Really, I'm ok, look I've got to go,' Juliette said and went to move on along the pavement.

Ali then saw Luke over the road and a look of understanding passed across his face as Juliette kept looking furtively to the right.

'Okay, see you later,' Ali said, stepping out of the way to his right as Juliette walked past him.

It was too late, she could see the boot of Luke's BMW was up and Luke putting the holdall in the back. Even if she ran back across the road, he would be in the car and about to pull away and that would mean she would have to call out or wave and she had wanted it to be so very casual.

She was so hot now that she stopped in the middle of the pavement, took off her scarf and started to pull her arms out of her coat. She leant on a wall as she watched the BMW indicate to the left, pull away and drive off down Seapocket Lane.

Damn it, Juliette thought as she leant on the wall, *oh well, what will be will be.*

She gathered up her coat and walked along the rest of the lane to her little cottage and smiled as she saw the pink door with the huge wreath and the little electric Lucia candles flickering in the window.

Her breath nearly returned to normal and not feeling quite as hot as she had on the pavement, she walked up the path reaching into her bag for her keys and just as she was unlocking the door looked to the right. Sitting on the little chair with the lantern beside it was a bunch of flowers propped up against the back of the chair.

She picked up the flowers and looked inside the thick white paper - a posy of beautiful roses from White Cottage Flowers tied with a pale pink silk ribbon, a small white heavily embossed card tucked inside.

Thanks for the other night. It was amazing. Love Luke.

And right under that in small, scrawly handwriting was Luke Burnette's number.

Holding the bunch of flowers in her left arm, Juliette pushed open her front door, closed it gently behind her, leant back and screwed up every bit of her face.

'Yessssssssssssss!'

Chapter 30

Juliette had been thinking about it for a while. She was going to throw all caution to the wind and go for it with Luke. Well not all the caution, in all the wind, but she was going to have a go. There would still be deliberation - she had Maggie to think about and there would be care, but she was going to put herself in the game, fully one hundred per cent in the game.

However, she did not want to appear as if she was throwing herself at him - she still had to maintain a modicum of respect even if inside she could have quite happily walked around to his cottage, scooted up his stairs and fallen into his bed for a night, or six, of wild passion.

After the episode with the rollers and the flowers she needed to orchestrate bumping into him... that was what she would do to appear nonchalant. The accidental bumping into someone was something she was definitely not experienced in though, in fact she was more a professional avoider. She could spot someone she didn't want to see from ten paces and avoid them with deft skill and much expertise. She had mastered the art of pretending not to see someone on many different occasions over the years including, but not limited to, the school run and any number of Jeremy's political events.

She sat there at the pink kitchen table drinking a cup of tea while Maggie played with Lego and she wrapped orders for A Christmas Sparkle and put the product parcels into little white satchels. As she methodically wrapped vintage Christmas decorations in white tissue paper, gold stars and tiny little gold baubles threaded onto ribbon, her mind went over and over the situation with Luke.

Here she was just moved into a new house, it was her favourite time of year, Bella was doing really well at Oxford and she had finally put the whole Jeremy debacle behind her and all of a sudden she'd kissed a man in the hallway of his cottage, he'd left flowers on her front step and given her his number. All very strange. And all very exciting.

She got up from the table, arranged the pile of prettily wrapped parcels on the end of the table and took a piece of paper from the dresser and started to write things down - just where and how could she bump into him again without sending him a text and instead having the whole thing seem a bit more, casual?

There was work, the pool, the pub and possibly the laneway. Work was a problem, firstly, she wasn't doing as many shifts because of the shop, and secondly, he was on at different times to her. The ocean pool where apparently he loved to swim laps was not her favourite place; while Juliette loved nothing better than a little swim at the beach, getting into a swimming pool or going anywhere near it in the cold weather, was not on her preferred list of ways to spend time. Then there was the pub, if she could find out what night he strolled to the pub she could pop in too - or would it be odd for her to suddenly pop down to the pub? So many questions in romancing someone it seemed.

From the angle of the cottage front window she could just see down to the end of Seapocket Lane and Luke's house, maybe she could just keep an eye on it and find out when he went out.

'I'm just going to pop outside Maggie.'

'What for?'

'Just to have a look at something.'

Juliette crossed the sitting room, opened the front door and walked down the path. If she stood at the end of the path near the gate she could just about see his front door if she craned her neck, otherwise she couldn't really see his house so bumping into him in Seapocket Lane wasn't going to be so easy.

***

Juliette wrapped Maggie up in her pink coat and bobble hat, put on her own boots and coat, grabbed her basket full of parcels from the side and opened the front door. Cold air hit them and she sighed happily at Seapocket Lane looking all festive and pretty. Ali over the road had gone all out with lights on his fir trees now and all the way down the street lights twinkled and she smiled at the cottage next door with a huge wreath on the front door and pots of white poinsettias standing either side of the pathway.

'Right Maggie, let's go. We'll drop off the parcels, then we'll walk over to the other side of Pretty Beach and go to the swings - do you fancy that?'

Maggie nodded and skipped along by Juliette's side. They walked all the way along the laneway, White Cottage Flowers had had a delivery of fresh Christmas trees which were stacked up out the front. The gift shop was playing Christmas tunes and one of the staff was dressed up in an elf costume and giving out tiny little candles in exchange for a donation to Pretty Beach Lifeboats.

'Can we get some buns, Mummy?' Maggie asked as they walked up to Pretty Beach Bakery.

Juliette nodded and they walked up to the shop, gazing up at the beautiful shimmering reindeer on the roof and pushed open the door to the smell of mince pies and Christmas puddings. Holly had draped garlands of rich-looking thick silver tinsel from the ceiling and another shimmering reindeer had appeared in the corner.

Hanging from a vintage ladder on the left wall were hundreds of Christmas puddings wrapped in muslin and tied on the top with silver ribbon. A rustic timber shelf underneath was stacked with boxed Christmas cakes and a large blackboard under the ladder detailed all the specialities on offer.

Hand-wrapped, beautifully ribboned Pretty Beach Christmas Puddings - our own secret seaside recipe.

Juliette and Maggie got in the queue as Holly zipped around chatting to all the regulars and her girls worked quickly and efficiently through the line of people to the door.

'Ahhh, lovely Juliette, and hello Maggie! How are you both?' Holly enquired, came around from behind the counter and kissed Juliette on the cheek.

'We're good. I think we were after some buns, but that may have changed now,' Juliette said as Maggie peered into the counter, eyeing up the gingerbread men.

'You've been busy then, by the looks of it,' Juliette said, pointing to the ladder full of puddings and the Christmas cakes on the shelf.

'We certainly have, I can't get them out quickly enough - the shop in Newport has sold out already and the Seafolly shop is nearly out too.'

'I'm not surprised, they're delicious.'

'Don't worry, I've got the Locals Only ones all ready out the back. Anyway, a little dickie bird told me you were on the ferry the other night from Seafolly.'

'Pearl Beach, actually.'

'Ahh yes, that's right... and you were escorted home by a very nice chap,' Holly said, lowering her voice so Maggie couldn't hear, and winked at Juliette.

Juliette leant closer to Holly and whispered, 'How the heck do you know that? Holly you must have spy cameras all over Pretty Beach!'

'I have my sources. You find out all sorts in the Marina Club on poker nights.'

'I know, Captain Jones! He was on that night, it was a bit hairy through the Middles I can tell you.'

'I'm not saying a word,' Holly said, throwing her head back and laughing.

I've heard the chap who escorted you home goes to the Smugglers for the Locals Only lunch, not being a very good cook apparently and liking a hot lunch - not that you'd be interested in that or anything.'

Juliette started giggling, 'How do you know that Holly?'

Holly tapped the side of her nose and smiled, 'I know everything in Pretty Beach.'

Holly passed Maggie a gingerbread man, they said goodbye and pulled open the door and walked back onto the laneway.

Well, that was one thing sorted, the bumping into Luke may just have to be the Smugglers special lunch. Simple.

Chapter 31

Juliette drove along the coast road, thick white fog low on the ground and sparkly frost glittering in the middle of the road. On the way to Maggie's school, Christmas songs played on the stereo and Maggie was chatting away telling her all about the Christmas play. Arriving at the school car park, Juliette put Maggie's hat on her head and walked her up to the school gates.

'Okay darling, so daddy will be collecting you from school today and then I will see you tomorrow morning,' Juliette said, adjusting the collar on Maggie's coat.

Maggie kissed her and skipped off happily and Juliette thanked her lucky stars that so far Maggie loved school. She strode back to the car, turned on the ignition and her phone started ringing. She clicked the button on the steering wheel to answer.

'Hey Daisy, how are you? Sorry I missed your calls, I was at work and then I had drinks, it's been all go the last few weeks. I bet it's the same for you, right?'

'I'm manic, don't know my ass from my elbow at this time of year. I've got food everywhere and every night booked out at work. Any news to tell me? Any exciting happenings down in the world of Pretty Beach?'

'Well I might have just the smidgen of something to tell you,' Juliette said, as she sped along looking out over the sea, the Pretty Beach lighthouse way off in the distance peering out over the cliffs.

'Oh no, what's Jeremy done now?'

'Nope, all good on the Jeremy front but, well...' Juliette trailed off.

'I'm intrigued, do tell, Sparkles, do tell.' Daisy replied.

'I may have had a little incy-wincy kiss with a very tasty man, the tasty man I danced with at the Christmas dance.'

'You have got to be kidding me!' Daisy shouted down the phone in excitement.

Juliette was laughing as she stopped at a set of traffic lights in the direction of her storage unit.

'I know. I'm astonished to be honest. I can't even tell you the last time I looked at a man. I mean it's been years, like years and years and now this. Not only have I kissed him, I can't stop thinking about him. Of course, I'm only telling you this, to everyone else I'm completely not interested, but Daisy, I'm so, very, very much interested.'

'I did not see this coming Sparkles!' Daisy almost yelled down the phone.

'Nor me, I've been in an emotional vortex for precisely eighteen years and 8 months and something is happening to me that I cannot control,' Juliette joked, and they both laughed.

'When you walked out on Jeremy you said you'd never, ever have a man again and live the rest of your days out pottering around making Christmas decorations, with lots of pets and looking after your girls,' Daisy stated.

'I know I did and that was fully my intention. And I was telling myself that too and that I wasn't going to think about Luke and then I looked in the mirror and saw happy, plump, very much more relaxed Juliette and I thought well what have I got to lose?'

'Oh. My. God. Where's the popcorn. I'm taking a seat and getting comfy for the ride. Sparkles, this is going to be absolutely fabulous!'

'Ha! Well, there's no ride... yet, but I am orchestrating one.'

'Sorry, who are you? And what have you done with my friend Juliette?'

'I know, I know, it's all nuts, but I'm enjoying it Daisy. For the first time in years I'm relaxed and I don't even know how to describe it. But I'm sort of optimistic.'

'What's he like then, this Luke?'

'How many words do you want?' Juliette said, laughing.

'As many as you like, my friend.'

'Well, I'll give you just the one. Gorgeous. Absolutely gorgeous. Like he just stepped out of a movie gorgeous.'

'Wow! Okay, you need to send me pics. Look I've got to go, I'm up to my eyes but I was calling to say that I'm coming down soon for the weekend. I've got a weekend with no work and I'm getting on the train and coming down to the sea.'

'Okay, all good, the sofa bed is ready and waiting for you whenever you need it. It'll be nice to have you back in Pretty Beach.'

Juliette ended the call and thought about Daisy, her long-time friend who she'd first met in the bedsit when she had been heavily pregnant with Bella. They'd clicked from the word go and Daisy had got her through some tough times - the early days when Bella was tiny and Juliette didn't have a clue what she was doing, the schedules she'd had to adhere to when she was doing her training and mostly just being a really good friend.

Daisy was also the reason that Juliette had ended up in Pretty Beach in the first place. Daisy had been down in Pretty Beach to see her mum and had seen an advert for jobs in Newport Reef and they'd come down together in Daisy's tiny little car with Bella in the back. As soon as Juliette had seen Pretty Beach as they'd driven along the coast road she'd decided that a life by the sea was the one for her.

Daisy hadn't stayed in Pretty Beach though and when Juliette had taken the job, Daisy moved on from the tiny bedsit and alongside her hospital job had started cooking more in her spare time and it had taken off and at this time of year she was busier than ever.

Juliette thought about how good it would be to see Daisy. They would chat and eat and laugh for hours, and a dose of Daisy was always just what Juliette needed. She drove around the corner, parked her car near to the storage unit and walked in.

'Hi, how are you, Juliette? Cold enough for you?' Michael asked, from the front desk.

'It's certainly not warm. The nearer we're getting to Christmas though the more I'm wanting more snow,' Juliette replied.

'Still got a bit of a wait until Christmas! Though the decorations seem to be in the shops these days in August. The snow will come, don't you worry, I can feel it in my bones. What are you up to today, then?' Michael asked.

'I've got lots of orders to wrap and loads of case notes to write up, but I'm going to treat myself to lunch at the Smugglers,' Juliette replied.

'What, the LO lunch? Yeah, I've heard that's meant to be amazing.'

'I've heard that too. I certainly hope it is.' Juliette smiled and chuckled to herself as she passed the reception desk and made her way to her storage block. It wasn't just the lunch that she hoped would be amazing.

Chapter 32

Juliette poured the tea from the pale pink teapot into the mug, took three chocolate Hobnobs out of the biscuit tin, sat down and dunked them in her tea.

She'd worked out that if she steamed through her admin and dropped her parcels off at the post office she would have just about enough time to shower, do her hair and stroll nonchalantly over to the Smugglers and just so happen to have lunch there on her day off.

She had it all planned out. If Luke was there and he happened to mention that she was there alone she was going to say that she'd wanted some time alone after a busy week at work and looking after Maggie and that she wanted to take some pictures of the wonderful fire in the middle of the pub for a blog post on her website.

She finished her work, heaved herself up the steep stairs, had a long hot shower and put her hair in her rollers. She opened up the built-in wardrobe musing what the outfit was when hoping to bump into a man. Hmmm, tricky. She wanted to look nice, but not like she'd tried. Did regular men (not men like Jeremy who absolutely noticed) though, really notice what a woman was wearing? She tried on her favourite pink ruffle dress. No. The black wrap. Also a no. She then flicked through the tops at the end of the wardrobe. Yes, a pale blue, floaty top with a ruched bodice and small white polka dots with dark navy-blue jeans and her boots. Casual and pretty. She looked in the mirror and shuddered at the thought of the old super-thin, super-stressed, married to Jeremy Juliette who would never have gone out in a soft, floaty top.

She did her makeup, pulled out the rollers to big soft curls, put dangly little heart earrings in her ears and dabbed her favourite floral perfume at her wrists.

***

Juliette walked all the way along Seapocket Lane and glanced at Luke's cottage - no signs of life there at all. She then walked along the back and made her way through Mermaids to see if there was any further indication that Mr Jenkin's cottage was going to go up for sale.

She pulled her coat further around her, a cold window coming in off the sea as she approached Mermaids and squinted down towards the cottage. There were definitely signs of something going on - a bright yellow skip was sitting outside piled with an old mattress, a toilet and lots of building rubble. As she got closer she could see that the front door was open and she could hear a radio playing and what sounded like workmen inside.

She wondered what Nicky Jenkin had decided to do in the end. By the looks of it she was going to rent it out but maybe she was doing some cosmetic work before it went to market. Juliette doubted that though, the woman's attitude had been to get rid of it and get out of Mermaid Lane as quickly as possible.

She whipped her phone out of her pocket and took a picture of the cottage and the skip. The problem with it being done up though was that she was hoping for an old place to keep the cost down. If this Nicky was renovating then she would be hoping for the same price as the one over the road had gone for and that was way out of Juliette's price range.

Juliette carried on walking along the road, the cold breeze blowing her curls all over the place as she approached the Pretty Smugglers. The coloured lights swayed outside in the wind, and the car park was already packed for the lunch special. That was good she thought, at least it wouldn't be too obvious she was on her own hoping to bump into Luke if it was packed with regulars.

No doubt it would go around like wildfire with the locals and the likes of Holly that she just so happened to be in there for the LO lunch. Juliette smiled to herself at Holly, she knew everything about

Pretty Beach and on this occasion Juliette was quite pleased that she did.

She pushed open the door to the pub and looked around, lots of locals standing at the bar, the tables nearly all taken, a massive fire in the middle. The warm, cosy pub smell enveloped her together with the smoky scent of the fire and some of her Christmas candles were lit over on the far end of the bar.

Over in the corner one small table for two laid with knives and forks wrapped in paper napkins, bottles of brown sauce and salt and pepper was free. She walked up to the bar, ordered a lemonade and tapped her card to pay for it, taking a menu.

'Locals Only is mini-roast - it's pork and Yorkshires, baked pumpkin and gravy if you're interested, Juliette,' James the barman said quietly, 'Not too much of that left though, so if you're wanting it you're going to need to order soon. I have to say the Yorkshires are outstanding, and there's crackling and then there's John's crackling, he's outdone himself today.'

Juliette scrolled down the menu, she always fancied a roast but it seemed a bit strange on a lunchtime, more a Sunday dinner for her. She mulled over the homemade burgers, she'd had them before and they were delicious too.

'You know what, yes, I'll have the mini-roast please James.'

She handed him back the menu and paid, grabbed her lemonade and went all the way over to the free table in the corner. She took out her phone, checked to see if any more orders had come in for the shop and scrolled through some pictures Bella had sent her of a Christmas fancy dress party she had gone to as Mrs Christmas in a tiny little red suit, black tights and a red hat with a bobble on the end. She smiled as she scrolled through them. Bella was having the time of her life and everything that Juliette had wanted for her and it made her very happy.

Just as James was walking over with the plate of roast, the door to the pub opened, wind whistled in through the gap and there he was, Luke, standing there in a grey crew neck jumper and scarf. He unwrapped his scarf as he came in the door and looked around the pub and caught her eye. He walked over as James put the steaming roast lunch down in front of Juliette.

'Hello again. I've never seen you in here for lunch before.'

There were huge sparks going between them. Sparks tinged with a little bit of embarrassment as Juliette sat there looking at Luke, re-living the kiss in the hallway over and over again. All she knew was that she fancied the pants off him and who could argue with that? She sat there staring at him, his mouth moving but her not really hearing what he was saying.

'Juliette? Are you with us?' Luke joked.

'Yes, sorry. I've got a day off and needed a bit of breathing space and fancied the Locals Only lunch,' Juliette said, pretending that she just so happened to be there.

James shuffled the knives and forks around and smiled to himself and turned to Luke, 'Hey Luke, how are you? Can I get you the roast too? We're down to probably the last three.'

'I'd love it, thanks,' Luke replied.

'And a pint of your usual?'

'Indeed - that would be great, cheers James.'

'No problems, I'll bring your pint over and put it all on your tab.'

Juliette could have sworn that James had orchestrated the whole thing, getting Luke to order the roast and offering to bring his pint over - she couldn't really have done it better herself.

'Looks like you've got the only chair left in the place,' Luke said, pointing to the chair.

'Have a seat. I'd love someone to chat to,' Juliette said, fluttering her eyelashes and curling her hair over her shoulder.

What the heck am I doing? Did I just flutter my eyelashes and play with my hair? Get a grip! Breathe and calm.

'Great, thanks,' Luke said, and sat down.

A couple of minutes later James brought a pint of ale to the table and another roast dinner and Juliette and Luke tucked into the food and chatted about the hospital.

'So how are you getting on with your shop? That must be really busy at the moment.' Luke asked.

'Yeah, thank goodness. It's turning out to be my best year ever and every single penny will be going into the pot for a deposit on a house.'

'So where are you looking?'

'Well if possible I want to be in Pretty Beach or somewhere close. But yeah Pretty beach is the preference, I've loved it here since I first came here years ago.'

'I can see why. I feel the same already.'

'There's a cottage over on Mermaids that might be coming up, but I just walked past this morning and it looks like it might be being done up, so that would put paid to that idea.'

'It's a tricky old thing buying a house, isn't it?'

'Yep, and I want something old and with character so that cuts out a lot of stuff that I could afford.'

'It's like a waiting game and then once you actually find something you like it's then like gambling - all the offering and then other people offering,' Luke said, draining his pint.

'Another drink?'

'Yes please, a lemonade.'

'Great, I'll be back in a sec.'

Juliette watched as Luke with the very pert bottom in his jeans strolled towards the bar, the dark musky scent that seemed to do something to her brain wafted past her nose and she sat back in her chair and smiled to herself. She didn't know what was in that aftershave, or indeed where he got it from, but goodness did it set her veins on fire.

Luke came back to the table with the drinks, the pub had started to empty out a bit, people on their way back to work, the lunchtime food trade now dwindling away. Juliette looked into the flames of the fire as Luke chatted about how he still hadn't decided whether or not he was going to go to Sweden or Spain after Christmas.

'Have you sorted out your plans yet?'

'No, I'm still waiting to hear from Jeremy and what his mother is doing as to what days he's going to spend with Maggie and then I can get things organised. Bella has been invited to go to America with someone from uni so if I can help her out with the flights I'm going to tell her to go for her life. So, there's a possibility that I could actually be alone!'

'Well that would be a bit sad.'

Juliette finished her lemonade. 'Oh, I'll be fine. Right Luke, I'm going to get going.'

'I'm going to stay for another drink actually, have a sit at the bar and read the news.' Luke replied.

Juliette picked up her bag and coat, 'Thanks for joining me for lunch, I thoroughly enjoyed it. I need to make it here more often.'

'No, thank you. By the way, I was wondering if you would like to come to the cinema? The Orpheum over at Pearl Beach, I've heard it's really good and they do special themed movie nights there. What do you think?' He looked at her earnestly with the big brown eyes and flop of hair.

Juliette spluttered, and replied, 'Wouldn't mind that at all Luke, not at all.'

Juliette looked at Luke standing there looking at her in his navy-blue scarf and jumper and ever-so broad chest. Her heart raced as she heard herself replying that yes she would very much like to go and watch a film.

'The Orpheum. I haven't been there for years. It's magical at Christmas time. Thanks, I'd love to.'

'What are you up to at the weekend? Any free days? What about Maggie, is she at her dad's?'

'Yes, the weekend would be fabulous. Maggie is at her dad's and my daughter Bella is coming down from uni. She's going out with her old school friends on Friday night so that would work.'

'Deal. I'll book the tickets and message you.'

'Okay, well thanks for a nice lunch.'

Luke leant over and kissed her on the cheek, resting his hand on her waist and the musky smell wafted past her again. Juliette stood there in the floaty top and curled hair and didn't move for a second, lost in thought. Lost in the thought that for so long she'd thought that she was too old, too sensible and had too many responsibilities to think about something as silly as romance in her life. But the tingly thing that happened to her skin when she had first laid eyes on Luke Burnette had seemed to put paid to all those sensible grown-up feelings that had been sitting at the front of her head for eighteen years. She didn't move for a second until he looked at her quizzically.

'Juliette? Are you ok?'

'Oh, yes, sorry, yes, just a lot on my mind,' she said, shaking her head and bringing herself back to the moment.

'By the way,' Luke said, 'the other night was amazing.'

Breathe and calm.

Juliette just looked at him and nodded, backed away, heard herself saying goodbye in a ridiculous sing-songy voice and crossed the pub to pop to the loo before she left to walk home. She walked into the toilet, locked the door, closed her eyes tightly together, squished her fists up to her lips and did a little squeal.

James the barman who was walking past the loo door with an armful of glasses heard the little squeal and smiled to himself.

Chapter 33

Juliette finished packing her midwifery equipment into the back of her car and as she put it into the boot suddenly thought about Ashley who had delivered on the bathroom floor in the cottage next door to Luke, and was doing well now she was home - time since that beautiful birth seemed to have flown by. She drove home to Pretty Beach and parked outside her cottage on the lane. Christmas lights swayed in the breeze coming in from the sea as she locked the car, walked up her path and let herself in.

'How was it? Lilly, her friend Nina's nanny, who had been babysitting when Juliette had been called out to a birth, asked.

'Ahh, it was lovely, a beautiful water birth, I'm pretty tired though. How was Maggie?'

'Fine. She tried to con me into three stories though before she'd go to bed and she even tried getting the tablet in bed with her to read another story,' Lilly replied.

'Little toad!'

'It didn't work and she was sound asleep by seven. You must be shattered.'

'I am and I'm going out tomorrow night so I need to get a good sleep in.'

'Where are you off to? Another Christmas party?'

'Actually no, I'm going to the Orpheum for a special showing of a Christmas film - the one where they swap houses - the LA house and the house in the Cotswolds.'

'Lucky you! I heard the tickets sold out for that really quickly - were you on a waiting list or something?'

'I don't know actually, I didn't buy them.'

'Right, who are you going with then?'

'Actually, keep it to yourself Lilly, but I'm going with Luke who moved into the end of the lane.'

'Oooooh gossip. I won't say a word Jools.' Lilly said laughing, and gathering up her laptop and books, putting her coat on and walking to the front door.

'I'll be seeing you then. Have a fabulous time tomorrow night.'

'I hope so,' Juliette said smiling.

Juliette walked across the sitting room and stepped down into the little kitchen, put a portion of leftover spaghetti bolognese in the microwave and just as she had sat down at the table a message came in from Daisy.

You're not going to believe this!

What?

I've only got an extremely famous American wife of a huge politician booked in for dinner at work next weekend - can't name any names, I had to actually sign a non-disclosure!

Interesting, can't wait to hear more on that.

Exactly what I thought. Any news from you? What's happened since the kiss and pert-bottomed man?

I may or may not be going out with him tomorrow night. Juliette typed with one hand while she carried on eating her bolognese.

Sparkles! You didn't tell me!

Sorry, I've been so busy, I did ring but you must have had your phone off.

So, my god, so many questions! What are you wearing?

I don't know.

How did all this come about then?

I just so happened to be in the pub when he was in there - I may have accidentally on purpose bumped into him.

Wow, who even are you?

I know. It's crazy and I'm loving it.

Right, I'll ring you in the morning. I want a full run-down and full details, possibly a video-call while you're getting ready. Plus I want communication while you're there. Does Bella know yet?

Not yet. No one knows anything.

Chapter 34

Juliette sat at her desk in the consultation room at Pretty Beach surgery and mentally went through her checklist - Maggie was sorted, she was up-to-date with all her orders for A Christmas Sparkle, and she had two more ante-natal appointments to finish and she was on time, which was a miracle considering how busy it had been all morning.

She sat there thinking about the date with Luke and all her previous bravado and ideas about going for it had slowly withered away and she had asked herself quite what she thought she was doing.

As more and more doubts crept in, she tried to talk herself out of them and kept repeating over and over to herself in her head. *Open mind, confident attitude, optimistic outlook.*

The doubts got worse as the day went on and as Juliette started getting ready she got more and more nervous. A whirlwind of emotions were traipsing in and out of her brain and every time she thought of another reason why she was crazy to be going on a date with Luke with all her responsibilities she opened the fridge and comfort ate something else. She'd already had a pork pie, a tube of crisps, a toasted cheese and tuna sandwich, a slice of apple cake and half a jar of olives.

She had a mixture of excitement, anticipation and nerves, but mostly she really had the jitters. She'd primped and polished every part of her body in anticipation and kept thinking that she shouldn't be even thinking about primping, or more importantly, be thinking about what primping would lead to.

For goodness sake I've birthed two babies, been married and run the life of a high-flying politician while holding down my own career - I should be able to cope with going on a date.

As she pottered around the cottage more thoughts ran through her head at a hundred miles an hour.

Oh my goodness, who will pay the bill? Oh my goodness, will it be awkward? Oh my goodness, what will I do if he wanted it to go further than the kiss in the hallway?

She had washed and curled her hair and put on her makeup, but with all the thoughts and emotions jangling around her head she'd ended up sitting on the floor of her bedroom leaning up against the bed staring at the wall for fifteen minutes persuading herself that she would be fine.

Open mind, confident attitude, optimistic outlook.

After having picked out the dress she was going to wear days before the Orpheum date, once she was getting dressed she'd looked in the mirror, hated her new curves, felt frumpy, dumpy and old, and had promptly removed the dress and had started to frantically rummage through her wardrobe. She had gone through nearly every item of clothing, discarding everything in a heap on the bed and wondering what on earth she was going to wear. The whole bedroom looked like a tornado had whipped through it when she'd finished and then she'd picked up the original dress, tried it on again and wore that anyway.

Juliette had wasted so much time trying on different outfits and sitting on the floor trying to allay her butterflies-up-to-her-throat nervousness that she was now going to be late if she didn't get going. She looked in the full-length mirror one more time and decided that firstly, it was as good as it was going to get, and secondly, it would have to do. Luke probably wouldn't be looking at her clothes anyway, with any luck he would be looking somewhere else.

Juliette rushed out of the cottage in Seapocket Lane pulling her coat on as she ran down the pathway and headed down to the ferry. Just as she got to the top of the wharf she saw the ferry coming around the corner and slowed her pace knowing that she'd made it.

All of a sudden she panicked. *Oh my Christ! Did I put deodorant on?* She thought as a bead of sweat ran down her back and she undid her coat and tried to frantically sniff under her arm as she walked along.

***

Juliette got on the ferry, sat up the top, held on while it went through the Middles, waves crashing into the hull and answered a text from Daisy.

What was I thinking? I'm all sorts of nervous.

You'll be fine.

I think I forgot to put my deodorant on and now I think I stink!!!

Get a grip, it's just a date.

Just! Just a date! Daisy I haven't been on a date for eighteen years. I mean you can't include meeting Jeremy as a date.

True. Deep breaths. Breathe and enjoy.

Juliette, with her coat over her arm in the freezing cold air and now convinced that her armpits were not pleasant, walked along the road to the spot where she'd arranged to meet Luke, who was coming from Newport Reef on the way home from work.

Breathe and enjoy, breathe and enjoy, she repeated over and over to herself as she walked up the wharf to the meeting point and saw Luke standing under the light from a lamppost in a navy-blue jumper, dark jeans and a big scarf.

Breathe and enjoy, she said again to herself as she approached him.

'Hey, hello,' she said, sounding a whole lot more casual and calm than she felt inside where she could have sworn everyone in a two-mile radius could hear the banging of her heart against her ribs. *He looks absolutely gorgeous,* she thought as she looked up at him.

Luke touched her arm and leant down to kiss her hello on the cheek. She breathed him in and all of her thoughts and worries about it being difficult or awkward disappeared as with a tiny movement he pulled her just that little bit further into him and stroked her tenderly on her back. She felt his chest through the thin fabric of her dress and loved how he made her feel, loved how all of sudden the trombones started to boom.

'No coat? Was it warm on the ferry then?' Luke asked, pointing to her coat over her arm.

Juliette pretended that her dress was warm and not that she had taken off her coat because she was petrified that she'd forgotten to put her deodorant on.

'Oh this dress fabric is really warm, really warm indeed.' She heard herself say as she tried to stop herself shivering in the icy wind coming in off the sea.

He nodded and she fell into step beside him as they walked along underneath the Christmas lights of Pearl Beach. He asked her all about Maggie, a few pointed questions about Jeremy and he told her that he was ready for a break what with starting a new job and moving house.

They walked up to the Pearl Beach Orpheum, its bright lights lighting up the whole street, three Christmas trees stood to attention on top of the Art Deco awning. Multi-coloured Christmas lights encased poles outside and huge old timber doors with brass plates were propped open at the top of the red-carpeted steps.

'This is gorgeous. I'd forgotten how lovely it was,' Juliette said as Luke found the tickets on his phone and they queued up behind a red rope barrier to a young lad dressed up in an old-fashioned suit. Luke scanned his phone over the tablet on the stand and the lad unhooked the rope and let them through.

'Popcorn, sweets and drinks over there. The bar is over on the right and there will also be an interval with refreshments. Enjoy The Orpheum,' the young man said.

'What shall we have then?' Luke asked. 'Do you like popcorn?'

'I love popcorn,' Juliette said, smiling at the booth with the popcorn, but seeing the candyfloss machine behind the glass counter she continued, 'I love candyfloss more though.'

'I thought it was just me who liked candyfloss - I'm like a five-year-old still. I love the stuff!' Luke said as they stood in the queue and watched the young girl dressed in an elf costume behind the counter scoop fresh popcorn into buckets and wind sticks round and round the candyfloss machine. The girl looked up at them with a huge smile, her hair braided into two tight plaits and pinned up on the either side of her head.

'What would you like?' the young girl asked them both.

'We would like two of those please - the largest you can do,' Luke said pointing to the candyfloss. The girl reached behind her for two sticks and started to wind the pink candyfloss onto the sticks until she was done and passed the two huge clouds of pink over to Juliette. Luke paid and they walked along to the cinema.

Juliette could barely see over the candyfloss as they walked into the dimly lit cinema and found their seats. Heavy, thick red velvet curtains covered the screen and in the corner a man in a dinner suit played the piano.

'This is gold. I didn't realise it was going to be as authentic as this,' Luke whispered over to Juliette as they squeezed along the packed row of seats.

'It's amazing, isn't it? I love it. I'm always surprised at how popular it is. I've never been here when it's not sold out,' Juliette replied.

'Yeah, apparently there were only five tickets left when I booked these.'

They sat down in the old-fashioned, burgundy, velvet seats with timber arms, and fifteen minutes later the film began. Juliette sat there with the candyfloss, feeling like bolts of electricity were running between her and Luke where their arms touched on the armrest. Luke's long legs were out in front of him and she kept thinking about touching one of them, seeing what it felt like, wondering how hard the muscles were.

Ridiculous, get a grip on yourself, a voice said in her head. *You have a teenager of your own, an ex-husband and a little girl in primary school, get a grip.* Juliette had absolutely no idea what to do and it wasn't even as if she had asked for all this.

She sat there looking at his leg and thinking about all the feelings and ludicrous day dreaming she was now having about the man who lived down her road. Before he'd arrived she had been quite happy thinking about house hunting for her own little house in Pretty Beach and concentrating on her Christmas shop. Now she was ordering dresses, shaving in places she'd even forgotten were there, having meltdowns about outfits and prancing around in sparkly shoes.

Breathe and enjoy, breathe and enjoy.

She continued to shovel candyfloss into her mouth at an alarming rate and stare up at the screen as snow fell on the beautiful cottage in the Cotswolds and the handsome movie star did all the right things on the screen. She stared up at the tiny little cottage in the film and hoped she'd have her own lovely little home very soon too.

Halfway through the film interval time came around and the thick red, gold-edged curtains closed, and a young girl in a black uniform with a white shirt and black cap walked around with a tray strapped to her shoulders selling more sweets, popcorn and ice creams.

'I'm just going to pop to the loo,' Juliette whispered, gathering up her dress, getting up from her seat and making sure she had her phone in her pocket. Luke moved his long legs out of the way and touched her gently on the arm as she went past.

Juliette pushed open the toilet door, opened her phone and sent a message to Daisy.

My god, I have no idea how to behave! This is lunacy. He's gorgeous! I've made myself feel sick stuffing candyfloss down at a hundred miles an hour.

The three little dots on the screen flashed as Daisy typed back a response.

Exciting! I've been wondering how it was going.

But what do I do Daisy? You are the one who has been on a million dates. I'm sitting there bolt upright like an ironing board thinking about touching his leg. Fantasising about him.

Just be you Sparkles. It will all work itself out.

Ok. Yes, of course. This is nuts. I wasn't even looking for a date and now I'm in a cinema with a blimming god.

Hahahahaha! I'm loving this - it's the best thing that's happened all year. I want a full report on the rest of the evening when you get home - if you get home.

Don't be ridiculous! I'll be going home. I haven't had sex for years - there's no way I'll be doing that. And anyway, I've forgotten what to do.

Never say never Sparkles, text me later.

Chapter 35

Luke Burnette said thank you to the girl dressed in an elf costume standing in the foyer seeing people out and held open the art deco door of the cinema for Juliette. Juliette strolled through clutching onto her bag handle and trying to stop herself from jabbering on about nothing. Whatever was happening to her was weird; she'd moved on from stuffing in candyfloss to now talking incessantly. *Breathe and enjoy.*

They walked out onto the red carpet covered stairs and looked up at the sky as tiny little snowflakes swiftly fell from thick heavy clouds.

'I didn't know snow was forecast,' Luke said as Juliette started to put her coat on and he helped her to pull it over her shoulders.

'I thought it was forecast to rain. Aren't you going to freeze without a coat?' Juliette asked.

'Nah, I'm good.'

Juliette rummaged around in the bottom of her bag, 'I've got a mini umbrella in here somewhere.' She pulled out the spotty blue umbrella and struggled to get the catch open. Luke held out his hand, fiddled with the clasp and opened it, holding it over them both as they stood on the steps of the old cinema peering out at the dark snowy night. A group of twenty-somethings in Christmas hats strolled by on their way to the pub and a couple wrapped up in coats with tinsel around their necks ambled along hand in hand clearly on the way home from a work party.

'What do you fancy doing then?' Luke asked. 'Straight back to Pretty Beach, or shall we go for something to eat?'

'Well, I've nothing to get home for for once, no babysitter or anything...' Juliette said, thinking that she would absolutely love to go out for something to eat with Luke and sit there and stare at the chiselled jaw and the eyes and try to stop herself from stroking his leg, his arm, or for that matter any part of his body at all.

'I'm not really sure what's here, not being a real local yet. Are there any good places nearby?'

'I haven't been to Pearl Beach to eat for a long time, but there used to be a really good Chinese down by the wharf. We could walk all through the High Street and look at the Christmas lights on the way down. The restaurant is on the way to the ferry. It used to be open really late because it's next to Pearl Beach Halls so lots of people go there after a show.'

'Sounds perfect. I love Chinese so we're all set,' Luke said as they stepped onto the pavement under the spotty umbrella in the snow.

Strings of oversized Christmas lights hung in garlands over the cobbled high street as Juliette and Luke strolled past shops, looked up at the beautiful clock tower and watched a rather drunk man stumble out of a pub and heave himself onto an old, seen better days, black bike. Gentle flurries of snow fell down onto the road and disappeared as quickly as they fell.

They gazed into shop windows at Christmas displays and Luke chatted about his flat in London and how he wasn't missing the London traffic, long hours and noise. They peered into an old-fashioned sweet shop decorated with hundreds of tiny sparkly snowmen and stopped at a tiny cobbled alleyway on the left.

'Now if I remember rightly, this alleyway comes out right down the bottom near the restaurant,' Juliette remarked.

Overhead down the narrow, winding alleyway clusters of tiny white lights hung from one side to the other, the cobbles shimmered from the melted snowflakes and window boxes outside tiny little cottages with doors opening straight onto the pavement were draped with icicle lights.

'How pretty is this? I'd forgotten just how sweet and quaint Pearl Beach is. I'll have to bring Maggie over on the ferry to go and see Father Christmas once it gets a bit nearer.'

Juliette walked along beside Luke, her hands deep down in the pockets of her coat, with Luke holding the umbrella over them both as they made their way down the cobbled lane. The ferry horn sounded far off in the distance and they could just make out the sound of the sea, the air cold and brisk.

As they came to the end of the cobbled alley Juliette looked around, 'Yes, here we are, it's over there tucked in the corner.' She pointed over to the left where bright pink Christmas lights flashed all the way along a tiny parade of shops tucked off a pedestrian square.

They walked over towards the Chinese restaurant and peered in the window. Every table was taken, a queue of people stood at the desk and the seats waiting for takeaway were full.

'Hmmm, not looking too hopeful to get a table in there,' Juliette said, gesturing over to the Pearl Beach Halls. 'Maybe a show's just finished and it's Christmas party time after all.'

'I'll go in and ask,' Luke said, handing Juliette the umbrella and pushing open the door to the noise of the restaurant.

Juliette stood under the awning of the restaurant holding the umbrella, whipped out her phone and sent a message to Daisy.

All going well. Having something to eat. Still thinking about stroking any part of his body.

Chapter 36

Juliette slipped her phone back into her bag and folded up the umbrella whilst waiting for Luke to come out. She looked in to see him standing at the desk talking to a tiny woman who was pointing to the rear of the restaurant and nodding her head up and down frantically. He opened the door and came out.

'There's a small table at the very back near the toilets. I'm thinking it's a no. What do you think?' He pointed down to the end of the restaurant to the table. Juliette cupped her hands over her eyes, leant up to the glass window and looked down through the packed restaurant to a tiny table squashed in the corner with a toilet sign above it.

'Not looking that welcoming is it really? Plus, everyone will be squeezing past it every two secs.'

'Exactly what I thought.'

'Well how hungry are you?' Juliette asked.

'Pretty hungry even though I think I consumed my weight in candyfloss in the cinema.'

'How about we stroll along by the beach and then get fish and chips? There's a chip shop down there by the wharf.'

'Perfect,' Luke replied as Juliette smiled to herself at Luke's reply - Jeremy wouldn't be seen dead in the street with food and they would never have been able to do something as simple as walk along with a bag of chips.

'Let me have a look and see when the next ferry is too,' Luke said looking down at the app on this phone.

'I think they are fifteen minutes and forty-five minutes past the hour at this time on the weekends.'

'You're right,' Luke said, studying the timetable on the app.

'Great, then we don't have to worry about getting home either. Have to say I love living here and being able to get the ferry here and there, it's so easy.'

'I know, you really get used to it.'

Juliette pulled her coat tighter as the snow continued to fall all around them.

'Cold?'

'It's not warm Luke, I can't believe you don't have a coat on and seem immune to it.'

'This scarf works wonders.' Luke said and started to unwind the scarf from his neck and stopped and put it round her shoulders and tucked it into the collar of her coat and she walked along breathing in whatever the smell was on the soft scarf and wished that if nothing else she could bottle the smell and keep it by her bedside forever.

Breathe and enjoy, breathe and enjoy.

They walked along to the wharf and pushed open the door to the brightly lit Pearl Beach Fish Shop. Jingle Bells was playing loudly on the radio, a bright red Santa danced on the top of the counter and an old plump man in a Christmas jumper with an apron over the top called out to them.

'You've just made it. I'm nearly finished. What can I get you lovely pair?'

Luke looked at Juliette with his eyebrows raised in question.

'Share a large fish and chips?' Juliette said.

'Yep.' Luke turned to the man in the Christmas jumper. 'Your best large fish and chips please mate.'

'Coming right up. Where've you two been this chilly evening then?' the man asked as he busied around getting the chips and loading them into the paper.

'To the Orpheum to see a Christmas film.'

'I haven't been up there for years! What was it like?' The man asked.

'Fabulous. Really lovely,' Juliette replied, leaning on the heat of the counter and letting it seep through her coat.

'I might just have to treat my wife to some tickets.' The man said and passed over the fish and chips wrapped in thick white paper. Luke pulled open the door and the man followed behind them, said goodbye and locked the door.

Juliette and Luke strolled down to the wharf and sat on a bench in a shelter overlooking the crashing sea, protected from the wind with the fish and chips on their laps, and a can of drink on the bench beside them. Little flurries of snow fell all around them and slowly began to settle turning the whole scene a soft white.

They finished the fish and chips and sat there watching snowflakes flutter down onto the sea, a couple of seagulls swooping in from above and the Christmas lights on the wharf blowing in the wind.

Juliette looked out to sea through the snowflakes and sighed at the beautiful dark, cold night. She wondered if Luke was also feeling the way she was, like the space between them was on fire.

Her eyes widened and she didn't move a muscle as Luke put his hand on her leg and leant over. Juliette turned and Luke bent his head and kissed her gently. Juliette moved her hand and placed it at the top of his leg and could feel the soft wool of his jumper underneath her fingertips. *Breathe and enjoy, breathe and enjoy.*

She inhaled that same musky smell and closed her eyes as Luke moved his hand up from her leg and pulled her closer to him as they sat in the tiny shelter surrounded by snowflakes gently floating to the ground.

Juliette could hear the ferry in the distance, the wind whipping about her feet, the trombones marched into her head and whatever it was that was happening to her she didn't want it to ever go away.

Chapter 37

A few days after the Orpheum date, Juliette opened up the back door and walked all the way down the garden to the old timber summer house, which was really a glorified shed tucked into the corner at the bottom of the garden.

She opened the right side of the double doors and warm air hit her - whoever it was who'd thought of installing a heater in there had been a genius. It worked nicely as an extra room and since she'd painted all of the interior and put little blue curtains with pink roses up at the small windows either side of the door and a rug under the table it had become quite the cosy little spot. And here she was preparing it for a candlelit dinner for two.

She dragged the old timber table nearer to the double doors, covered it in a white tablecloth, set two hobnail glasses at each setting and placed a large vase filled with holly into the middle.

The day before, on the evening when Maggie was at Jeremy's, she'd climbed up onto a ladder and weaved tiny little Christmas lights all through the exposed beams in the roof. She'd bought a potted Christmas tree in White Cottage Flowers and placed it on the top of a small side table in the corner and it had filled the room with a lovely Christmas scent.

Standing on top of the table she'd hung an oversized candle chandelier and on the door had hung a large fir wreath peppered with pine cones and tied it with a huge red velvet bow.

Now, as she pottered around finishing it off she folded two tartan rugs and put them on the backs of the chairs and made sure the little fondue set was ready. As she prepared everything she revelled in this new feeling of being with Luke. She loved it and was embracing it wholeheartedly.

When she'd been with Jack, Bella's father, as a teen it had been so very different. And as she looked back now as an adult she'd felt concern about that young girl then. What she'd felt for Jack now she could see had been complete and utter obsession. Unhealthy infatuation in fact. As an adult, she could see that you had to be quite obsessed with someone to think that if you got pregnant at eighteen at least you'd have a little part of him with you for the rest of your life.

As Juliette pottered around she reflected on that young girl then and how her home life had been hideous compared to how she was bringing up Maggie and Bella. Her staunchly religious parents, who were perfect pillars of the community on the outside, were very different behind the scenes. And all their moral codes and strict beliefs had to be upheld on the surface at all costs, and when Juliette had finally told them she was pregnant they'd given her the options in no uncertain terms - to use all her savings to make the problem go away or leave.

And so with her building society card and one suitcase Juliette had ended up in a tiny bedsit very frightened and very alone.

As she moseyed around the shed getting it all ready she thought about how different she was with Bella now than her parents had been. Her and Bella were super close even though Bella was now in Oxford. Juliette couldn't imagine throwing Bella out and never speaking to her again like her own mother had done.

The best thing about it all though, had been that Juliette had learnt from being on the receiving end of her own mother's hideous failings how to be a very good mum or at least she hoped she was. She'd done everything in her power to make Bella and Maggie feel loved, safe and secure, which was a far cry from the miserable, sorry home she'd come from where everything had looked so perfect on the outside. Sadly, behind closed doors her mean, negative mother did her best to always put Juliette down, restricted what she could wear, spent her life running people down and enjoyed telling Juliette that she would never make anything of herself. Added to the whole sorry farce her father supposedly devoted to his church and his marriage had a whole string of women at work he was stupid enough to believe no one knew about.

Unbelievably, Juliette felt herself smiling at it all now. She felt pity for the horrible pair, the arrogant misogynist man and the mean tight-lipped woman and wondered what they were doing now.

She'd first heard from her mother years after Bella had been born when Juliette was in the newspaper as Jeremy's wife. Her mother had sent her a message saying that now that she was married and lived in the very respectable Seafolly they would allow her to come back to the house.

Juliette had thrown the letter onto the fire and thought how it was the last place she would ever go back to. The barren house, bare of any niceties, with sickly green paint and a depressive aura was not somewhere she wanted to revisit... ever. You couldn't pay her a million pounds to go back there with her beautiful girls.

It was all now almost like it was someone else in another life who had grown up in that bleak, oppressive environment. Now she had her two girls, a lovely cottage, a good career and was happy with her lot in life.

She put the ceramic fondue pot and stand on the table, set the wine glasses at the places and folded white napkins with gold spots and placed them on top of each plate.

Juliette carried on fussing around the little shed to make it feel cosy and festive. She wove ivy in and out of the slats around the two small windows and placed storm lanterns at the door. An old timber outdoor chair she'd found in the shed sat on the porch and she'd tied jam jars with wires, popped in little battery tealights and hung them from the tree branches outside.

She wanted it to all look pretty and dreamlike and as she pottered around getting everything ready she thought about how when Luke and her had got back from the date at the Orpheum they'd kissed on the doorstep in the moonlight.

Now she was ready for more, for more Luke and more magical things.

Chapter 38

Juliette was ready - Maggie was safely with Jeremy's mum for the night for a sleepover, everything was done with work, she'd been wrapping and sorting orders for A Christmas Sparkle for most of the day and she'd cleaned the little cottage from top to bottom, including changing all the sheets, disinfecting the fridge and vacuuming the sofas.

She stood in front of the mirror in the tiny bathroom at the top of the cottage. She was definitely looking her years, she thought, as she touched her hands to the sides of her cheeks and pulled them back a bit to make them more taught. They weren't as gaunt as they once were a few years before though, and she recognized the plumper cheeks as another very good side effect to the weight gain of the last couple of years. The emaciated look around her high cheekbones had gone and even the fine lines on her forehead and around her eyes seemed to have plumped out a bit - always a bonus.

She pulled out the rollers from her hair, sprayed the roots and clipped back the top layer away from her face. Sprayed on copious amounts of shine spray so that it picked up the glints of gold at the bottom of her hair and curled the ends over her shoulders. That would have to do.

She walked over the little hallway on the top floor of the cottage and stepped into her bedroom, the fairy lights around the iron bed twinkled and the clean linen she'd put on earlier was all ready. Not of course that she was intending on ending up in there with anyone, of course not.

She opened the chest of drawers she'd painted a very soft antique white and opened a glittery box and pulled out white silky knickers edged with delicate lace, a matching white bra and a camisole top with tiny little diamante butterflies on the straps. She put it all on and stared at herself in the mirror running her hands over her stomach and loving her new curves. She chose her red tea dress with the puffy sleeves and ruched top and tied the tie tight to her waist.

After finishing her makeup, layering herself in body lotion and perfume she walked over to the creaky double doors, opened them up and looked out over Pretty Beach, the boats behind the Orangery and looked down at the garden at the twinkling lights and lanterns she'd put down there the day before. The radiator had been on all afternoon so it was toasty and warm, and she'd popped out there with one of the diffusers and pumped essential oils into the air so that it smelt divine. Everything was ready for a night with a delectable man.

She carefully made her way down the steep stairs of the cottage, all the way through the kitchen, opened the back door onto the terrace and walked down the pathway. It was a surprisingly warm night, as she went to check everything was ready in the shed she heard a tapping on the front door, she walked back through the cottage and opened the door.

There he was, lovely Luke, in a navy-blue jumper with a pale blue button-down shirt underneath, jeans, boots and in addition to what he was wearing he came with the smell that made her almost woozy.

She invited him in, trying to remain casual, calm and cool while inside she wanted to take his hand, pull him through the sitting room, drag him up the stairs to her bedroom, rip off his clothes and put him in her bed.

Calm and in control, calm and in control she repeated to herself in her head over and over as Luke kissed her on the cheek and gave her a bunch of flowers and took off his scarf. She took the flowers and the scarf, hung the scarf on the coat hooks beside her pink coat resisting the urge to stick her whole face in the scarf and take an almighty breath in.

'Smells amazing, I could smell it from the end of the path,' Luke said.

Juliette was staring at the scarf, lost in thought.

You mean you smell amazing don't you? Juliette said to herself.
'Juliette?'

'Oops, yes sorry, oh you could smell it from outside. It must be the roasted garlic.'

'Whatever it is, it smells amazing.'

'Good.'

'And you look beautiful,' Luke said, touching her on the arm as they walked through the sitting room.

Calm and in control. Calm and in control. Juliette repeated as she said thank you and glanced up the steep stairs thinking about running up there with him and not emerging until after Christmas.

They walked into the conservatory, the smell of the roast chicken and garlic permeating throughout the whole kitchen, and Luke sat down.

'What can I get you? Glass of wine or I've some craft beers in the fridge - not sure what they're like but Ben bought them over when he was here for dinner a while ago, apparently they're some new brew.'

'Sounds right up my street, I'll try one of those then please.'

Juliette came back in with a small glass of wine for herself, the beer and a glass and handed them to Luke. His arm touched hers as she passed the glass to him and she took a breath in as sparks seemed to fly in the air between them.

Juliette leant back into the velvet sofa, popping her drink down on the table and letting her skirt drop to the side of her knee. The conservatory was warm and comfy, the little flames from the pot belly stove leaving dancing shadows all over the wall and the Christmas tree beside her twinkled.

'Well cheers, it's been a busy month. I have to tell you I'm looking forward to Christmas getting here.'

'Yep, I'm exhausted, I feel like I've had something on every night and we're not even near Christmas yet. Cheers Luke, I'll drink to a happy, calm, relaxing Christmas,' Juliette said laughing. 'Though with Maggie's excitement levels, I don't know how relaxed it's going to be.'

Juliette sipped on the wine and leant forward on the sofa to the coffee table and helped herself to some olives.

'So, how have you been finding life in Pretty Beach then?' Juliette asked.

'Fabulous - though I have to say I can't wait until the weather warms up and I'll be able to swim more in the sea. I've joined the open water swimming club but some days I don't last long out there - it really isn't that warm.'

'Brrr, you must be crazy, I suppose swimming is in your blood, though.'

Luke started to tell her about how he'd swum in London all year round at outdoor swimming baths on the heath, and how he'd played water polo when he was younger. Juliette thought to herself that she already knew that - she noted that he hadn't included the tiny little detail that he'd represented the country in water polo. He continued to tell her that the swimming club was about the only thing he really missed about London, and even that wasn't too bad.

Juliette popped another olive into her mouth and contemplated everything for a moment, looking over at Luke, his floppy bit of hair at the front falling down into his eyes, the broad chest seeming to take up a large proportion of the sofa.

'Well, I've had quite the busy year this year Luke. Few years actually - since I left my husband, ended up in a flat and I haven't really been up for air since... until now that is.'

'And the ex? Are you on good terms?'

'On the whole - I gave him quite a hard time really, but he's okay overall. You might know him actually, the surname might have given it away.'

Luke looked back at her with a frown, confused.

'Sparkles as in Jeremy Sparkles, MP for Newport and junior member of the Cabinet.'

Luke sat upright on the sofa.

'Well I never. Sorry I didn't put two and two together. So that was something to walk away from then.'

'It absolutely was Luke,' Juliette said, and sank back into the down-filled cushions of the velvet sofa hoping she wasn't saying too much, hoping that she didn't sound as if she was coming with a shed load of baggage - which she definitely was.

'Ha, you're going to run a mile now I've told you all that,' Juliette said, chuckling.

Luke shook his head vehemently and finished pouring the last of the beer into his glass.

'I don't think you get to this stage in life without some history, I suppose.'

'I make you right. Okay, I think we're ready to eat then, shall we go into the kitchen?'

***

An hour or so, and a few more drinks later, Luke and Juliette had polished off the garlic chicken and roast potatoes and Juliette had piled all the plates into the sink and suggested that they go out to the summer house for the chocolate fondue.

Juliette opened the back door onto the terrace, switched the lights on and their glow lit all the way down the old block-paved pathway to the end. The lights from the Orangery shimmered just over the top of the trees and cool air whipped in from the sea.

Juliette, her arms full with a plate of strawberries and chocolate and her drink, led Luke down the pathway to the summer house. She put her drink down on the arm of one of the outdoor chairs, unlocked the door and pulled it open. Heat hit them both.

'Wow, it's boiling, I really didn't think it would get this hot out here at this time of year!'

Luke walked in and fanned his face, put his drink down on the table and started to roll his sleeves up and pulled his jumper away from his jeans. Juliette got a glimpse of an extremely toned set of abs as he went to sit down.

Calm and collected, Juliette, Calm and collected.

Juliette lit the candle underneath the ceramic dish and the chocolate began to melt and as they sat there in the little summer house which was really a glorified shed, surrounded by Christmas lights and the Christmas tree on the right they both relaxed, the conversation turning to chat about the DJ at the dance and what had happened the next day when he'd come to pick up his equipment.

'Will you be attending the Pretty Beach Carols, then?' Juliette said, dipping another strawberry in the chocolate and popping it into her mouth.

'I don't think I've had a better offer for a long time - only if I can go with you. Pretty Beach carol singing with a very beautiful woman, I like the sound of that,' Luke said laughing.

The heat in the room, the scent of the Christmas tree and the sugar rush from the chocolate had all made Juliette feel very happy, topped up with a couple of drinks she sighed out and continued to dip the strawberries in the chocolate and her mind wandered to how this was going to end.

A tiny little gong went off from a Christmas clock she'd popped on a shelf at the back of the summer house. It was already eleven, she couldn't believe the time.

'Excuse me for a bit, I just need to check my phone, sorry I didn't realise the time. I always check-in with Jeremy's mum before she goes to bed when Maggie is over there.'

Juliette took out her phone, there was a message telling her that all was okay that had come in twenty minutes before. She replied, saying thank you, checked her phone was not on silent, closed it and put it on the table.

'Goodness, I didn't even realise the time.'

'Time flies when you're having fun,' Luke said, laughing.

Juliette didn't need to continue to tell herself to be calm, with the text from Jeremy's mum confirming that all was good with Maggie, and with the lovely evening she was having with Luke, she felt calmer than she had in years. Sitting in the back of the garden of the prettiest little cottage in Pretty Beach, in a soft floaty dress, stuffing her face with whatever she liked and not worrying about a thing was absolute bliss.

'I bet you didn't think you'd be sitting in a Christmas grotto dipping strawberries into chocolate in the middle of a shed at the end of a garden when you moved to Pretty Beach did you Luke?' Juliette mused and giggled.

'I didn't. Has to be said though, I've been sat in worse sheds in my life.'

'Really, not sure if I want to hear about that. What sort of sheds have you had in your life then?'

'When I was at medical school I was in this dump of a student house - it was like your worst image of student digs multiplied by fifty - filthy, grotty place. Anyway, outside next to the patio was a shed and, umm, it was named The Dope.'

'Right. As in smoking?'

'Yup. It stunk the whole street out. My one and only visit to it was short lived. I never did really get on well with the smoking scene.'

'My shed sounds a whole lot nicer than that.'

'I can assure you it is,' Luke said, leaning back in the chair and stretching out his legs.

'I just need to pop to the loo Luke, I'll be right back.'

Juliette walked all the way through the garden, went into the downstairs loo and when she came back five minutes later re-spritzed with perfume and her hair spruced up Luke was sitting outside the shed on the steps.

'I couldn't take it in there any more - you need to rent it out as a sauna,' Luke said, explaining why he'd moved outside.

Juliette sat down on the step next to him.

'Reminds me of the night I saw you out the front, surrounded by Baileys and broken glass,' Luke said and put his hand on her leg.

'I'll never live that down will I?' She replied, turning her head to him and looking into his eyes as he pushed his flop of hair at the front out of the way.

'I remember wondering then what was happening to me when I looked at you Juliette. It was the same feeling as when I saw you the first time in the car park - remember?'

Juliette stared at him, lost in the stirrings, wondering what to do now. She gazed at him, saying nothing, loving the feelings racing through every part of her body and put her hand on top of his. She imagined him picking her up and carrying her all the way to the top of the tiny cottage and never being seen again.

There was no way she was initiating this going further, she wasn't anywhere near confident enough and was certainly not used to sitting with men in sheds thinking about taking them up to her bedroom and stroking intimate parts of their bodies. Juliette was not used to the feeling that she wanted to, quite frankly, jump on the man and never let him go.

Luke put his other arm around her waist and pulled her close to him as they sat there on the steps and he bent down and kissed her hard on her lips. Her whole body relaxed and she moved along the steps closer to him, intoxicated by his dark, musky smell. She moved her hand up over his chest and then back down and stroked her hands up and down his back.

Luke pulled her into him and put his hands up into her hair and caressed the back of her neck. He started to press closer into her, more insistent and she slid her hands underneath his shirt and felt the strong thickness of his abs.

Trombones began to play and Juliette Sparkles felt things going on inside her she hadn't felt or thought about since she was eighteen, and she lost herself in the kiss, lost herself in the smell, the feel of Luke under her hands.

She felt ecstatic with happiness that she'd decided to let herself feel again, because she knew one thing for sure, this Luke with the good bottom and very pleasing chest felt very, very nice indeed.

Chapter 39

Juliette woke up to a video call on her phone, she grabbed it quickly not knowing what the time was and suddenly thought that she had forgotten to pick Maggie up. Then she remembered that Maggie was with Jeremy's mum. Then she remembered the night before.

She opened the front flap on her blush pink phone cover and pressed accept on the video call and held the screen away from her face.

'Wow, you've got sex hair!'

'Very funny Daisy.' Juliette said, sitting up and leaning back on the pale pink linen pillows. She looked back at herself, it was fair to say that her hair did look like she'd been hung up by her ankles and blown with a leaf blower.

'Right, I want all the inside information. Every single bit of it in minute detail.'

'Not much to tell...' Juliette said, plumping up the pillow behind her and giggling.

'Oh no, no way are you getting away with that. I've counselled you through a marriage, nigh-on co-parented your newborn baby and held your hand when you cried all night about Jack. You owe me, Sparkles, and you owe me big.'

'What about all the times I've listened to you waiting for Doctor D to leave his wife? Held your hair up over the toilet when you saw him on Valentines with her. Fed you soup when you hadn't eaten for a week when he took her to the Maldives.'

'True, you still owe me though. Shoot.'

'Well, all I can divulge is it was nice.'

'No way, I want details. Movie script details.'

Juliette sighed and started giggling, 'Well, he arrived looking absolutely gorgeous, and whatever it is that he sprays on does something to my nether regions.'

'Sparkles, who are you? I thought your nether regions were closed! This is awesome!'

'Then we had drinks and dinner and we chatted and it was amazing.'

'And then?'

'And then we went outside to the summer house for melted chocolate and strawberries.'

'Oh wow, this just gets better and better. I'm thinking molten chocolate in places other than strawberries.'

'And then I went to the loo.'

Juliette sat up, pulling her messy hair into a scrunchie and continued, 'When I came back, he was outside on the step with his jumper off because it was so hot in there and then...'

'Here comes the good bit!'

'And then, I sat down next to him and he put his hand on my leg and we kissed, well we did more than kiss and it was delicious.'

'And then he carried you up those super steep stairs and spent the whole night sending you to heaven and back?'

'And then he left because he had an early shift in the morning and well because I got the jitters and I sort of stopped it all.'

'What? You did what, Sparkles? Cripes, you can't make this up. So you're telling me that after a long sex drought, a very handsome, very hot and may I just add, younger than you doctor makes a play for you, kisses you by the stairs, takes you to a vintage cinema and feeds you candyfloss and then comes round for dinner and when it gets to the crunch point you back off?'

'Yup. I know.'

'Sparkles, I don't know what to say.'

'You say well done best friend, well done for ending the night well, not having casual sex with the newest member of Pretty Beach and thinking about your little girl.'

'Okay Sparkles, you do have a point - it's hardly casual sex though, I mean it's not the first date.'

'Daisy, I tell you what though. I'm in, hook, line and sinker. The stirrings were out of this world.'

Chapter 40

Free to come out for dinner at all?

That was all the text from Luke said.

I've got a free night on Friday, where were you thinking?

I'm thinking I'd like to take you out, treat you to a lovely dinner and then kiss you all the way home ;) The Old Bell Hotel does a Christmas menu - I had an advert flash up on my phone and thought it looked nice.

I'd love to.

Juliette closed her phone, smiling from ear to ear and hugged it to herself while she sat in the car in the Monday afternoon queue in the drizzle waiting for Maggie's class to come out of school. She'd not stopped thinking about Luke since the fondue and the summer house. She may have been wishing that she'd done something else with the chocolate but the sensible part of her was pleased it had ended where it had. She had Maggie to think about and after her sex drought she really did think that if and when it happened it really would be nice, really would be more grown-up, if her initiation back into that world was somewhere a bit more salubrious than what was essentially a fancy shed.

Juliette and Luke had been out a few more times since the fondue, to the pub down the end of Seapocket Lane for a quick drink one night when Maggie was at a Christmas party at Jeremy's work. When Luke had dropped her off at home he'd come in and it had all been very glorious standing in her little sitting room kissing him, her hands under his jumper, his mouth kissing her neck. And they'd been for afternoon cake in the laneway where they'd ordered huge mugs of hot chocolate, topped with copious amounts of real whipped cream and shavings of hand-made chocolate and large slices of Christmas cake and he'd told her how much he liked her.

Luke had also walked all the way along the beach with her one morning before Maggie was dropped off and they'd chatted for hours in the freezing cold air coming up off the beach. When they'd got right to the end where there weren't any houses and the sea crashed in against the sea wall Luke had pulled her into his arms and kissed her for what felt like a lifetime and she'd kissed him back hoping no one in Pretty Beach would see.

***

Juliette had an hour for her lunch to fly to the lingerie store in Newport Reef's out of town shopping centre. If truth be known, she abhorred the place and avoided it as best she could, preferring to keep her money in the economy of Pretty Beach, but when you were planning, with a bit of luck, to get naked with a very nice, younger-than-you man you wanted to at least look the part.

She parked her car, locked the door and hurried into the shopping centre and into the lingerie shop. Things had clearly moved on in lingerie - rows of underwear with strange names stared back at her and it had put her right off the whole idea. Who knew there were Miami, Brazilian and bustiers in the regular old high street stores these days? She took one look at the tiny bits of string everywhere and went to turn around and walk out.

'Can I help you?' A small woman, in her mid-fifties with extremely tanned skin, a short brown bob and name badge announcing her as Jennifer asked.

'Umm, no not really. I was after something I don't know, sort of pretty and flattering... not as much skin on show but still, well a tiny bit, umm, sexy too I suppose.'

Jennifer smiled, 'Come with me - Brazilian is just all the rage at the moment so it's all out the front, you want to come through here to our other collections. Is it for a special occasion? Anniversary or something?'

'Not quite. I'm well, put it this way, I'm hoping to find myself in a situation where my underwear is nice.'

'Right, and you want it to be silky or lacy and what sort of price point are we thinking?' Jennifer asked.

'I haven't really thought about it, I thought I'd run in and out quickly. I want something pretty and girly, maybe a frill, silky would be nice and not too expensive.'

Jennifer led her over to a rack of silky camisole tops edged with lace and red ribbon.

'Nope, nothing like that.'

'Something more understated?'

'Yes, and I don't think I want black.'

Jennifer led her to another stand. 'This is lovely, it's mid-range budget-wise,' she said, pointing to a beautiful pale pink camisole set with little lace ruffles over the cups, thin straps with a tie detail at the back and delicate little bows on the straps. Jennifer pulled out the matching camisole knickers in the same pretty pink and topped with delicate bows.

'Perfect.'

Juliette left the shop fifteen minutes later with the underwear beautifully wrapped in tissue paper and a wish of good luck from Jennifer. She walked to her car, put the bag inside her handbag and drove back to work.

Chapter 41

Juliette turned left out of her pathway, walked to the end of Seapocket Lane and rang the bell on Luke's front door.

'Hello gorgeous, how are you?' Luke said, and Juliette stepped inside the hallway and he kissed her gently on the lips. She stood there lost in his smell, in the feel of him and thought she could quite happily forget all about the meal at the Old Bell, go upstairs, rip off all his clothes and spend the night doing things with him that she'd been thinking about since the first time she'd seen him in the car park of the hospital.

'Ready?' he said, picking up his phone from the hallway table and grabbing his keys.

'Yep, I'm looking forward to this meal, Luke, I've heard a lot about this place.'

'It certainly looks nice and it sounds nice so only time will tell.' He grabbed her hand and walked across the hall, 'You're sure you're ready to be seen by the locals of Pretty Beach in my car?' he said, laughing.

'It's not a joke Luke, you don't know what they're like, as soon as we are spotted together in your car, the gossip will go around like wildfire. I'll probably have a text from Sallie or the girls from work by the time we've pulled out of the end of the lane.' Juliette said, laughing and pulling her hand away as they stepped out the front door.

Juliette got into Luke's BMW, the lovely new car smell all around them, the leather seat comfy against her back. She could feel the silky pink underwear under her dress and smiled to herself. Had she, Juliette Sparkles, boring old midwife who hardly ever went out really gone and got herself dressed up in sexy underwear? It seemed as if she very much had. She slipped her hand inside the wrap on the front of the dress and felt the silky fabric on the camisole top - it was so soft and made her feel pretty and relaxed. What was she hoping would happen?

Twenty minutes later and they arrived at the Old Bell Hotel, greeted by a huge front door with a fresh garland on the front, a Christmas tree touching the ceiling in the foyer and Christmas tunes from a woman singing next to a piano in the corner.

They were led to the restaurant of the hotel, Luke behind Juliette and as she took her seat he kissed her on the cheek. 'You look stunning,' he whispered in her ear.

'Thank you,' she said, giggling and picking up the menu and reading down all the way to the end.

'Goodness Luke, I didn't realise it was a six-course dinner with different wines for each course. I'll be under the table and asleep before the dessert.'

'I do hope not, I was hoping you'd be very much awake later,' Luke said, and looked her right in the eye and smiled. Juliette felt the stirrings and what had now moved on from feelings she hadn't had before to full-blown, one hundred percent lust. There was no beating around the bush, she wanted Luke Burnette very, very badly.

They finished the meal a few hours later with full stomachs, too many wines and Luke having moved his car into the hotel car park and checked that he could leave it overnight, intending on getting an Uber home to Pretty Beach.

The waiter brought over cheese and biscuits and Luke got his phone out of his pocket. I'll see how long it is for an Uber or taxi - it's probably ultra-busy this evening.

Juliette, the wine, the evening, the Christmas tunes, the soft underwear beneath her dress all gone to her head, leant over the table and whispered to Luke that they should get a room.

Luke's eyes widened and he started to laugh, 'You're kidding me, what happened to the not being seen?'

'Stuff that Luke, you only live once right?'

'Are you seriously propositioning me and asking me to go out to the foyer and check if there is a room free in the hotel?' Luke asked her, taking her hand into his.

'I seriously am,' she said back, giggling. 'Luke, it's Christmas, I've not got Maggie for once and, you, you're the best thing that's happened to me in a very long time,' she said and clinked her water glass to his.

Luke started laughing, 'I've never done anything quite like this Juliette - I'm a respectable doctor and I have to say that I like you very, very much too. I'm so incredibly glad I saved you from a pile of Baileys in the street.'

Ten minutes later he came back to the table with a room card and a very big smile.

'The last room apparently and it's the, wait for it, Honeymoon Suite.'

Juliette burst out laughing, but a tiny little bit inside her suddenly felt extremely ridiculous. She had not only thrown caution to the wind, she had propositioned someone to spend the night with her in a hotel and the last time she had done anything anywhere near as crazy eighteen years prior it had not ended at all well. So much for calm and sensible.

As if reading her thoughts Luke got up from the table and held her gently on the arm, 'Come on, let's go and have a post-dinner coffee by the fire and think a little bit more about your crazy idea. I'll wait all year for you if I have to.'

Chapter 42

Juliette sat back in the huge, leather Chesterfield and sipped on her coffee. She could have sat there all night drinking in Luke - his eyes, his long legs, his beautiful chest. Yet, a tiny voice in the back of her head was telling her to get in an Uber super quick, get back to her cottage, lock the door behind her and get into her own bed. But relaxed Juliette was telling her to go to the hotel room and have the best night of her life.

Juliette followed behind Luke, her hand tightly clasped in his as he led her to the lift. It felt like an eternity before it arrived. They stood in the lift saying nothing as Luke pressed the button to the top floor, held Juliette's hand closely and then as the lift doors opened he led her along to the door of the room.

He pushed the card into the little slot and nothing happened - the light stayed red.

'You've got to be kidding me! The card isn't working,' Luke said, grinning. 'What are we doing Juliette?'

'I think there's a knack to it - push it in and pull it out slowly,' Juliette said leaning against the doorway giggling and looking down at the card.

Two more goes and the door light suddenly turned to green and they heard the lock on the door click and Luke heaved the heavy hotel room door open with his shoulder and pulled Juliette into the room. It slammed shut behind them and Luke pinned Juliette to the back of the door and kissed her gently on the lips and then moved slowly down to her neck. His hands rested on her waist and she pulled him more urgently towards her, feeling her way up under his shirt to the muscles of his back.

Luke slowly pulled up the soft folds of Juliette's silk dress and caressed the skin underneath the soft fabric of her knickers and he kissed her again gently, taking his time. She lost herself in his touch, in his smell, allowing herself to take pleasure in every single second.

After what felt like ever, he gently lifted her up, she wrapped her legs around him and he carried her to the bed. Juliette laid back against the thick heavy hotel pillows as Luke slowly undid the buttons one by one on the front of her dress to reveal the pretty pink ruffles on her camisole top.

'Juliette, you are absolutely beautiful,' Luke said, as Juliette reached for the belt on his jeans and allowed herself to feel things that were out of this world.

Chapter 43

Juliette hummed as she walked into Pretty Beach Village Hall holding Maggie's hand as children in Christmas party clothes ran around playing. They lined up in the queue to sign Maggie in for the party, added her name to the list and Maggie went through the gate of the hallway in her blue velvet dress and sparkly tights, heading straight for the bouncy castle.

Juliette walked out of the hall, past the wharf and along through Mermaids as little snowflakes started to fall and catch in the wind coming in off the sea. She strolled along wrapped up warm in her coat and gloves looking in at the lovely little cottages at the end of their front gardens.

A big, bright Shane Pence sign on the right announced that number 34 had sold and Juliette felt her heart sink a little bit. Even at this time of year houses in Pretty Beach were snapped up. Who was she kidding that she thought that a house in a mess would go for a reduced price? It seemed as if any house was snapped up regardless of the condition. Heck, she'd even heard that people bought houses off the internet without even viewing them - Pretty Beach was that sought after.

She continued to walk along and approached Mr Jenkin's house. There were no signs of life at all, no skip, no workmen and as she tried to peer in the window at the front it looked as if all the furniture had been removed. The old front door still looked shabby and unloved, but the wheelbarrow growing weeds had been emptied and was now standing up by the side of the door and the cracked window had been repaired.

Juliette stood there looking at it, unfortunately, Nicky Jenkin was very astute. It was on the right side of Mermaid Lane for the sun at all times of the year and its position on the street was one of the best.

Just as she went to move forward something caught her eye on the pavement, she bent down and picked it up. A tiny little pink iridescent heart that sparkled in the light. She popped it in her pocket and hoped it was a sign of good luck. Whatever happened at least she was out of the grim flat with the hundreds of downlights and now safely in the cottage. Her life had taken a turn for the better and she was going to be positive and upbeat.

She walked along the road thinking about everything and wondered just what was going to happen at Christmas. She'd had a good mind to pull up Jeremy on his deciding what he was going to do and what day he would be with Maggie, but after he'd just paid the last set of school fees without complaining and had also deposited some money to pay for ballet she'd decided to keep schtum.

Plus, she had the other little secret up her sleeve that no one really knew about. The secret that was making her giddy, making her glide around in a state of pure glee. The secret that was Luke and that fact that they had been meeting up at any and every available second and were not exactly sitting around drinking cups of tea.

Chapter 44

Juliette was standing at the sink in the bathroom on the first floor of the cottage while Maggie was sitting on the edge of the bath in her pale blue nightie brushing her teeth when her text pinged.

She assumed it would be Bella, she normally phoned or texted at this time of night - Luke's name flashed up on the top of her phone.

Hey, not sure if you've seen it or not but that house you like in Mermaid Lane, well it's online and there's a video tour of it.

I hadn't seen it! Thank you.

Looks like it's going to be a good price - it's in a right state. Have a look.

Juliette finished off sorting out Maggie, laid out her clothes for the next morning, padded down the stairs to the sitting room and opened her laptop to the website and in the top right-hand corner put Pretty Beach in the search bar.

She scrolled down the listings and there it was with a little ticker in the corner saying 'new'. She looked through the pictures and almost shuddered. Holly had been right about Nicky Jenkin, the place was in a right mess - how could she have let one of her parents live like that?

It now looked as if some of it was half-ripped out. Whatever Juliette had seen happening on the day she'd walked past with the skip outside had come to an abrupt end.

She looked at the pictures and then realised that it was up with Shane Pence. That was weird, firstly, Shane knew about her situation and said he would call her about anything that came on, and secondly, she had been told that Nicky Jenkin had left him at the altar so she was very surprised to see him representing the house.

She clicked on the video and watched as Shane led the way around the house. It was in a terrible way, damp on the walls, a cupboard hanging off the wall in the kitchen, it looked like it had very old central heating installed and threadbare, filthy carpets were on the floor.

Out the back an old conservatory had one of the walls falling down and the whole of the left side of the garden was not only overgrown but it looked like a health hazard.

She shut the laptop and saw that she had a message on her phone from Shane Pence Estate Agents. Juliette knew Shane and his wife and had delivered their babies, she'd known him for years and he was well aware of her story and her situation.

Hi Juliette. Shane here. Look, sorry I have only just got to message you, hope it's not too late in the evening, but Mermaid Lane has come on. I'm not sure if you heard but Mr Jenkin passed away, very sad and sudden and there were things in the will that came out about the house. Anyway do you want to come and view it? I think you should come and have a look at it. It's in a terrible state but I do know it will go for a good price.

Thanks Shane. My goodness I'm so sorry to hear that, how sad. I'm working mornings tomorrow - what time will you be there?

I was thinking about 2pm if that suits you?

Yes it does, but the one over the road went for loads more than I can afford so is there any point?

Yes there is. This is going to go for a good price that's why I'm messaging you. I'll fill you in on it all when I see you.

OK, thanks, see you then.

Chapter 45

Juliette waited at the end of Luke's path as he finished off a call, and looked all the way down to the end of Seapocket Lane to the sea. Big, crashing waves broke out the back and the wind whipped seaspray on the top of the water.

Juliette sighed, she really, really wanted to stay in Pretty Beach and if she could she would rather it was in an old house, no matter how tiny it was. She wondered what it was with Mr Jenkin's cottage and thought it was strange that Nicky Jenkin had put it on with Shane Pence in the end, and even more strange that Shane had agreed to it when years and years ago Nicky had jilted Shane at the altar. She wondered if the horrid woman with the long pointy finger-nails and ever-so perfect hair would be there again looking down her nose at them all. She doubted Nicky would look down her nose at Luke though, she hadn't seen any woman yet who had been able to take her eyes off him.

Luke came out of the house, walked down the path, put his arm around Juliette's waist and kissed her on the cheek.

'Sorry, I had to get that sorted out. Right, let's go and look at this cottage.'

Juliette fell into step beside Luke and desperately wanted to hold hands with him, and although they were certainly not taking it slowly, she had seen him every day since the hotel, she wasn't going to be broadcasting it around Pretty Beach that she and Luke were very much an item.

She was pretending on the outside that it was all going slowly but in reality her and Luke had gone full throttle into the relationship since he'd carried her over to the bed in the hotel. It was like that night had sealed it for both of them. He'd told her he wanted to spend every minute he could with her and had said she drove him crazy and that he was thinking about her all the time.

218

Since that night when she'd felt like her head had blown off she'd not looked back, and the only reason she hadn't stood on the top of Holly's bakery next to the glittery reindeer and shouted from the rooftops that she loved stroking every single part of Luke's extremely well-toned body was because it would be a whole different ballgame letting Luke into the Maggie part of her life. There was one thing she did know though, Luke blew Jack and Jeremy out of the water and left them in his wake.

They walked under the Christmas lights of the laneway, Christmas carol singers stood outside White Cottage Flowers and as they got to Holly's bakery her staff were standing outside dressed in stripy red and white tights and flashing Christmas jumpers and giving out mini-mince pies.

'This really is some town - how many places do you know that give out mince pies?' Luke said, as they strolled along.

'Ahh, she's a clever one our Holly - giving out mince-pies is part of her business plan. She knows everything in Pretty Beach, what bread you like, how much you earn and whether or not you're good enough for Pretty Beach. Don't you think the council runs Pretty Beach Luke,' Juliette said laughing as they both took a mince pie and continued down the road.

At the bottom of the laneway, Sallie and Ben were coming out of the Boat House, Ben with their friend Nina's baby girl Ottilie wrapped up in a carrier on his chest.

'Hi Sparkles, how are you?' Ever-so charming Ben said to Juliette, kissed her on the cheek and held out his hand to Luke.

'I'm good, really good actually. Did you hear about Mr Jenkin?' Juliette said, stroking the hair on the baby's head.

'Yeah, Holly told me a few days ago, so sad, isn't it?' Sallie said.

'Really sad and even worse is the state that the house was in. It's unbelievable, but it might be good for me though. Shane thinks it's going to go for a great price.' Juliette told them.

'Oh, right, I thought there was something between Shane and the daughter and he wouldn't be selling it?'

'You and everyone else in Pretty Beach, but apparently there was something that came up in the will.'

'Ooh, I wonder what, I bet Holly knows.'

'We're on the way there now to have a look. I doubt I'll be able to afford it but you never know...' Juliette said and Luke smiled at her.

'Okay, we're off then, behave yourself Sparkles,' Ben said and raised his eyebrows to Luke and Juliette as they walked off down in the direction of Mermaids. Just as they went to turn down the lane Juliette turned back and Sallie was turning back too and gave Juliette a secret little thumbs-up sign under her coat.

***

Juliette walked alongside Luke loving how it was feeling to be beside him, she'd never felt that feeling when she walked along with Jeremy and she'd certainly never had the chance with Jack.

They walked all the way along the first part of Mermaid Lane, Juliette told Luke all about the house on the left side of the road which had sold way out of her budget and then they approached Mr Jenkin's house and Shane Pence was sitting in his white BMW outside. The gate was blowing backwards and forwards in the breeze coming in off the sea, and a dog barked from the house next door.

Luke looked up at the narrow, three-storey terrace house and the bowed wall of the ground floor, the tiny in-built sun terrace that ran all the way across the width of the first floor and the basement down below. The once bright blue front door was old and peeling, the pressed tin to the roof on the terrace on the first floor was hanging off, and the sea air had corroded the plaster by the window.

Shane Pence jumped out of his car, approached Juliette and Luke, kissed Juliette on the cheek and held out his hand to Luke.

'Hey, how are you? I remember you house-hunting down here earlier in the year, that's right isn't it?' Shane said to Luke, smiling.

'Yes, Shane this is Luke, he lives down the end of Seapocket Lane not far from the Orangery.'

'Oh yes, that's right I remember.'

'So, let's get in and then I'll tell you all about it,' Shane said, pressing the remote to lock his car.

They walked in through the front black metal railings and looked up at the front door, a bird flew out from under the porch roof and the wind blew leaves and an old crisp packet around their feet. Juliette's fists were tightly closed in her pockets and she was holding her breath as Shane fiddled with the keys to the front door.

He twisted and turned the lock as they stood there in the biting wind and when he finally got the lock to turn and the door to open it creaked noisily and stale, dank air hit them. As they stepped in the smell of dogs and urine and mould added to the dank smell in the air.

'Oh dear,' Juliette said, and almost gagged.

'It's not pleasant, sorry, but it's got a lot of potential,' Shane said, waving them in.

Luke squeezed Juliette's arm and followed Shane through the long narrow hallway and through an archway in the middle. An old radiator had fallen off the wall and was propped up on the left and Shane opened a door to a sitting room with bay windows looking out onto the road.

Stained brown carpet, green swirl wallpaper peeling off at the top and an electric fire in a boarded-up fireplace were to the left and on the right there was an archway to what looked like a dining room. Juliette looked up at the peeling ceilings and down at the grotty carpets.

'I don't know if I want to see further inside - this will be too much for me Shane, I'm not a property developer.'

Shane turned to Juliette, 'I wouldn't have shown it to you Juliette, unless I thought it was worth it. It's mostly cosmetic, honestly, this is a great buy and it's always a funny time of year to buy a house so that's in your favour too. Come on, just have a look around.'

'I'm having a hard time imagining it, to be honest,' Juliette said, holding her hand over her mouth to stop herself from gagging at the smell.

It got worse as they trooped through - a long narrow kitchen with old pine cupboards opened out onto a terrace which was more mud than brick. A door under the stairs led down to a dark basement which looked like it hadn't been used for a long time, an old stained mattress leant up against a wall and old, open rusty shelving lined the walls of another room.

Steep turning stairs led to the first floor with a bedroom, a box room not much bigger than the width of a bed and a bathroom, then up a further set of stairs to two more rooms.

Luke was walking around pulling back carpet, tapping on walls, opening cupboards and looking up into the fireplaces.

They followed Shane up to the top to a room with bay windows looking out over the sea, a fireplace on the far wall and a small door on the right. Shane walked across the disintegrating carpet, the smell of dogs and mould rising from the floor as he strode over.

'This could be a bathroom, it's just an old toilet at the moment' he said opening the door to a room with an avocado green sink and plastic toilet, a sash window with a crack right through the middle and from the smell it had not seen any disinfectant in a very long time.

Juliette put her hand to her chest and gagged.

'It's awful. I can't move in here with Maggie.'

'I think it's got a lot of potential,' Luke said quietly. 'It's a great position, the building is sound, it's just an absolute mess, inside and out.'

'I couldn't move in here and I wouldn't have enough money for a kitchen renovation,' Juliette sighed, and almost felt angry with Shane for showing her the house at all.

Shane touched her on the arm, 'All you would need to do would be to rip all the carpets out and stain the floors, that wouldn't be too much money. The kitchen could be painted as it's pine and with a bit of fixing here and there it would be fine as it's actually beautifully hand-crafted. Plus, if you did one room at a time you could pretty much shut off the rest of the house until you were ready and able to improve it.'

'You seem to have thought it through Shane,' Juliette said, shaking her head, disillusioned.

'Of course. I love houses and I see hundreds - this is wonderful and then you've got that whole other bit downstairs in the basement with its own entrance which you could rent out, you would even have an income - stick in a tenant or do it as a holiday let.'

Juliette walked over to the window and looked out at the sea beyond, 'I don't know, I just don't think I've got it in me to take it on.'

'Why don't you get Sallie to come and have a look at it with you? She knows her stuff and does everything on a super-tight budget and she's got great vision. Makes me look like an amateur,' Shane said, smiling.

'Maybe, look I don't know Shane, thanks for thinking of me.'

'Not a problem, you really should think about it. This won't come up again and definitely not at this price.'

'Anyway, how come you got the house?' Juliette asked.

'I'm sure you know what happened all those years ago with Nicky Jenkin - well her old dad had clearly been thinking about it too... the will not only stipulated that Shane Pence Estate Agents sell the house but he left it to his nephew who was the only one who visited him in the last fifteen years.

'What a turn up for the books!'

'You're telling me and trust me I will take great pleasure in dealing with Nicky should it arise.'

They walked back down through the house and stepped outside, Juliette said she would think about asking Sallie to come and have a look and Shane got in his car and drove off.

Juliette looked up and down Mermaid Lane at all the other beautifully kept houses and turned back and looked at Mr Jenkin's sad and dilapidated place. Luke put his arm around Juliette and gave her shoulders a squeeze.

'It'll work out. I really think you should seriously consider this, I'll be here to help out. I'm quite handy with a drill.'

Juliette looked up to him and smiled.

So, Luke was planning on sticking around.

Chapter 46

'Hey mum, how was it?' Bella said from the end of the phone.

'Two words: absolutely awful!'

'Oh no!'

'Yep, it was just awful everywhere you looked. The smell was disgusting, the floors vile, the kitchen would be condemned I think and the bathrooms were dreadful, if you can even call them bathrooms.'

'What a shame, Mermaids though, it's so nice down there and you love those old houses.'

'I know, but it's so much to take on and the budget would mean I wouldn't have much left to do anything at all.'

'Is there anyone else interested?'

'Not at this stage apparently. Shane said it was a funny time of year the time before Christmas and with the state it's in, that knocks out a whole load of buyers. I mean it's not just bad Bella, I can cope with that, it's awful.'

'That's so disappointing, mum.'

'I know, but Shane knows what he's talking about and thinks it's a good house, which I suppose is right. He said I should go and have a look with Sallie.'

'That's a good idea - remember the Boat House before she got hold of it? We used to walk past there with Maggie in the pram years ago and it was nearly derelict in those days and now look at it.'

'Hmm, I hadn't even thought about that. You know, you're right, that was probably in a similar state as this place and she turned it round and on her own too.'

Maggie was sitting on the sofa next to Juliette.

'Is it the house next to the pretty blue one we walked past, mummy?'

'No darling, it's the one where we saw that lady in the red coat and gave her the note.'

225

'The sad one?'

'Yes Maggie, the sad one.'

'We could live there and make it happy again,' Maggie said, and Juliette smiled.

***

Daisy was sitting in the little white outdoor chair under the porch when Juliette pulled into Seapocket Lane, parked her car, opened the car door for Maggie and pushed open the gate to her little cottage.

'Sorry, I realised I took the spare key in last week and didn't put it back. I keep forgetting to put the back-up spare key out. So good to see you!'

'Not a problem, after that journey I thought I'd sit here in the fresh air for a bit and enjoy all the Pretty Beach Christmas lights.' Daisy said, jumped up and hugged Juliette and picked up Maggie and gave her a huge cuddle.

'Miss Maggie, my princess, you just wait and see what I've got for you. Lots of beautiful presents all for you!'

'Yesssssss, Aunty Daisy,' Maggie said excitedly.

'It feels like ages since I've seen you both!' Daisy said, picking up her bag as Juliette started to open the front door.

'Well, you haven't even seen the cottage, the last time you came we were in the flat still. Where does the time go?'

'I know and now you're here in this gorgeous cottage, I can't believe it. It's absolutely lovely, I've been peering in the window and went for a little walk down the lane. The sea in the background and all these sweet little cottages. I used to walk down Seapocket Lane on the way to the bus to school,' Daisy said.

'I'm so pleased to be out of that flat I can't even tell you.' Juliette said, opening the door.

Warmth, lavender and the cosy smell of the Christmas tree in the corner greeted them as they stepped in leaving their shoes in the porch. Juliette flicked the Christmas tree lights on, took off her coat and hung it on the coat rack.

'Come on then, Maggie, I want you to show me round,' Daisy said as Maggie took her hand and pulled her through the sitting room and up the first step of steep stairs.

Juliette went into the kitchen, filled the kettle with water, switched it on, emptied the teapot and rinsed it out. She opened the cupboard, pulled out a pink polka dot tea caddy with Assam written on the front and put three tea bags into the pot. Daisy and Maggie came back into the kitchen just as Juliette was pouring out the tea. Juliette handed Daisy a floral mug and passed a small plastic cup to Maggie.

'It's divine. My goodness, I want to live here - you've done it up beautifully too. All the lovely girlie things you've wanted for so long. It reminds me of the bedsit in a weird way. I recognise some of the bits and pieces from back then.'

'Yep, I've had a lot in storage. Jeremy didn't like the girlie stuff at all, but there was no way I was throwing it out.'

'The eiderdown in Maggie's room - it's beautiful and I can't believe how nice the wallpaper looks and that you did it yourself! It looks so much better than it did on the video.'

'Let me show you your little room for the weekend then,' Juliette said.

Juliette walked over the kitchen, up the two little steps to the middle room with the window overlooking the terrace and opened the door to the tiny office. Sallie had painted the whole room a soft white and Juliette had added to it with thick linen curtains with tiny pink flowers, a pale pink sofa bed was pushed up against the far wall and an old desk she'd found outside one of the flats she had painted with pale pink chalk paint and topped each end of it with white fabric lamps.

'It's delightful, just right for me - you decorated it for me, yeah?'

'Of course.'

'I'll go and get my other bag out of the car.'

Daisy went out to her car, and two minutes later, breathless, came flying back into the cottage.

'I think I've just seen him! Black BMW. Grey jumper. Very, ahem, nice bottom encased in very nice jeans.'

'What? Oh my goodness.'

'Yes, he was just parking his car, so I ducked down in the back seat, waited until he'd walked past and then took a very good look, analysed the bottom, the jumper and the swagger.'

Juliette started laughing as Maggie came in.

'What are you laughing about?'

'Just silly Aunty Daisy, she didn't believe me that the sofa turns into a bed, she thought she might have to sleep on the floor.'

Chapter 47

Juliette stood in the garden in her dressing gown, her hands cradling a mug of tea as she looked down past the Orangery at the waves crashing in and out onto the beach. Winter sun and a pale blue sky warmed the tiny suntrap on the patio Sallie had told her about when she'd first moved in. Maggie was sitting there with a bowl of porridge, chattering away about the Christmas crafts she was making at school.

Juliette was listening to Maggie with one ear but her mind was racing with other thoughts. She held her face up to the sun and thought about the last few months, the last few months where a handsome doctor had all of sudden catapulted into her life, swept her off her feet and left her reeling and wondering quite what was going on.

As she stood there and looked around at her surroundings it was like moving out of the flat and into the cottage had given her a whole new lease of life and every single thing was looking up. Jeremy seemed much less annoying these days, her savings were slowly but surely building and everything just seemed more stable, and so much more relaxed. There might even be the chance of a house on the cards.

And then there was Luke. She'd let herself be swept up in it all and it felt absolutely amazing. Trombones, heck in fact, a whole brass band of happiness followed her around playing in her ears. She'd loved every single second of it - the wining and the dining, the Winter-y walks where he'd kissed her leant up against the lighthouse, the secret meal in Seafolly Bay when Maggie had been on a sleepover, the kissing in the car when they'd driven to Pearl Beach to look at the Christmas lights down by the canal.

She picked up Maggie's bowl and spoon and walked back into the kitchen, putting them in the dishwasher and thought more about

Luke. He filled every moment of her thoughts and it was as if he felt the same. The sex was amazing like nothing she had experienced before, not that there had been much to compare it with, but Luke made things happen that dragged her into a whole other world. It was like their bodies were made for each other.

She tidied up the kitchen thinking about their lunch date that afternoon, she couldn't wait to see him, she hadn't seen him for a few days. The last time was when Maggie had been at Jeremy's and she'd snuck round to Luke's early evening and spent a wonderful night with him. It had ended up with her creeping down the road the next morning just in time for Jeremy to drop Maggie off and her opening the door to Jeremy as if she'd just come down the stairs when she had in fact only just walked in. She had been sure that her guilt had been written all over her face and she'd cringed with embarrassment about walking down the lane the next morning. But there was also a little bit of her that was loving the whole clandestine thing, the secrecy and the pleasure... it had been so very long since she had such joy in her life.

Luke had been glorious in every way - texting her just the right amount of times, turning up with flowers, leaving notes on her windscreen and making her feel special and gorgeous and wanted. It was like he'd read a manual on how to make her feel like she was the one and had followed it to the letter.

They'd been together at every opportunity they could; she'd been out with him to restaurants, they'd walked and talked over the fields at the top of Strawberry Hill, they'd been for lunch on a canal boat and up to London on the train. He was handsome and kind and seemed to have fallen for her just as much as she had him.

She thought about it all as she sprayed down the kitchen with disinfectant and wiped everything clean. He had been perfect in every way and she loved how they just got on, how time with him seemed to go in a flash and how she felt giddy when she was around him. She couldn't wait for it to move further on, couldn't wait to introduce him to her girls.

Hugging her secret to herself she pottered around the cottage and got Maggie's bag ready for horse riding, went up to have a shower, curled her hair and put on a black silk tea dress with a ruffle at the bottom and soft flowing sleeves. She looked in the mirror as she went to walk out of the room and stopped dead in her tracks - how different she looked, so much happier, so much more at ease. It was like the last few months, the extra weight and the new love of her life had plumped her out and made her look... jolly. Jolly was a whole lot better than gaunt and incessantly hungry.

It was amazing what love and carbs had done for her, a few years ago she was miserable, hated how she looked and felt, and every waking minute of her life had been about control. Now she could barely wait to get dressed in the mornings and celebrate her new self.

'Have you got your hat Maggie?' Juliette called out as she came down the stairs.

'Yes, it's on my head,' Maggie said, looking at her, giggling and pointing to her hat.

'Oh yes, silly me,' Juliette said. 'Right, so I'll drop you off and daddy is picking you up.'

Maggie nodded, they put on their coats, shut and locked the pink front door and walked down the path.

'Hello Maggie,' Ali, standing with his wife Deepa, called out.

Maggie waved and Deepa looked left and right and crossed over the lane.

'You look fabulous, Juliette, where are you off to? You smell gorgeous too!' Deepa exclaimed.

'Just a bit of Christmas shopping this afternoon for me and Maggie is off horse riding and then to Jeremy's,' Juliette said, as she opened the car door for Maggie and helped her to get in.

'Very fancy for a bit of Christmas shopping,' Deepa said, smiling and crossing back over the road to Ali, she waved, 'Enjoy the horse riding and the, errrm, shopping, Juliette.'

Juliette thought about Ali and Deepa as she pulled out of the lane - their looks had been sort of knowing, had they witnessed her waiting to go in Luke's front door or seen her skipping along the road one morning just in time before Jeremy arrived? Maybe they had, not much went without being noticed in Pretty Beach.

Chapter 48

The Pretty Beach ferry was all dressed up for Christmas with rows of fairy lights at the front and big garlands of red and gold tinsel tied on the inside. Juliette and Luke got off the ferry, made their way through Newport Reef, ambled through the industrial estate with ugly squat beige buildings and out onto a main road lined with big old houses with black railings.

They walked down the road, Juliette's arm tucked into Luke's, looking up at the sky and wondering if it was going to rain. They stopped to gaze at the dancing Christmas lights from a house covered in decorations and a tiny black cat sitting on a wall meowed at them as they walked all the way along the road to find the pub Sallie and Ben had recommended for lunch.

'If these directions are right it should be just down here on the corner.' Luke said, looking down at his phone.

'That looks like a pub down there, hope so because I'm ready for lunch now after this walk and no breakfast,' Juliette said, peering down the road.

They turned the corner and a lovely old pub with leadlight arched windows and dark grey window boxes full of white poinsettias stood in front of them. Luke pushed open the door with intricate glass inlay and they walked into the pub, greeted by a long curved antique bar stacked behind with rows and rows of gin.

'Wow, Sallie said this was amazing, it certainly is!' Juliette said, pulling off her scarf and looking around.

'I'll see where our table is,' Luke said, strolling up to the bar as Juliette was taking off her coat. He came back a minute later.

'Over there on the left in through to the conservatory, table in the corner.'

They walked into the conservatory off the back of the pub to the only available table, filled with noise, a tall Christmas tree in the corner, succulents hanging from the ceiling, plant pots tied with gold Christmas bows cosied between the tables and a man in the corner playing the piano.

'This is delightful, it's exactly like Sallie and Ben said, what a lovely place to come for lunch. I bet it looks beautiful in the evening too,' Juliette said as she sat down and looked around at the overly warm conservatory.

The waitress asked them what they wanted to drink, Luke ordered a half pint of ale and Juliette a raspberry water and they scanned down the menu chatting and deciding what to have for lunch.

An hour later after chatting over tiny little canapes and polishing off roast turkey with pork and clementine stuffing with red wine gravy and bread sauce, Luke and Juliette sat back in their chairs full, relaxed and happy.

'That was delicious.' Luke said, and held Juliette's hand.

Juliette touched his foot with hers under the table and the same stirrings she'd had the very first time she'd seen him in the car park at the hospital began to surge through her veins. She felt drunk on happiness - whatever it was that Luke did to her she was loving it, loving him and very much wanting it to continue. She was even beginning to think about how she was going to introduce him to the girls and he'd mentioned it too.

Luke ordered coffees and liqueurs and they sat there as the patrons in the conservatory began to slowly dissipate and the light went down.

Luke looked at Juliette across the table, 'Who would have thought this would all be happening before Christmas... when I moved into Pretty Beach I didn't know a soul and now I've got you.'

Juliette felt time freeze. What was Luke saying? Where was this going? She'd let herself be completely swept away by it all and was loving every single second of the ride but now he was cementing it all.

'I know, it's been amazing, Luke.' She smiled, looking into his eyes.

Luke was holding her hand and looking out towards the pub when a strange look crossed his face and he continued looking out of the door.

'Luke?'

Luke didn't say anything back.

'Luke? Are you okay?' Juliette asked as Luke pulled his hand away and pushed back his chair.

'Yes, look we should go.'

'Okay, I'll just finish my coffee.'

Juliette finished her coffee and they got up to leave.

'I need to pop to the loo,' Juliette said as Luke stood at the entrance of the conservatory, tapped his card against the machine and said thank you to the waitress. He all of a sudden seemed anxious to go, edgy almost.

Juliette walked across the pub, and noticed a very pretty woman in her mid-thirties with wide-leg pants, long blonde hair and a sparkly diamond necklace talking to a man at the bar.

Juliette came back out of the toilet to Luke who was standing at the entrance of the pub, his back to Juliette and holding Juliette's coat from the rack. He pulled open the inner door, holding it open for Juliette to walk through.

Just as Juliette went to walk through the blonde woman in the sparkly necklace who had previously been at the bar opened the outer door, not looking where she was going and bumped straight into Juliette. The woman looked up.

'Sorry!' She said and then as she looked across from Juliette to Luke the woman's eyes widened, she gripped the side of the door and her face went white.

Juliette looked at her confused.

'Karen,' Luke said quietly and took a step back. The stunning woman looked back at him and then to Juliette, her eyes darting from left to right.

'I'm sorry Luke,' she said, stumbling over her words, her face drained of colour, her eyes wide.

'Luke. Sorry, have I missed something. Are you okay?'

Luke nodded, his face grim, his lips set in a straight line.

'Do you two know each other?' Juliette asked awkwardly, the three of them standing between the two doors.

'You could say that yes,' the woman Karen replied.

'I'm Luke's wife.'

Chapter 49

Juliette pushed her way past the woman with the blonde hair and out of the pub, blood rushing to her face. She held onto her coat, ran outside into the rain and started running down the road. Running and running and running until she was out of breath and couldn't run any further.

She finally slowed her pace, her coat and dress soaked through to the skin, and held onto some railings out the front of a huge house and tried to catch her breath. This couldn't be happening, could it? She'd just spent the last few months falling in love with a married man.

Thoughts raced through her mind; *if he had a wife why didn't he live with her? If he had a wife, why hadn't he mentioned it? They'd talked about everything under the sun but he'd forgotten to include that he was married, who even did that?*

Juliette leant on the railings her breath slowly returning to normal and closed her eyes, her whole body trembled as she bent over. All sorts of feelings were galloping through her brain - anger, confusion, upset, but most of all she felt betrayed. Betrayed that she'd let him into her tight little world and stupid that she had abandoned reason. Hurt that she'd let Luke into her life, her lovely new little life with Maggie and Bella and let him be part of the happy, relaxed new Juliette. Hurt that she'd let him even witness her new self - whatever this all was he hadn't deserved to be part of her new world.

'Why, why, why did I not wait?' she whispered to herself as she looked in her bag for her phone to book an Uber. There was no way she was getting the ferry home or going anywhere where there was the chance of bumping into Luke. She was going to go back to the cottage, lock the front door, close the curtains and potentially would never come out again. She knew she was being on the rash side, there was possibly an explanation from Luke, maybe she was being immature, but she didn't want to know the whys and wherefores, she just wanted to hide.

He hadn't even said anything, he'd just let her walk out. He hadn't called after her or tried to catch up with her - he'd been quite happy to let her go. She didn't know what was worse.

Five minutes later an Uber turned up and she got in the back.

'Been anywhere nice?' enquired the driver.

'Well, the place I went to was nice, but the company, well the company turned out to be a complete and utter shark.'

They got home to Seapocket Lane and Juliette glanced all the way down the end, at least there wasn't a clear view of Luke's place, at least she would be able to somewhat avoid him.

Juliette felt numb, it would possibly have been better if she had burst into tears and let it all out, but she was just stunned and reeling from having the very nice rug with the nights of fantastic sex, the cosy chats and what she had thought was falling in love, pulled directly out from under her, screwed up and thrown into the corner in a heap.

Opening her front door, she carefully and quietly closed it behind her, put her coat neatly on the hooks by the door and slipped off her shoes.

All she could think about was the look on the woman's face. It played over and over and over in her mind, like a scene from a film that you replay again and again reliving the good bits. And as much as she continued to go over it she couldn't quite work out what the look was on the woman who appeared to be Luke's wife. The woman hadn't said anything, she'd just sort of stalled in the middle of the entrance hall and almost looked... embarrassed, that was it, or it could possibly have been shame. There was one thing it absolutely wasn't and that was anger and if you'd bumped into your husband out with another woman wouldn't you be angry?

She opened the fridge, pulled out some leftover lasagne, heated it up in the microwave, went into the conservatory and sat on the floor leaning up against the sofa shovelling the lasagne into her mouth as quickly as she could.

How could she have put herself into this situation? Why had she not been more cautious? A new man had swept into town that no one knew anything about and she'd not only been out with him, but been very much in his bed.

She cringed as she remembered that she had suggested to him that they get a room in The Old Bell Hotel. And then as she thought more about that memory she shuddered to herself at how she'd woken up the next morning with him by her side and she'd brazenly lusted after him again.

She knew why she'd been that way; it was because he was handsome and gorgeous and the thing with the stirrings had made her lose her mind. The stirrings had made her forget that she had so many responsibilities and had had them for so very long.

When she was with Luke, sensible Juliette who worked hard and saved money and worried about her daughters was put away somewhere in a drawer and relaxed happy Juliette came out to play. When she had been with Luke it was almost like she was the Juliette of eighteen years ago, the Juliette with hopes and dreams and silly thoughts about pretty houses and lovely things.

And with Luke it had just all felt so relaxed, so easy, so lovely. He'd been sweet and perfect and seemed to feel exactly the same way about her as she did about him. Exactly the same way but with a little addition, a very much alive and kicking wife.

Chapter 50

Juliette adjusted the little red pom pom reindeer nose on the front of Maggie's Christmas jumper and put Maggie's coat on over her sparkly grey tulle skirt and walked her through the gates of the school.

Juliette held tightly onto Maggie's hand, head down, clutching a tin full of Christmas fairy cakes topped with silver sprinkles and avoided catching eyes with any of the other mothers. After what had happened at the lunch the last thing she wanted to do was to have to stop and talk to anyone, not that anyone really even knew that there was a thing going on, but if there was one thing she knew about Pretty Beach and its surrounds it was that everyone, sooner or later, found out your business, and she wasn't giving anyone the opportunity to find out hers.

'Morning Juliette, how are you?' Feony called out from the other side of the path.

'Morning,' Juliette said, and quickly carried on walking.

Fifteen minutes later, Maggie safely deposited with Miss Henshaw and the cakes delivered, she was back in the car. As she indicated to turn out of the car park her phone started ringing, she pressed the answer button on the steering wheel and Daisy said hello.

'Sorry I couldn't get back to you yesterday - everything okay?'

'No, not really, everything is definitely not okay,' Juliette replied, keeping her eyes on the road in the heavy traffic.

'Oh no, you sound awful. What the heck has happened? I only spoke to you the other morning and you were really looking forward to going out with Luke.'

'Well, there's no two ways around it really and no other way to say this other than bluntly - Luke has a wife.'

'What!' Daisy yelled down the phone.

'Yes,' Juliette replied quietly.

'What do you mean he has a wife? Like a wife he doesn't live with?'

'I don't even know, that's the worst bit. All I know is this extremely pretty, and I mean, Hollywood pretty, woman with long blonde hair bumped into us in the pub and it appears that she is his wife.'

'What do you mean you don't know? Sorry, this is very confusing.'

Juliette continued filling in Daisy on what had happened - the woman in the foyer of the pub, the look on Luke's face, and that the woman seemed to be embarrassed by the whole thing.

'This is all very odd. What is she like some secret wife he hadn't told you about? What a scumbag.'

'I know, after everything he knows about me too.'

'I can't understand it though, I mean he seemed just so into you and just so lovely; the flowers, the texts, the thing at the lighthouse.'

'The whole thing was weird. Sort of creepy weird, I think that's why I just bolted.'

'And you ran and ran and what he didn't come after you and hasn't called or texted?'

'Nup, nothing, well actually I don't know that because I've blocked his number. He could have called me a million times for all I know.'

'This is most bizarre, I'm so sorry. What are you going to do? I mean, sorry and don't take this the wrong way, but you've blocked him? You're not eighteen, you need to talk about it, like adults.'

Juliette sighed, she'd thought exactly the same and when she'd unblocked his number and gone to message him, she'd changed her mind. She felt like her lovely little world had been tipped up, given a shake and poured back out again by the addition of Luke's secret wife and she didn't like how it made her feel. She didn't like it at all and so she'd felt it was much easier to wrap it up, lock it in a little black box and shove it to the back of her mind.

'I don't think there is much for me to do, is there? A lurking wife is not quite the romantic fairytale I had set myself up for here.' Juliette said with a sad, resigned laugh. 'I'm just going to go to ground, keep my head down and keep well out of his way - I know what you are saying, I'm being immature, I just don't want to handle it.'

'I can't believe he's not been round or texted you... or said sorry.' Daisy almost screamed the last bit.

'I know, it's like the whole thing was a dream in my head, not the last lovely few months of getting to know him and then, you know, the night in the hotel... all the other nights. God, I feel so stupid,' Juliette said as she sat in a queue going down Strawberry Hill.

'You don't want to knock on his door and ask him for an explanation?'

'Not really - what will he say? Oh yeah sorry I have a wife, I normally keep quiet about her and no one is any the wiser. Sorry you had to find out about her Juliette.'

'Yep, I have the t-shirt on that situation... at least I knew about the wife though, not that I knew in the very beginning.'

'And look where that got you.'

Daisy sighed, 'Tell me about it. Try and forget about it I suppose, it's not even worth getting an explanation if he's the sort of person who forgets to tell you something as big as the fact that he has a wife.'

'Exactly. It's not as if we're teenagers either, I mean I know I bolted like one, but I was shocked. I presumed that we were both grownups and I assumed that he liked me as much as I did him. Well, to be honest Daisy, I think I love him, or loved him. Where did that even come from? I feel like crap now, that's all I know.'

Daisy, had gone quiet from the other end of the phone.

'Are you still there, Daisy?'

'Yeah, yeah I am. I don't know Sparkles, but I could tell this was all very different that very first day you told me about him. I was like, my goodness, Sparkles has only gone and fallen in love.'

Chapter 51

Juliette walked down the laneway under the crisscross of beautiful Christmas lights and bunting. How ironic the picture-perfect scene of it all felt - the Pretty Beach Christmas dream wasn't feeling quite as rosy as it had when she'd walked the exact same steps the week before. Then, she'd hugged her little love secret tightly to her chest, and imagined herself kissing under the mistletoe, Bing Crosby in the background. She hadn't thought there would be three of them under the mistletoe though, and certainly hadn't envisaged that one of them would be Luke's wife.

She was on her way to see Holly; Holly knew everything about Pretty Beach, and over and above that she always seemed to just be able somehow to give sensible, relevant advice. Juliette pushed open the door of the bakery and the familiar comforting smell of fresh bread combined with Christmas pudding and mince pies enveloped her. Was it possible that the smell of baking bread could make you feel better? It certainly seemed to work for Juliette.

Juliette waited for a couple of customers to be served and then catching Holly's eye she leant over the counter.

'Holly, I need to talk to you.'

Holly, seeing the look on Juliette's face indicated for Juliette to go behind the counter.

'Come back here, are you okay?' Holly ushered Juliette into the back of the bakery, gestured for Juliette to sit down on a chair and put the kettle on for a cup of tea.

'Not really, actually no, no I'm most definitely not okay.'

'Oh no, what's Jeremy done this time?'

'Not him for once,' Juliette replied, smiling wryly. 'I need to ask you if you know anything more about Luke.'

'Like what?'

'I don't know, you always seem to know everything in Pretty Beach.'

'For once, I don't, I mean he just turned up out of nowhere at the back-end of Summer, got everyone talking but didn't really say much himself. I did chat to James about him when he came in for his bread, but he said that he was a great bloke by the sounds of it, that's all I really know.'

'Exactly. I've realised the same thing - I don't actually know much about him at all. I was swept away by him always being interested in me, always being kind, always doing lovely things, so that, well, I don't actually know that much about him and who he is.'

'What's happened then? Apart from the fact that you've been seen with him on multiple occasions, that he went to see Mr Jenkin's house with you, that you came out of The Old Bell in last night's clothes and that you were seen going into Newport for lunch.'

Juliette started laughing, 'See, you do know most things about Pretty Beach!'

'It seems not enough.'

'So, yes, we went for lunch and it was wonderful and I was really loving every second of it, loving every second of Luke. We were even sort of hinting at what was going to happen in the future.' Juliette stopped talking as Holly put their cups of tea down on the table and cut open a mince pie.

'Go on.'

'We were sitting at the table and Luke all of a sudden looked very strange - like he'd seen a ghost strange.'

'Right.'

'And then I went to the loo, came back and he was already standing by the door and as we went out I bumped slap bang into a woman.'

Holly looked at Juliette intently, her chin resting on her hand, her mug of tea in the other hand.

'Well it turns out that this other woman was, is, Luke's wife.'

'Oh. My. God.'

Chapter 52

Juliette crossed over the tiny little bridge over the stream to the Boat House to Sallie's house right at the end of the laneway. The lighthouse beam swept across the bay and the twinkly lights on the marquee at the end of the drive sparkled in the dark night. It all reminded her of the Christmas Dance where she'd positively hummed with anticipation at seeing Luke. The very same Luke with the very pretty wife.

Sallie opened the door in black jeans and a sparkly black jumper and kissed Juliette on the cheek. 'Come on up, we need a very long talk,' Sallie said hugging Juliette and patting her on the back.

'Holly and Xian are already here,' Sallie said as they walked up the steep steps at the side of the Boat House.

Juliette stood at the top of the stairs and looked around at the beautiful scene in front of her. Tiny white lights shimmered from the old-fashioned sash windows and in the corner a huge tree sparkled.

'Goodness, it looks and smells amazing in here!' Juliette exclaimed as she took off her coat.

'It's the clementine cider, I've had it simmering away all afternoon just for you, it will hopefully make you feel better.'

'You've got your hands on Locals Only cider? My, this is indeed an occasion - I must be needy - I bet the whole of Pretty Beach has been wondering about me,' Juliette said, smiling.

'Not me, I'll give you one guess who got it,' Sallie said, pointing a finger at Holly.

'Holly, you're the gift that keeps on giving. I love the stuff,' Juliette said as Sallie came out of the kitchen with a cocktail glass full of the warm clementine cider topped with slices of orange and a cinnamon stick stuck on the side.

Juliette sat down on the opposite side of the sofa to Holly and Xian, Sallie brought in a huge sharing platter of nibbles and they chatted about all the goings-on in Pretty Beach and how their friend Nina was getting on now that she'd started to recover from a nasty complication with asthma.

'So, anything further on the Luke situation?' Holly asked, as Xi-an took a large sip of her special drink.

'Nothing. To be fair I've blocked his number on my phone so I wouldn't know even if he had tried to get in contact with me. I've not had any shifts at Newport either as I'd petered them out for the busy bit in the shop, so there's been no chance of bumping into him there.'

'You don't want to find out what the story is?' Sallie asked.

'How does one explain they had a wife they had forgotten about?'

'True,' Sallie said, topping up their glasses with more of the clementine cider. 'Let me get this straight again - she said she was sorry to him and he looked like he'd seen a ghost?'

'Yeah, it was all very weird now I look back on it. It was like she was the one apologizing. He didn't say anything or in fact do anything, he just stood there looking dumbstruck.'

'So what are you going to do then? I mean just running out of there you don't know the full story.'

'I just feel like if I ignore it, it will just go away. I feel like such an idiot that if I bury it, it won't be quite as bad. I won't feel like quite as much of an idiot.'

All four of them sat there, saying nothing. They all knew Juliette had fallen hook, line and sinker for Luke. They all knew about her past and that it had been a huge thing for her to let someone in and so then to be sitting around discussing the fact that he had a wife left a very bad taste in everyone's mouth.

'I don't know, it all seems a bit odd to me though Juliette. He was so into you, he seemed nice and caring and then boom he suddenly has a wife. Like where was she then? He moved to Pretty Beach, and what, just left her behind? Ben said the same,' Sallie questioned.

Xian, who had sat for most of the evening checking her shares on her tablet, looked up.

'There's more to this story Juliette - you don't just bump into someone's wife in a pub and he reacts like that. None of it adds up, not at all. You need to put your big girl pants on and listen to his side of the story.'

They all turned and looked at Xian.

Of course, she was right.

Chapter 53

Luke placed his empty pint glass down on the beer mat and as James the barman walked back up to his end of the bar he ordered another pint.

James pulled the pump on the ale and they both watched it swirl in the bottom of the glass and waited for it to settle. Luke had become quite friendly with James since he'd been in Pretty Beach, strolling to the pub a good few times a week and often popping in for dinner in the evening. James had invited Luke to join the Pretty Beach Open Water Swimmers Society and had heard bits and bobs of the Juliette and Luke story from Luke's side. Bits and bob that hadn't included Luke's long-lost wife.

'I've been really stupid, haven't I?' Luke said, contemplating the situation with Juliette.

'Mate, I'm no relationship expert but I think you're up the creek without a paddle. You swept into town, swooped onto Pretty Beach's only and very much loved midwife, took her to bed and forgot to tell her you had a wife. You're lucky your balls are still intact and your house hasn't been burnt down if you ask me,' James said, alarming Luke by the fact that he was only half joking.

Luke shook his head and sighed. 'I know. I just kept bottling out when I had to tell her I had a wife from ten years ago who packed up and left one day and told me she'd never loved me anyway. I mean it's not the kind of impression I was trying to give to a woman the first time I saw her... well mate, you know the rest.'

James leant on the pump while Luke swigged his beer. 'Yeah, not sure this is a bunch of flowers situation here Lukie-boy. You're going to have to do two things; one, come clean as a whistle, tell her everything and two, throw everything you can at her. Make old Sparkles feel special - I'm talking diamond special. I can't say it'll work though,' he said and shook his head, 'I mean mate, what were you thinking?'

'Small problem. She's obviously blocked my number, she hasn't answered the door when I've rung the bell and when I did see her parking her car in the lane, she saw me, got Maggie out of the car, bolted into her cottage and shut the door so quickly I was barely even approaching the gate.'

'You're going to have to think of something, but I tell you one thing: make sure you are sure what you are doing first. If you mess her around twice, you'll be toast in Pretty Beach. Put it this way, you won't be sitting in this pub having a beer, the locals will make it quite clear you're not welcome.'

Luke sighed, 'I just don't know what to do, I feel like the biggest idiot ever and all because I was too much of a coward to tell her and the further it went on the bigger it got.'

James went to serve another customer and came back five minutes later.

'I'm going to have to ask you Luke - how does one have a forgotten wife, though?'

'Like I said, she upped and left me one day, as in I got up and went to work as normal one morning and when I got home all her things were gone and there was a note on the worktop in the kitchen.'

'Crikey, that's a low blow if ever I've heard one,' James replied, raising his eyebrows and shaking his head.

'It was a complete and utter shock, but after that wore off and I thought about it a bit more it was obvious she'd been planning it for a long time.'

Chapter 54

Juliette pushed open the door as she and Maggie got home from Maggie's horse riding club Christmas Party. Juliette had come straight from work, was still in her uniform, Maggie was over-excited from all the sweets and running around and all Juliette wanted to do was get Maggie ready for bed and go all the way to the top of the cottage and have a long, hot, soak in the bath.

'Right darling, we're going to go straight up to the shower, get you in there and get your nightie on.'

'Another Christmas card,' Maggie said, picking up a white envelope from the floor and holding it up to Juliette.

'Okay, yep, put that on the table and we'll go upstairs and get you in the shower.'

Maggie put the envelope on the little table beside the lamp and they walked up the steep stairs. Juliette went and got changed out of her uniform while Maggie was in the shower and half an hour later Maggie was in her nightie and they were sitting on the floor of her bedroom leaning up against the bed and finishing a story.

'Right, hop into bed and I'll tuck you in.'

Maggie was not looking in the slightest bit tired, 'Can I have my nightlight on for a while?'

'Ten minutes and that's your lot,' Juliette said, smiling and she switched on the little ceramic mushroom glow light, tucked Maggie in and kissed her goodnight.

Juliette went downstairs to the kitchen, made herself something to eat and then went up to the bathroom, ran a deep bath pouring in eucalyptus muscle soak and emerged an hour later in her polka dot dressing gown. She went down the first set of stairs, checked in on Maggie, made herself a cup of tea and went and sat in the lounge to watch Netflix.

She sat down on the sofa and as she put her mug down on the table, saw the envelope Maggie had picked up from the doormat. Another Christmas card - she was so behind with hers and this would no doubt be another one to add to her list. She picked it up and opened it. It wasn't a Christmas card. She pulled out a small white card with an embossed heart on the front and opening it up a piece of folded white paper fell out onto her lap.

Dear Juliette

I don't really know what to say apart from I am so very sorry.

I realise you don't want to see me or talk to me, I've tried to call you and text you many times and I've knocked on your door too.

The woman we met in the pub was my wife. She still is my wife.

I haven't seen her for ten years - she left me with all her things out of the blue one day and hasn't been back since. I've had no communication with her, or from her, and until I saw her in the pub with you, I haven't seen her for years.

I can't say much more other than the fact that I am truly sorry that I didn't tell you and that I have hurt you. I wanted to tell you but I just couldn't find the right time.

Please let me talk to you, we have/had something really special and I want to please make it up to you and explain.

Luke x

Juliette closed the letter and put it back in the card and placed the card on the table. She picked up her mug of tea and sat there thinking about it all. Her mind was racing, tears pricked at the back of her eyes and thoughts of Luke and images of them together went in and out of her mind as she held the mug of tea up looking into the bottom of it as if it could give her the answer.

What did it really change? He was admitting he had a wife and hadn't seen her for ten years, but he hadn't addressed why he'd not told her about it at all and what person in their right mind would want to carry on with a relationship where the other person went into it without telling the truth?

Chapter 55

Juliette watched Maggie skipping along by the water as she walked along with Sallie on the shoreline, the waves crashing in and out on the beach. Breathing in the sea air she hoped it might do something to unwind the tight knot in her stomach and unravel the coiled-up thoughts in her head.

'So, when did the letter actually arrive?'

'It must have been sometime yesterday, Maggie picked it up when we came in the door, I thought it was just another Christmas card and didn't even open it until later on in the evening when I was sitting down with a cup of tea.'

'Right.'

'You can read it if you want,' Juliette said, taking the envelope out of her pocket and handing it to Sallie.

Sallie pulled the piece of paper out of the envelope, flicked it open and as they strolled along by the sea she read it quietly.

'What do you think?'

'I really do not know what to say,' Sallie replied. 'Have you told anyone else?'

'Nope. Daisy is phoning this evening so I'll tell her then, not that I need all my friends to tell me what to do, we're not twelve. It's just so, I don't know, strange. You know I'd fallen for him and I thought he felt the same way.'

'I guess he could feel the same way, just because he has a wife doesn't mean anything. Look at my ex-husband, we had been what I thought quite happily married, and then one day he informed me the neighbour was moving in. I mean it really was as drastic as that.'

'You can't make this stuff up.'

'Then the story of David - his wife left him for their carpet cleaner. So it does happen, people do fall in love with other people when they are married to someone else.'

'Why did this happen to me? I was quite happy pottering along without any complications and now I feel like I was at the top of a beautiful romantic ferris wheel and someone shoved me off the top.'

'It says he hadn't seen her for ten years, that would make sense of the look he had on his face in the foyer,' Sallie said, peering through her glasses at the letter and reading the line out again to Juliette.

'I know, I thought that too - the look on his face was the weirdest thing about it all, he looked like he'd seen a ghost.'

'Well if he hadn't seen her or heard from her for ten years and she left him out of the blue, it would have been quite the shock. I'm not defending him at all, but that's quite traumatic.'

'I hadn't thought about it from that side.'

Sallie folded up the piece of paper, put it back in the envelope and gave it back to Juliette.

'I just don't want to see him, it's almost like I haven't got the will to even listen to it and all the complications, crikey I've had my fair share...' Juliette trailed off, looking out onto the purple-grey sea crashing and breaking right out at the back.

'I know what you mean. When my ex-husband announced he liked the neighbour better than me, part of me couldn't even be bothered with it. I was exhausted by it all. Like mentally exhausted and physically ground down - that was part of the reason he managed to get away with getting so much of the money and left me with next to nothing.'

Juliette nodded, 'I'm just so tired, so tired of everything being complicated, worrying, thinking things over. I just don't need it anymore. There's a problem though Sals.'

Sallie looked over at Juliette with her eyebrows raised in question.

'I love Luke.'

Chapter 56

The few days before Christmas Eve came around really quickly and Juliette had been to pick up Bella from the station, had driven her home, dished up a casserole from the slow cooker for dinner and put Maggie to bed. Bella had then gone out with some old school friends and was staying the night over in Seafolly Beach.

Daisy, who had arrived a few days before had gone up for a shower and to read Maggie a story and made a cup of tea for herself and Juliette and in her dressing gown brought it into the sitting room.

Daisy sat on the corner of Juliette's sofa and dunked a biscuit in her tea with the letter open on her lap.

'Hmm.'

Juliette sat back on the opposite sofa watching her intently as she read it through.

'Not being funny, but just talk to him.'

'It's not quite as easy as that Daisy!'

'Why not? It's all written down here in black and white. He hasn't seen her for years, and he wants to talk to you about it.'

'I'm not sure I want to get involved further with someone who forgot to tell me he had a wife.'

'Sparkles. Look. Do I have to spell it out to you? You're in love with this man. I've known you for eighteen years. I've helped you with a puking newborn, I've been your bridesmaid to a man I told you not to marry, I've sat with you while you signed your divorce papers and I've driven you around in tears when Bella broke her leg and I have never seen you like I've seen you over the last few months. When I was here for the weekend it was the happiest I've seen you look, like ever! I couldn't believe the difference in you and it was standing there right in front of my eyes.'

Juliette looked back at Daisy and wrung her hands together over and over again.

'It's true. I actually love him. It's ridiculous, but I think I thought that in the car park that day as he jogged over the flyover without a coat.'

'It supposedly can happen, they say, love at first sight and all that.'

'That's why I'm stalling though, because it's like I don't want to admit it to myself.'

'Remember when you told me to talk to Matt? You said that the only way through it was to actually talk to him, ask him, see what he said and then I'd know, I would really just know.'

Juliette looked up from her hands.

'Yes, yes I do remember that, but this is different.'

'This is no different at all, you'll know, you'll know as soon as he starts to speak, by the look in his eyes, by the way he holds his hands, by the words he uses. It's exactly what you told me and it's exactly how I knew, after ten years, that Matt was never going to leave his wife and never loved me like I did him.'

Juliette leant forward to the coffee table and put her mug of tea down and looked back at Daisy.

'It's true, you're actually right. I'm going to need to do something about it.' Juliette replied, sighing and looking out at the Christmas lights on the lane.

Chapter 57

Juliette stood with Bella on one side, Maggie on the other and Daisy holding onto Maggie's hand as they all stood under the crisscrossed twinkling lights of the laneway and looked up at the sparkling reindeer which had now been joined by a giant crystal snowflake sitting on the roof of Holly's bakery.

'It's all so lovely, girls, isn't it?' Daisy said. 'I remember the laneway when I was a little girl just like you Maggie and the Christmas Carol Service meant Father Christmas was finally nearly going to arrive. My mummy used to sing in the Pretty Beach choir too.' Daisy continued wistfully, speaking to no one in particular, memories flooding through her head.

The four of them crunched over the recently fallen snow and made their way to the Old Town to the church. Daisy pulled her hat down over her ears, the bitter wind off the sea biting through her coat and Bella adjusted her scarf so it covered her nose. They walked through the churchyard and cemetery, up the old path to the church door and hustled in from the cold.

'Sallie said she'd try and save us some seats, but we're early enough that they're quite a few left anyway. Milly should be here somewhere too,' Juliette said, peering into the church as they walked in and she showed Roy Johnson on the door their tickets on her phone.

They took off their hats and scarves and made their way up the aisle of the warm, cosy candle-lit church. Pretty Beach's Choral Society all dressed in black and Christmas hats were bustling around with their last-minute preparations as they all sat down in a pew behind Sallie, Ben, Holly and her mum Xian, and Jessica and Camilla the owners of Pretty Beach Fish and Chips.

Sallie in a beautiful black coat with a velvet collar and matching velvet clip in her bun, turned around from her seat, 'Hello, isn't it beautiful? I love carols and it's been snowing!'

'I know, it's like the front of a Christmas card out there, better than the last few years when we had lashing down rain. We got soaked last year on the way home from this and ended up all stripping in the foyer of the flat,' Juliette said, laughing at the memories.

Sallie leant forward so that no one else could hear, 'Any further developments on the Luke front?'

'Nope, I've completely chickened out, Sals, I just can't deal with it, what with the girls here and everything.'

'Well, don't look round now, but he's just walked in and he's just walked in with what looks like maybe his brother or sister and partner, perhaps an au-pair and two little children.'

'Hopefully not another of his wives,' Juliette whispered back.

'I have to tell you, Sparkles, stuff me, he is absolutely gorgeous. I mean that jumper and that bottom.' Sallie joked and giggled.

'The bottom who has a wife.'

'You're going to have to talk to him, you cannot give that up,' Sallie said, as she watched Luke over Juliette's shoulder take a seat a few rows back. They both laughed, 'All joking aside, you need to sort this out - you can't say he's not tried and everyone in Pretty Beach saw what you looked like when you were, well, whatever you were doing with him was clearly working. You were radiant.'

Daisy leant in and whispered, 'I've told her to get round there and talk to him.'

'Talk to him and then do whatever it was that they were doing that made her sparkle like her name,' Sallie whispered to Daisy.

'I know Sallie - I've been friends with Sparkles for eighteen years and never, ever seen her like this,' Daisy whispered back.

The church began to slowly fill up, Milly joined their pew, sitting down next to Maggie, Pretty Beach Choral Society took their positions and the church rang with bells before the carols began.

An hour and a half later, after singing their hearts out, listening to a solo performance from Julie from the council and Silent Night as the final tune, they all filed out of their pews and started to make their way over to the church hall next door for mulled wine and mince pies.

Juliette stood next to Ben chatting about the Orangery decorations with a glass of mulled wine and a mince pie and Daisy was chatting to Shane Pence about how much the housing market had changed since the fast train had reached all the way to Pretty Beach.

'Hey Juliette, how are you? Any news about Mermaid Lane?' Julie from the council asked, as she passed by with a huge tray of mince pies.

'There's a delay until well into the New Year, but I'm keeping my fingers crossed,' Juliette said, smiling and helping herself to another mince pie.

'I'll do the same. Merry Christmas!' Julie said, and continued walking around with the huge foil platter of mince pies.

Juliette tried to look around to see if Luke had come in, the place was packed, but as she nodded to Ben about the decorations she couldn't see Luke anywhere. Secretly disappointed she sighed inside, even though he'd done what he'd done just seeing him made her realise she liked him a hell of a lot more than any of these people who had offered her advice thought. Which scared her even more.

After they'd had a couple of glasses of wine and mince pies, Bella had taken Maggie home, the hall had slowly cleared out and Juliette, Daisy, Ben, Sallie and Holly were standing by a trestle table finishing the last of the mince pies.

Roy Johnson came up to the table with a bin bag and started collecting all the rubbish.

'Need a hand with all that?' Julictte asked, full from the mince pies and ready to give a hand.

'Actually, if one of you could sweep and the others bring out all the plates and cups into the kitchen, it will be done in no time.'

Juliette took the broom which was leaning up against the stage and everyone else started to walk around the hall picking up cups, plates and bits of rubbish. Fifteen minutes later and most of it was done.

'Thanks guys, that's been a real help,' Roy said, as he loaded the recycling by the front door.

'Right, we'll be off then,' Ben said, walking out the door with Sallie and Holly, Juliette and Daisy following not far behind.

'I'm just going to pop to the loo before you lock up Roy, I'll catch you up Daisy,' Juliette called out over her shoulder and turned to the toilets.

Juliette washed her hands and looked in the mirror, her face was flushed from the sweeping and the mulled wine. She opened the door of the toilet, walked across the hall and heaved open the big old side door as Roy quickly clicked the lights off from the other side.

As she stepped down the steps Luke suddenly appeared from the right and came bounding up the steps from the bottom, she stopped right where she was. What was he doing? What was he going to say?

'Errr, hi, damn, sorry, oh dear, I'm the last person you want to bump into on the steps of the church hall. I've been sent back for a soft toy, going by the name of Fluffy and crucial to my two-year-old niece getting to sleep.' Luke said, stumbling over his words and looking up at Juliette.

Juliette just looked at him, didn't say anything back and went to walk past him when she got a hint of his strong, musky, beautiful scent. It took her breath away and she nearly slipped on the bottom step.

'Juliette!'

'I'm sorry Luke, I just can't do it. I don't want to know.'

Juliette pushed past him and started to walk briskly down the path of the church hall, desperate to get as far away from Luke as she possibly could.

Chapter 58

Juliette sighed heavily, looked for a spot outside her storage unit, parked her car and walked into the brightly lit reception area.

'Morning Michael,' she said, as she approached the desk.

'Morning,' Michael said, and offered her a plate of home-made mince pies. Juliette shook her head and said no.

'Refusing my wife's mince pies. Are you sick?'

Juliette shook her head.

'You alright, Jools? You look absolutely terrible. Do you need to sit down for a bit?' Michael asked.

'Not really Michael. In fact, I'm not good at all, but I'm not sick.'

Michael came around the other side of the desk and put his hand on her arm.

'You look awful. Come on, let me make you a nice cup of tea.'

Juliette followed Michael into a back room with a mini-fridge and kettle. He took two mugs off the side, popped in two teabags and poured in milk and then the boiling water.

'What's up, lovely? I've never seen you looking so down in the dumps.'

Juliette who over the years had become quite friendly with Michael ended up telling him the whole Luke story from the Baileys on the pavement to the wife in the foyer.

'Woah, that's a bit off,' Michael said, scratching the bald patch on the back of his head.

'And now he's sorry and explained it all, but I don't want to forgive him, but then I'm like what am I letting go? He's said he wants to be with me, that the wife is nothing. Plus, there's another thing, I feel like I was meant to be with somehow, I can't explain it, it's weird, he does something to me.'

Michael sighed, looked out the window, contemplating what Juliette had just relayed to him and sucked his breath in through his teeth.

'All I can tell you is I only knew my wife for three weeks when I knew she was the one. In fact, it was only nineteen days as it goes. I've known her now for forty-one years, married for thirty-one and we've not been apart for a single night other than when my mum passed away and I spent the night at her bedside.'

'That's lovely, Michael, you never told me that before.'

'Aye well, I don't go around telling people my business, Jools, mind it wasn't lovely before I met her. I'd been married before for thirteen long months of dread and hell.'

'Oh what? Wow. So, you were married before and only for that short time?'

'Yep, it was our parents, sort of pushed us into it, goodness knows why... and just over a year it lasted and then we split. Then I bumped into Mandy one day coming out of the Spar, like knocked into her and her bag of apples went flying all over the road. Been with her ever since,' Michael said, reliving the memory and chuckling.

'That's so sweet, you old romantic,' Juliette said, as Michael got up and picked up the mugs.

'Thing is Jools, I felt for Mandy exactly as you're saying now - like I never wanted to let her out of my sight again. If you've got that feeling I reckon you take it by the you-know-whats and hang on for dear life.'

Chapter 59

Juliette finished wrapping the bacon around the cocktail sausages for the pigs in blankets, put them in the fridge and checked on the defrosting turkey. All she had to do was make the trifle and everything would be ready.

Jeremy had finally decided on his movements for Christmas and Maggie was going over to Jeremy's mum on Boxing Day and then they were all going away for a week in January to their house in France which coincided nicely with Bella going to her friend from uni's place in America. Leaving Juliette a week in January to do exactly as she pleased.

She thought about it as Maggie helped her to put the sponge fingers in the bottom of the trifle dish and pour the jelly on top. Juliette couldn't remember the last time she'd had any time on her own.

'Rightio Princess Maggie, get your coat on and we'll go and see what are the best Christmas lights we can find in the whole of Pretty Beach,' Daisy said, handing over Maggie's coat as Juliette finished off the trifle.

'Anything else we've forgotten?' Daisy asked Juliette.

'The only thing I haven't done is the brandy butter, because I've run out of brandy - I'll just stroll over to Jeddos while you're out on the walk, then I think we're all ready for Father Christmas as long as we're all good tonight.'

'Let's go then, Maggie,' Daisy said, and they walked out of the kitchen to go out for their walk to look at the lights.

Juliette sprinkled the top of the trifle with hundreds and thousands, covered it with clingfilm and put it in the fridge. Tired and ready for a sit down she'd wished she'd just bought the brandy butter in the supermarket.

She put on her coat and scarf and opened the front door to the cold dark evening, stepped outside and shut the door behind her.

Crossing straight over the road to avoid Luke's place, she waved to Ali who was just getting out of his car with two very over-excited grandchildren and strolled along to the laneway.

Pretty Beach was still bustling with last-minute shoppers in Jeddos off-licence and White Cottage Flowers had only just started to close, the last of its trees now sold.

Juliette pushed open the door to Jeddos, Silent Night played loudly from the speakers and lots of men stood around contemplating labels on wines. She went straight over to the brandy section, picked out a small half bottle, added two bottles of champagne and got in the long queue to pay. Four staff were behind the counter with a highly-efficient wrapping and scanning system and Jeddo's wife was walking around in a lit-up Christmas hat giving out tiny little morsels of Holly's Christmas fudge.

'Merry Christmas, Juliette. How are you? Haven't bumped into you for ages. All at home for Christmas?' Jeddo's wife, Celia, asked.

'Yes, Bella is home, Maggie is with me and Daisy's here, all the girls together.'

'Lovely!' Celia said, and carried on dishing out the fudge to the line of people behind.

Juliette finally got to the head of the queue, handed over her brandy and two bottles of champagne.

'Good evening, Juliette! Merry Christmas to my favourite midwife!' Jeddo bellowed as he scanned her bits and bobs and handed them to the right to be wrapped.

'Merry Christmas, Jeddo, have a lovely time.' Juliette called out as she took her bag and walked back through the shop, past the line of people and out of the door. She stood outside fumbling with the buttons on her coat when a woman came rushing out the door behind her.

'Excuse me!' the woman said, looking at Juliette.

'Yep, are you okay? Oh, did I drop something?'

'Look, sorry, you don't know me, but I just had to say something when they said your name is Juliette and well I overheard too that you're the midwife - I put two and two together.'

Juliette continued to look at the petite woman with the short hair dressed in an expensive-looking coat and a pair of diamond drop earrings sparkling in her ears.

'Only I'm Luke's sister-in-law. Luke Burnette that is.'

Juliette still didn't say anything, shuffled her feet a bit and nodded.

'It's none of my business but I just had to speak to you. Luke will kill me - he's at the pub with his brother, but so be it. I had to say something.'

'Look, sorry, it's Christmas Eve and I don't think there's much you can say.'

'It's just that I've known Luke for a very long time and I wanted to tell you that it's the truth about Karen, not that she calls herself that any longer, apparently she changed her name completely not long after.'

Juliette smiled, it was awkward and the woman was standing right in her way.

'Luke really hadn't seen her for ten years and she really did do the dirty on him. Just upped and left with their car and all their savings for a house. No one liked her and the marriage was awful from the word go. We all told him not to marry her and then when she left he just let it go. Didn't try and sort out a divorce, didn't try to find her. It was awful and he barely even mentioned her ever again.'

'Right.'

'And sorry if I sound nosey, but when he moved down here to Pretty Beach he got on the phone to Louie one night - they're so close and well I was listening too and he told Louie all about you, like all about you. He told us he was head-over-heels about you, but he couldn't pluck up the courage to tell you about Karen and the longer he let it go on the worse it got.'

'That's not really my problem though, is it? He wasn't honest with me from the start.' Juliette replied, putting her hand on her hip and head to the side.

'No, I get that, but Juliette, Luke is a good man, Luke does not mess about with women especially after what went on with Karen. When he told us about you it was so good to hear, to see him like that. And then he told us you'd told him how much you liked him and that you were sneaking in seeing each other all the time, well we were both so pleased for him.'

Juliette just stood there, shoppers coming in and out of the off-licence with bags, the cold wind whipping her hair around. The woman put her hand on Juliette's arm.

'I really think you should give him a go. He loves you, Juliette, he told us he loved you from day one...'

Chapter 60

Juliette bolted along the laneway, her hair trailing behind her in the wind, grabbing onto the off-licence plastic bag tightly, her feet pounding along the pavement. What Luke's sister-in-law had said kept going over and over in her head.

He loves you Juliette, he told us he loved you from day one.

She weaved in and out of people strolling along the pavement, pulled the belt of her coat open and as she could see the Christmas lights of the Smugglers in the distance slowed from her run trying to get her breath back.

He loves you Juliette, he told us he loved you from day one.

She pulled her coat off as she walked along, taking huge breaths to calm herself down and as she got to the Smugglers she cupped her hands over her eyes and pressed her nose up to the window. Condensation ran down the inside of the glass and she peered in to see if she could see Luke and his brother. They were at a spot at the end of the bar, Luke leaning up against the very end of the bar on the left. James the barman was standing in front of them wiping down the top.

Juliette opened the outside door to the pub, put her coat and plastic bag on the bench in the little porch, pushed open the inner door and was hit by the noise, by the heat of the fire and by the familiar pub smell.

She could just see Luke's back, he was leaning on his left elbow, a pint in his right hand and talking to his brother and James. Ben Chalmers was on the other side of him chatting to Suntanned Pete, Holly and Xian. Streams of gold decorations brushed the top of her head as she pushed her way through the tables and made her way to Luke.

She finally got to the bar and stood there behind Luke. Ben had stopped chatting to Suntanned Pete, Holly had taken a step nearer and James had ceased what he was doing and was looking straight at

Juliette. Luke's brother stopped talking and looked over Luke's right shoulder. Luke turned slightly to his right confused and looked back at his brother. Louie tapped him on the arm, raised his eyebrows and gestured towards Juliette who was standing behind him, her arms at her side, puffing.

'Luke.'

'Juliette.'

'Your sister told me,' Juliette said, breathlessly.

'My sister?' Luke said, confused and looked back to Louie.

'You mean my sister-in-law. Sorry, Juliette, I'm not sure what you mean,' Luke said, and gently touched her on the arm.

'Yes, yes, your sister-in-law, she told me about your wife and what happened.'

Luke didn't say anything, and Ben, Holly, Xian, Louie and James all stood there waiting for what Juliette was going to say next.

'It's just.'

They all looked at her expectantly.

'It's just,' she repeated, standing there looking up at him, wringing her hands over and over.

'It's just what, Juliette?' Luke said gently, standing up straighter.

Juliette looked up at Luke into his eyes, 'It's just she said that you said you loved me.' Luke went to reply but Juliette carried on, 'She said that you said that you loved me from day one. In the carpark with the biscuits.'

Luke took Juliette's hand and moved closer towards her.

'I did say that Juliette, and I loved you when you looked up at me from the pavement sitting in the middle of a pool of Baileys with black running down your face, the birthmark on your cheek and you started to laugh.'

'Okay, well right.'

'Well right?'

Juliette now didn't know what to do, she'd run all the way across Pretty Beach on the spur of the moment to find Luke and to tell him that she loved him too, that she didn't care about his wife and that she wanted to be with him every single day for the rest of her life, but now she was lost for words.

James moved from behind the bar and walked around into the pub, a bunch of mistletoe in his hand. He smiled and held it above Juliette and Luke's heads.

Luke stepped forward to Juliette and kissed her, she breathed in his gorgeous musky smell, trombones boomed in her head and she looked up at him.

'Luke Burnette, I love you too.'

***

The next in the series - A Pretty Beach Dream

Books for Babbettes

The Boat House Series

    Book 1 (Trilogy 1) The Boat House Pretty Beach (Sallie & Ben)

    Book 2 (Trilogy 1) Summer Weddings at Pretty Beach (Sallie & Ben)

    Book 3 (Trilogy 1) Winter at Pretty Beach (Sallie & Ben)

  A Pretty Beach Series

    Book 4 (Trilogy 2) A Pretty Beach Christmas (Juliette & Luke)

    Book 5 (Trilogy 2) A Pretty Beach Dream (Juliette & Luke)

    Book 6 (Trilogy 2) A Pretty Beach Wish (Juliette & Luke)

  Secret Evenings In Pretty Beach Series

    Book 7 (Trilogy 3) Secret Evenings in Pretty Beach (Lottie & Connor)

    Book 8 (Trilogy 3) Secret Places in Pretty Beach (Lottie & Connor)

    Book 9 (Trilogy 3) Secret Days in Pretty Beach (Lottie & Connor)

A Pretty Beach Dream

(The second in the 'A Pretty Beach' series.)

Have you loved absorbing yourself in all the goings-on in Pretty Beach, the delectable Luke, up there on his perfect podium, and the lovely Juliette?

Well, you'll adore the next in the series, A Pretty Beach Dream - the lovely little sequel to A Pretty Beach Christmas.

We delve back into the ins and outs of Juliette's journey as she continues the ride in what she thought would be a much less complicated life - but with ups, downs and all sorts in between, plus the unwanted presence of someone not so nice in town, Juliette wonders if she's done the right thing.

In A Pretty Beach Dream we delve back into the wonderful seaside town and as Pretty Beach blooms and comes back to life after being all tucked up in the cold, Spring is in the air and we find out what happens to Juliette, deal with a tragedy and immerse ourselves further into the sweet little town by the sea.

As the daffodils bloom we find out that for a pair who pretty much fell in love from the day they laid eyes on each other, it's not always quite as easy as living the dream... but Juliette and Luke are solid as a rock and the utterly gorgeous setting, plethora of heart-warming characters and dash of intrigue is perfect to curl up with on the sofa.

If you love romance for a new year, a gorgeous old house by the sea, all the awakenings of Spring and sweet, funny romcoms you'll love the next part in the Pretty Beach story.

Immerse yourself back into the cosy little town by the sea, guaranteed to brighten your day and leave you pondering a new life on the coast.

***

'Addictive, absorbing and does the trick to get you lost in a whole, new delightful world.'

Author's Notes

I hope you enjoyed the world of Pretty Beach and if you are reading this in the Silly Season I do hope you've been tucked up beside a Christmas tree with your feet up and a nice warm drink with little snowflakes floating down outside.

I wrote A Pretty Beach Christmas mostly sitting at the huge old table in the conservatory at the back of our house looking out into the garden, the window open for copious amounts of fresh air and rather a lot of pots of tea. I have to tell you too, there were these little Swedish biscuits my daughter found in a local cafe and they got me through lots of writing with my cup of 3pm tea. I am currently on the hunt for a good recipe for these biscuits, they're sort of like shortbread and covered in a very fine iridescent food glitter. OMG divine - please if you know of them and a good recipe let me know...

It was Spring when I wrote this book and the huge old wisteria that runs all the way along the back wall was out, plants poked up through the ground, and to be quite honest I adored going into the conservatory every day looking at all the activity going on in the garden whilst immersing myself in all things Christmas.

I'm not really sure where Luke came from (or Jeremy for that matter), he just seemed to speak to me as I started writing about Juliette. I wanted him to seem and very much look perfect... but then for there to be a teeny little secret that knocked him off that perfect podium of his. I believe he did quite well climbing back onto it though, don't you?

Juliette had very much been looking for a house for quite a while when she moved into Sallie's cottage and I really thought it would be good if she could actually afford to stay in Pretty Beach after what she had been through with the divorce. I got the idea about the state of Mr Jenkin's house from a house we looked at a few houses before the one we are in now - it had been owned by a lady who had kept her dogs (Alsatians to be precise) in one of the bedrooms and the smell was diabolical, overpowering is an understatement, and made all of us viewing the house, including the estate agent, gag. Always a nice start to home ownership - yes we did go on to buy the house, unbelievable but true.

I'm sitting here typing these notes in the same spot in the conservatory as all that time ago, with my planner by my side as the light is fading and I'm very much wondering whether or not to do yoga tonight or just get into bed extremely early with a huge pile of books from the ever-growing pile by the side of my bed.

By the way, do please come and chat on social media - I'm on Instagram or Facebook (or join us at my reader group) and would absolutely love to see you there. Oh, and please, if you have a minute, I would really appreciate it if you wouldn't mind leaving a review.

Love

Polly

PollyBabbington.com

Be part of Polly's World!

If you've loved reading along...
You might want to be part of the Babbettes and the Polly Babbington Reader Club - little bits and bobs from Pretty Beach, excerpts from upcoming books, pretty things and covers and the like that I'm working on... we'd love to have you over there. Xxo
Just go to Polly Babbington Reader Club group on Facebook and request to join.

Want to chat?... send me an email at pollybabbington@gmail.com or even easier send me a message - Instagram & Facebook @pollybabbingtonwrites

If you want a little bit more on the wonderful world of Pretty Beach sign up to Polly's newsletter Babbington Letters.

Follow Polly on Insta/Facebook @PollyBabbingtonwrites
PollyBabbington.com

Thank you!
If you've enjoyed all the lovelies at Pretty Beach please leave a review
xxx.

Printed in Great Britain
by Amazon

35355556R00159